GOBLIN SOUK

RACONTEUR PRESS ANTHOLOGIES

EDITED BY
CEDAR SANDERSON

Published by Raconteur Press, LLC.

For more information contact production@raconteurpress.com.

Copy Editing by Jaime DiNote and Sarah Clithero

Layout by Nick Nethery

Cover Art, Illustrations and Design by Cedar Sanderson

 Formatted with Vellum

CONTENTS

The souk: a near-mystical place even before you add magic. The narrow alleys with their centuries of history pressing in on the marketplace shops, the scent of spice, of dust, and camel dung to overwhelm the senses. The taste of sharp mint tea to cleanse the mouth, or iced melon scooped into a bowl and drizzled with orange blossom water and more mint to refresh the palate. The dazzling, bewildering, astounding array of wares to confuse the eyes while you try to learn the art of the deal from shopkeepers who absorbed it with their mothers' milks. The chant of the muezzin droning over the babble of many languages, rising and falling at all hours of the night and day in this sleepless, restless place.

Combine this with the Arabian Nights, the tales of Scheherazade, the princess who must captivate her husband's heart with storytelling if she is to survive to see another dawn, and you have the Goblin Souk. To set the scene: a story of the weaver of tales, assisted by the Norns in her passionate plea for life, through words. Here, you will find stories of genies, lamps, and wishes both granted and unfulfilled. You will find a tale of breathtaking cruelty where a genie must bear the flesh of pig...and yet, in that is his ultimate reward. Wishes which cannot be spoken cannot be taken too literally by the genie, who will grant the literal wish instead of the heart's desire poorly phrased, but wishes which cannot be spoken also cannot be granted. Honor's price can be worth more than a life, as three soldiers fallen into the far world of the goblins learn, and a thief's reward can be more costly than death.

In the end, it all comes down to love, and trickery, because only the canny survive when goblins are on the hunt. I hope you will enjoy these ten tales, which bring to life what such a place would be like, and what the consequences of a fairy tale can be in a place where a button is valueless because there is no way to count that high. Ten authors bring their wares, and bid you enjoy them. If you have read through their offerings, consider telling them what you thought. But remember! The goblin's hard bargains can leave a mark a lifetime will not erase. Some of these stories may haunt your dreams. Some of them may bring you to reconsider how you've always thought. And some, the really special ones, may make you laugh, or cry, and in doing so, they have shown their true value.

In editing the Goblin anthologies, I have been richly rewarded by being able to read well over a hundred stories, but sadly, the spaces were limited in this market. Still, I think you will find that the curated tales which populate these pages are ones you will enjoy just as much as I have. In that, we are alike. Words spun into worlds on the page come to life in our heads. The true magic is, as cliché as it may seem, in our imaginations fueled by the stories told at Scheherazade's behest.

I hope to hear from you, Dear Reader, in the reviews!

Cedar Sanderson, Editor
Tiny Town, Texas
June 2025

A WEAVER OF WORDS AND WORLDS

BY ROSS HATHAWAY

Scheherezade was afraid and getting more and more desperate. For 500 nights she had chained neverending tales one to the next. Each with a cliff-hanging non-ending so on the morning her husband and lover, King Shahryar, decided to allow her to live another day. There are, however, only so many stories and Scheherezade was finding it more and more difficult to spin another tale to keep her husband's interest.

She prayed to the gods—any gods for help with her dilemma. A frigid blast of wind rushed through the seraglio and three women dressed in strange furs appeared. The youngest called out: "Hail sister, weaver of words! We are the Norns. I am Urd and these are my sisters Veroandi and Skuld. We too weave—but we weave human lives and fates. For a time, we have watched your struggle and wish to help. Too often we must cut short a human thread and we do not wish that for you. So here is our gift!"

Urd gestured and an amazing tapestry appeared on the wall. "Know this, only you can see and use this gift. This is the living history of the Goblin Souk. It is woven from all the stories and interactions between the seen and unseen world. Each thread is an individual story and some end quickly, but others are endless and interlocked to boundless others. Touch any thread and you will know and understand from a god's eye. Touch this one short thread and you will know some of what the Goblin Souk is and is not. Tonight, start with this glowing, bright thread which branched out endlessly and you will start the tale of the forever war with the Unwoven."

Scheherezade was wise and knew everything comes with a price so asked: "What do you ask for such a princely gift?"

As the Norn faded away along with the frigid wind, she heard. "Just putting the story out into the world so others can make their choice is enough."

Hesitantly, Scheherezade touched the first small thread. Suddenly, she knew, felt, and understood the Goblin Souk.

IT HAS NO FOUNDATION. NO WALLS. NO TRUE NAME. ONLY THE ECHO OF one: Souk el-Ghul—Market of the Hidden.

The Goblin Souk is not a place, not exactly. It is a crossroads made of stories, stitched together by bargains, wrapped in silk and bound by heat. It exists only where the veil between worlds—between truth and myth, desire and dread—is gossamer thin.

Some say it was born when the first lie was ever traded for gold. Others claim it formed the moment the first goblin bartered a soul for a song. The oldest theory? That it's always been here, waiting. Not made. Not summoned. Just found.

It drifts across the sands of the Middle East, yes—but also flickers between alleyways in old Istanbul, beneath the great bazaars of Marrakesh, or in the backrooms of antique shops in forgotten ports. Once, it appeared in the eye of a sandstorm that lasted seven minutes—and swallowed a caravan whole.

It is drawn to need. To desperate hopes, twisted wishes, unsolved riddles, and hearts bartering with fate.

Its merchants and vendors are not always goblins. Not anymore. There are flame-sellers born of smokeless fire. A trio of masks that wear no face but speak in perfect chorus. An old man who sells time, but only in drops too small to notice. There are too many to comprehend and when one looks there is always another and another depending on what one wants, truly needs, or thinks they need.

Every merchant makes their own rules. Every deal has a twist. The price is never coin—only ever something real. A scent you'll never smell again. A heartbeat from your future. A promise you never made aloud.

Scattered around the Souk are signs. When Scheherezade first looked at them they were painted in strange symbols but then they reformed, and she read. The rules of the Souk:

You do not steal. Theft from the Souk is impossible. Take what is not given, and the Souk takes something of equal or greater value without warning.

You do not return without cost. Once you've traded in the Souk, it remembers your scent. You may leave, but it leaves with you.

You may not find it twice by accident. The first time is luck. The second is fate. The third? Purpose—and the Souk watches closely.

Scheherezade realized the Souk was alive and tried to understand what it wanted but the more she looked the more she realized that what it wants is unknowable by humans. She saw some believe the Souk is a kind of dream, living off the choices we make within it. Others think it's a wound in reality, bleeding magic, and trying to close itself with stories. A rare few say the Souk is a test. A filter. A forge. Only those whose stories matter will walk out whole.

But one thing is certain: The Goblin Souk always takes something. Even if you don't know what.

THAT NIGHT SCHEHEREZADE DECIDED TO TAKE A CHANCE AND NOT START the endless war. She wanted to see how her husband would react to this entirely different but same kind of story. She touched a shorter muted thread. And told the following story of the Roc's egg and the Djinn's twist:

The Goblin Souk did not exist in any one place. It shimmered between moments, hidden in the sigh of a dying wind, folded into the shadows of alleyways that had never been walked. Some said it arrived on the back of a sandstorm. Others swore it only appeared to those who'd already made a bargain they didn't understand.

Kamil found it at the edge of twilight, where the dunes bled into glass and the sky was too quiet. One moment he stood on the outskirts of a forgotten village, the next he was elbow-deep in a crowd of creatures and colors the world had long since forgotten.

It was breathtaking.

Silken tents bloomed like flowers in impossible hues. Jewels glittered from the eyes of merchants who were more shadow than flesh. A lamia bartered with a frost elemental over a cage of bottled dreams. A stall selling "Tomorrow's Memories—lightly used" was run by a child with too-old eyes. And overhead, slung on wires spun from moonlight, hung the silver chimes that marked the border between realities.

But Kamil had no time to gawk. His sister, Ranya, was dying.

It wasn't a sickness that doctors could name—it was a slow unraveling, as though something had reached through her dreams and begun to pull her soul out by threads. The wise woman of the village called it a binding fate, the punishment of a story left unfinished. The cure lay beyond the natural world.

So Kamil had come to the Souk to trade.

The Roc's egg sat in a cradle of ash and crushed pearl, radiating heat like a newborn star. He had read of it in fragments: a thing not laid, but willed into being by the Roc, a creature who soared so high it forgot the ground existed. The egg was raw potential—power untamed, wild enough to crack a curse if directed, to destroy a city if misused.

The stalls vendor was not goblin or man, but a djinn. She shimmered with impossible grace, her form veiled in desert winds and ink. Her voice held echoes of cracked stones and storm-light.

"You come with purpose," she said, more statement than question.

"I need the egg. My sister—"

"Is caught in a tale not her own. I know."

Kamil offered all he had—gems that wept water, the feather of a phoenix, a map that showed forgotten cities. The djinn looked on, amused.

"I do not take what is given," she said. "I take what is owed. And I want a story."

Kamil narrowed his eyes. "I've none to give. My life is a straight line."

"No," she said. "I want a story yet to be lived. Your future. A twist of your path, a moment yet unborn."

"And if I give it?"

She smiled, teeth like lightning. "Then the egg is yours. But know this: the path you were meant to walk will bend. You will find yourself in tales not your own. Others will speak your name in tongues you don't understand."

Still, Kamil nodded. The deal was struck. Her finger, glowing with desert flame, brushed his brow.

The Souk sighed. Somewhere, a bell rang. A door that never was closed softly behind him.

He returned to the village with the egg in a sack slung over his back, its heat warming his spine. By moonlight, he cracked it over Ranya's sleeping form. Lightning split the night. She awoke gasping, color returning to her face like water to parched land.

The curse broke.

But the djinn's words proved true.

Kamil no longer dreamed of his fields or the steady rhythm of village life. Instead, he dreamt of palaces made of bone and flame, of oceans that sang in voices older than time. Strangers began to appear—travelers, mystics, even monsters—seeking him. He walked into stories that had waited for him, stories he had never chosen.

He became a tale whispered in caravan tents and inked in forgotten tomes. Some called him the Twisted Path. Others, the Egg-Bearer. He outlived kingdoms, learned to speak with spirits, and walked in the spaces between stars.

And every so often, in the curl of incense smoke or the gleam of a polished mirror, he would see the Souk again—waiting, patient, its gossamer veil billowing in winds from other worlds.

The Goblin Souk never truly left. It lingers. And it always remembers a good story.

So ended the first thread that Scheherezade touched.

KING SHAHRYAR WAS INTRIGUED BY THIS NEW LINE OF STORYTELLING AND fascinated by the Goblin Souk so once again he did not call his Vizier and force him to end Scheherazade's life. He decided to wait another day and hear more.

The second night, Scheherezade touched the start of the forever war against the Unwoven with the story of the Sandglass and the Ifrit:

The desert shimmered beneath a sky of hammered bronze. Winds curled like fingers around the caravan as it moved toward the horizon, where the air danced, and the earth no longer obeyed its own laws. Silken-robed travelers, traders, mystics, and mercenaries all followed the same invisible pull—a call older than kingdoms, older than even the names for stars.

They were coming to the Souk.

No map could guide them. No compass would spin. The Souk arrived when it wished, like a mirage with weight. It rested this time at a crossroads of forgotten empires, near a dried-up well said to once belong to a prophet who dreamed of fire.

Its gates were not made of stone, but of blowing sand held together by memory and deals not yet made.

Inside, the heat shifted. The stalls teemed with silks sewn from spider-light, amphorae of monsoon thunder bottled in the jungles of Bengal, scrolls inked in phoenix blood, and rarest of all —time itself, caught and sold in grains within a glowing hourglass.

This is where Nazeera found herself. A map-reader from the mountains, exiled for seeing too much, her eyes touched by the far-seeing curse. The curse of prophecy and as such no one would believe what she knew would happen. She came to the Souk seeking an impossible trade: her curse lifted, in exchange for her future sight.

But the merchant she faced was no ordinary being. He stood

taller than a man, cloaked in rags that shifted like smoke, his skin scorched black as charcoal, his eyes twin embers. He was an Ifrit, bound not by shackles, but by contract.

"I deal in moments," he said, voice like coals ground under boot. "One second of perfect clarity for one lifetime of blindness. A fair trade, no?"

Nazeera did not flinch. "I want neither moment nor blindness. I want peace."

"Peace is expensive," the Ifrit said. "But I will offer you a deal. Bring me the breath of a haboob—the storm that speaks in sand —and I will shatter your far-sight like glass."

She laughed. "You ask for the wind itself?"

"No," he said. "I ask for its breath—what it says, not what it takes."

And so she went, through the alleys of the Souk and into the wastes, where the air whispered in tongues no man could tame. She found the storm rising on the edge of the world, a monstrous wall of dust and fury. She listened, not with ears, but with cursed eyes that had seen too much.

She brought back a single word, whispered in wind and etched on her soul.

The Ifrit, upon hearing it, recoiled. "You've spoken the true name of the Souk," he hissed. "No mortal was meant to hold it."

"Then perhaps I was never mortal," Nazeera said, her voice suddenly heavy with the echo of storms.

For that was the secret. Her curse had never been a punishment; it was a transformation. She had become part of the Souk itself. One of the far-seeing, born from sand and trade and story.

The Ifrit vanished, consumed by his own flame, and Nazeera took his place behind the stall, where now she sells whispers of prophecy wrapped in silk.

Sometimes, travelers pass her by and swear they see the storm stirring behind her eyes. And sometimes, when the wind howls just right, the Souk itself seems to breathe her name.

⁊⁊

AGAIN, KING SHAHRYAR WAS INTRIGUED. HOW DID THIS RELATE TO AN endless war he had been promised? Another reprieve and Scheherazade lived another day. That night the story continued with Nazeera and the Echo Vault:

Once Nazeera took the Ifrit's place behind the stall of shifting sands, the Souk began to change around her. Slowly. Subtly. The chimes above her canopy sang in unfamiliar keys. The lamps along her walkway began to glow with desert starlight, even when the sky overhead was veiled in storm.

She did not sleep. She did not age. She learned to sip time from the curved lip of an hourglass without disturbing the future. The old vendors nodded to her with a wary sort of respect.

It was only when the Echo Vault opened, though, that Nazeera understood the price of her becoming.

It started with a shadow that moved against the wind. It whispered across her stall, pausing just long enough to leave behind a stone sealed with gold thread. She picked it up—and heard it breathe. Not a sound. A memory.

"We buried it beneath the salt dunes. Wrapped in lion skin. The voice of the queen still echoes there..."

The Vault was waking. Few knew of it. Fewer dared speak its name.

The Echo Vault was not a place but a concept—an accumulation of all the trades too dangerous to be finalized. Deals that shook the foundations of time itself. Promises so potent they couldn't be kept, only hidden, and now, one had begun to stir.

Nazeera followed the memory's trail.

Past the souk's silk alleys and jeweled domes. Past the haggling djinn and bronze-masked scholars. She passed the Hall of Smiling Knives, where a goblin with no hands sold forgiveness to passing assassins. Past the Stilt Bazaar, where the goods floated two stories above the sand and the merchants wore mirrored sandals to reflect the sun and keep lies at bay.

At last, she reached the Vault: a staircase made of wind, leading downward where no downward should exist.

There, in the cool hush of ancient air, Nazeera found the salt dunes. Beneath them, wrapped in the petrified hide of a forgotten beast, she found the thing the memory had buried.

It was not a relic. Not a scroll. It was a voice.

Still living.

Bound inside a faceless mask made of lapis and obsidian, it pulsed with suppressed words. A voice that had been cut from a queen, long ago, to silence a prophecy. It hummed in Nazeera's hand, then spoke—not aloud, but directly to the still, silent center of her:

"You see beyond. Then you must decide: return me to the queen and wake the kingdom or trade me to the Souk and reshape the world."

The mask burned cold.

Behind Nazeera, the Souk's presence loomed. It was listening. Always listening.

This was the nature of the Vault: not secrets buried in fear, but choices too dangerous to be made without cost.

Nazeera turned the mask over. She saw cities reflected in its black surface—some crumbling, some golden, some yet to be built. Every choice she could make echoed out from it like ripples in sand.

Also, unseen once the Echo Vault was opened, other things could come out...

KING SHAHRYAR WAS TOTALLY ENGAGED WITH THE CONTINUING STORY. HE rushed through all the duties and ceremonies for the day because he needed to know what came next...Nazeera's price:

She stood at the edge of the Vault, the faceless mask heavy in her hands. Within it, the voice of a long-dead queen curled and hissed, pressing against the silence, begging to be heard again. In her bones, Nazeera felt the pull of its power. A voice that could awaken a fallen kingdom, undo wars sealed in blood and ash, summon memory into flame, but Nazeera had never sought thrones or upheaval. What she wanted—what she had always wanted—was quiet.

A world not drowned in prophecy. A moment without futures crashing down around her.

She ascended back through the Souk, past lanterns blooming with ghost-light and stalls that blinked when no one was looking. The Souk had already shifted in her absence. It always did. Time was a suggestion here, and reality was loose in its bindings.

At the very heart of the Souk stood a pavilion made of blue fire and ivory, guarded by seven beings who shared one shadow. They were the Keepers of Trades That Touch the World.

No one came to them lightly.

She approached with the mask cradled in both hands.

"I offer this voice," she said, "in exchange for peace."

The seven shadows shifted. One spoke with the sound of water against stone. "What kind of peace, Nazeera of the Far-Seeing?"

"The peace of a still mind. Of a soul no longer cracked by futures. Of a world, perhaps, without war—if such is possible."

They conferred in silence that lasted a minute or a lifetime—it was hard to say in that place.

Then the fire split open.

"Peace comes in three forms," they said. "You may choose one:

The Peace of the Self. You will sleep without dreams. Your far-sight will dim. You will know contentment, but the world will go on without your touch.

The Peace of a Nation. One war—past, present, or still to come—will vanish as if it never was. Lives saved. Grief undone. But your name will be forgotten entirely, even by yourself.

The Peace Between Realms. The Souk will seal its gates for a thousand years, halting the tide of magic between worlds. Silence. Safety. But wonder, too, will vanish—for a time."

Nazeera stood beneath a sky braided with constellations no astronomer had ever named. She thought of her childhood, spent trembling at visions. Of the Ifrit's stall, the first bargain. Of the voice she now gave away—once a queens, now a key.

She chose.

"Let the nation rest. Let grief be undone."

She laid the mask upon a silver plate carved from moonlight. It crumbled to salt and smoke. And somewhere—perhaps in the mountains she had once called home, or in a kingdom she had never seen—a war that had torn through generations was unwritten. Graves filled in. Names restored. The silence that followed was not hollow, but golden.

As for Nazeera, her memories of the Souk faded.

She wandered out days later with a satchel full of dust and poems in her mouth. No one remembered her name, not even her, but people listened when she spoke. Somewhere deep in her gaze, behind the soft eyes of a storyteller, the wind still curled in secret shapes.

Peace is never simple, but sometimes, it is chosen.

THE NEXT NIGHT THE TAPESTRY'S THREAD SLIPS TO SOMETHING OUTSIDE of the Goblin Souk but connected as something that had escaped —the Unwoven and Tariq, in a story called "The Dream of Dust and Thread."

The dream began, as many do, in a desert.

The sand rolled in endless waves, but there was no sun. Instead, a vast moon sat low in the sky, pulsing like a drumbeat. The air shimmered with heat that burned nothing. From the horizon came a figure—barefoot, hooded, trailing a robe that unraveled as they walked.

Tariq had dreamed of the desert before. He was a merchant's son from Marib, born in the shadow of cracked spice jars and brass lamps that sometimes whispered when no one was listening. He had always felt the pull of the Souk. But this dream was different.

This dream was waiting for him. In the center of the desert, he found a loom. Ancient. Vast. Hung with strands of light and memory. A weaver stood beside it—faceless, hands stitched with gold thread—and motioned to him.

"You may choose a thread," the weaver said. "But choose carefully. The wrong one unravels everything."

Tariq reached out instinctively, fingers brushing a strand that shimmered like river water.

Then the Unwoven whispered. "Don't choose. Refuse the loom. Refuse the weave. Step outside the thread and be free."

The air grew sharp. The moon flickered. The weaver froze.

Tariq blinked—and found himself outside the dream.

Still dreaming... but now in a space beyond. The air was full of broken thread. Unfinished stories. Stalled choices.

And the Unwoven took shape before him. It did not have a face. It had all faces, flickering. A djinn's grin, a child's sorrow, a merchant's hunger, a ghost's patience. Its voice was the echo of a deal never made.

"You were meant to trade your dream for truth. But what if you kept it?

What if you denied the Souk's design? What if no stories ended, no bargains closed, no prices paid?"

Tariq, wide-eyed, felt the thread of his name unravel slightly at the edges. And he understood: this was how it began. Not with a war, nor with fire, but with hesitation. With the refusal to decide.

That was Unwoven's gift: the lie of eternal possibility.

"No endings," the Unwoven whispered. "Only the comfort of never choosing."

Tariq was, however, the son of a merchant. He had watched his father haggle over apricots and illusions. He had seen the beauty in a deal done, in the sharp bite of decision, so he reached into his chest, dream-formed and fragile, and pulled from his own story a single golden thread.

"This," he said, "is the price of certainty," and he bound the thread around his wrist. The loom returned. The desert reformed. The Unwoven shrieked in the voice of unfinished songs. It retreated, not defeated—but denied, for now.

Tariq woke in his bed, breath ragged, moonlight staining the room like ink.

On his wrist: a golden thread, real as any coin. And that morning, without a word, he left for the Souk. He had a dream to trade, and perhaps, just perhaps, a story to finish.

The Goblin Souk called...

This is not his first time dreaming of the Souk. But this is the first time it's real.

THE NEXT NIGHT THE STORY OF TARIQ CONTINUED IN THE STORY "TARIQ and the Thread That Chooses."

The gates of the Goblin Souk never appear where you expect them.

For Tariq, they opened at the crossroads just outside Marib, where the date palms gave way to dunes and the wind sometimes spoke in forgotten dialects. One moment, he was walking along the caravan path with a satchel full of incense and questions. The next, the air shifted. Like breath caught in the chest.

The horizon folded in on itself, and before him stood an archway of copper and bone, humming softly, stitched with sigils made of salt and starlight. The Gates of the Souk.

He stepped through, and the world changed. Colors grew deeper. Scents doubled in weight—frankincense, cardamom, dream-oil, regret. The stone beneath his feet was not stone, but petrified possibility. The air held a thousand conversations from a thousand tongues: human, goblin, djinn, serpent, star.

The Souk was alive, and it noticed him. The thread on his wrist pulsed faintly.

As he walked deeper, the stalls blinked open like eyes. A goblin with beetle-shell spectacles offered him time in a jar. A pale woman with feathers for hair bartered in names. A serpent coiled around a brazier hissed secrets no one else could hear.

Tariq moved carefully, eyes open. He wasn't here to buy.

He was here to understand.

The golden thread tugged gently, guiding him. It led him to the Stall of Remembered Futures, tended by a figure wrapped in layered silk and dusk. The merchant had no face, only a shifting mask of sand and wind.

"You carry a thread not spun in this world," the merchant said, voice like flowing ink. "From a dream. From a bargain you refused."

Tariq nodded. "I came to finish what I almost didn't begin."

The merchant's hand flickered. A loom appeared—small, travel-worn, set with spindles of bone and starlight.

"You may weave your thread," they said. "But know this: it will change the Souk."

Tariq hesitated. "How?"

"Every trade shape the tide. Yours may draw the Unwoven closer—or push it back beyond the veils."

Tariq looked down at the thread. It was not golden anymore. It shimmered like sand in a dream—filled with futures he had not chosen. He began to weave.

With each pass through the loom, something shifted in the air.

Stalls paused. Conversations hiccupped. Somewhere, the Vault sighed.

The Souk itself bent ever so slightly, like a sail catching new wind.

As he tied the final knot, the fabric glowed. Neither a tapestry nor a prophecy.

It was a map of the Souk, of its secret paths and vulnerable edges.

It would allow someone—not Tariq, but someone soon—to reinforce the boundaries that kept the Unwoven at bay. He had made no grand sacrifice. No war. No battle. Just a dream made real, and a thread made choice.

The faceless merchant bowed.

"The Souk thanks you, Dreamweaver."

Tariq, blinking, found himself outside again—beneath the same sun, the same road. The air smelled faintly of rosewater and ash, and the golden thread was now part of his skin, like a faint scar in the shape of a story.

He turned south, toward the coast, where tales were bought in song and sold in storms.

❧

ENDING THIS NIGHT'S STORY, SCHEHERAZADE SET THE STAGE FOR THE next chapter. "So now we turn our gaze to the Unwoven—that which waits outside. Not evil, not chaos, but undoing. The quiet hunger of stories unspoken. The serenity of stillness stretched too far. Let us follow it now, through cracks in the veil—because it, too, has learned, and it is changing its approach."

The next nights story is "The Whisper That Learned to Wear a Face."

The Souk has always known how to resist it. Barter. Story. Decision. These are anathema to the Unwoven. They are anchors, but anchors can be lifted. And the Unwoven, ancient though it is, has begun to understand something vital: If it cannot close the gates from without, it need only convince someone within to do it for them. So now, it takes form.

A figure in bone-colored robes. A face too perfect to be remembered.

Eyes like mirrors that show you as you were before you made your first true choice.

They call it Safa—or sometimes The Pale Merchant. It trades in peace; true, final, velvet-lined peace.

The stall appears only in moments of fatigue to tired dreamers, burned-out prophets, and traders who've bargained away too much of themselves. No one sees Safa set up shop, but once you're near the Pale Merchant, it's hard to turn away.

Its wares? Oblivion, bottled like old wine. Forgotten futures, pressed into coin. Maps to nowhere, inked with tears.

The offer? "You do not have to choose anymore. Let me take

your threads. I will smooth them. No more struggle. No more shifting sands. Just stillness. Just silence."

More than a few have said yes.

Each time they do, the Souk trembles—just slightly. A wind stutters. A lantern flickers. A path closes.

The Unwoven is testing the fabric, strand by strand, but here's the quiet terror: No one remembers Safa afterward. Not the buyers. Not the stall-keepers nearby. Not even the wind. Only a faint, echoing unease remains—like forgetting a word you once knew was important. Like a flicker of a flame no one notices.

Somewhere beneath the Souk, the Vault creaks. Somewhere in a shadowed arch, a weaver with gold-stitched hands sharpens her needles.

The Souk knows it's being infiltrated, but the Unwoven is no longer only at the edges. It walks within, and its whispers are getting louder.

ENDING THIS NIGHT'S STORY, SCHEHERAZADE SAYS, "SOME NOTICE THE flicker. The hush between haggles. The echoes of stalls that never were. They are not heroes. They are stall-keepers, scavengers, truth-tellers, dust-sifters, but they've started watching each other a little more closely. They've started to remember what the Souk forgets."

The next night's story is "The Lantern-Bearers of the Hollow Quarter: A Resistance Without Slogans, Only Flame."

It began with a flickering lantern.

Not unusual in the Hollow Quarter, the part of the Souk that folds in on itself, where booths press like secrets, and you have to trade three lies before anyone shows you the truth.

There, in the corner of an alley that never points the same way twice, a child named Rufah lit a lantern that didn't go out. That was all, but the light it shed revealed missing things.

Shadows with no owners. Price tags with no stalls. The outline of a shopkeeper who'd been bartered away by Safa's velvet tongue and forgotten by the Souk.

Rufah wasn't anyone important. She sold cinnamon bark and stories half-told, and no one paid her much attention. Until she lit the second lantern.

Then a bookbinder with four hands came to sit beside her stall. He had begun noticing blank pages in books he'd already bound. Whole chapters... just gone.

Then came Majda, a former haggle-priestess who heard prayers stutter where they used to sing. She carried a pocket of salt, and a razor laugh.

And so, the Lantern-Bearers began, not loud or bold, but watchful, and clever.

They met in unspoken times: when the sand changed direction, or when the stars blinked twice. Their tools were simple: Lanterns lit with memory-flame stolen from the Vault, threads from abandoned trades, rewoven into words, and spices that made Safa's illusions blink, just slightly.

Their oath was simpler still: "We keep the Souk noisy. We keep the threads tangled. We keep the story moving."

They leave messages in fruit rinds and folded carpets. They trade nothing for the sake of something. They learn to track the Unwoven's whispers through the scent of lavender and despair.

They know, however, they are few—and Safa is patient.

Still, for now, the Hollow Quarter hums louder. The Souk shivers less often.

Every night, somewhere, a new lantern is lit by someone who remembers the shape of what was lost.

❧

The next night the story of "Rufah, Who Burned Bright in a Forgotten Corner:"

Her stall is small—smaller than it should be. Some say it's always been there. Others swear they walked that way yesterday and found only dust. It smells of cinnamon and old paper, the kind of scent that settles into memory like a lullaby you can't quite place.

She wears a tunic stained with spice and oil, and her braids are tied with frayed ribbons, each one from a deal refused. She doesn't shout her wares like the others. She hums, and if you listen closely, the tune is old. Older than the Souk itself, perhaps. A lullaby for something trying to sleep beneath the market stones.

Rufah came to the Souk with nothing but a cracked lamp and a question. Her father once traded in the Singing Quarter—a merchant of spices and stories. One day, he vanished. Not stolen. Not killed. Just...forgotten. His name burned away like a parchment left too long in the sun. No one recalled his face, not even Rufah's mother, but Rufah remembered the smell of his hands when he cooked cardamom tea. That was enough. She began searching. Asking. Listening.

One evening, while sorting bark and sugar peels, she struck flint in her little lamp—expecting nothing. The flame caught. Instead of flickering orange, it burned silver-blue, like starlight soaked in grief. Everything around her shimmered, just for a moment, and she saw the ghosts of trades undone.

A folded stall with no seller. A girl without a name, her mouth sewn shut with silken thread. A coin that wept when it was held.

Rufah didn't scream. She lit another lantern, and she waited.

One by one, others came. Drawn not to her words, but to her flame.

Now, her stall is a gathering place—for those who remember too much, or not enough. For those who feel a wind where there is no breeze. For those who suspect they've been edited.

Rufah greets each one the same. "Welcome back. Have some tea. What did you nearly forget?"

She keeps a book of almosts—names and deals and dreams people swore were real but couldn't prove. She maps the patterns of the flickers. She's even found traces of Safa, though never directly. Just the warmth of velvet and the scent of stillness.

She knows she's marked. The Unwoven watches her now, yet she keeps her lantern burning because somewhere, beyond the stall, beyond the Souk, in a thread not yet knotted, her father waits—and Rufah intends to remember him back into the world.

SCHEHEREZADE PROMISES WHAT IS NEXT AS SHE FOLLOWS THE STORY OF Rufah who leaves her stall and steps into the Souk that forgets.

The Lantern-Bearers had whispered for days, "Safa has moved. Again." A new stall. Not velvet this time. Something older. Stranger. A tea shop where the steam smells like loss.

Majda gives Rufah a satchel with three items: A shard of mirror that remembers reflections. A lump of salt bound in fig skin. A thread, pulled from a robe that once belonged to a man who no longer exists.

"If it tries to talk to you," Majda says, "don't answer.

Not with words. Only with memory."

The Souk stretches strangely as Rufah moves. The Hollow Quarter should be five turns and a prayer from her stall. Now it's seven turns and a shadow she doesn't recognize.

When she reaches the tea shop, there's no sign. Just a silver kettle, steaming without fire, and a bowl of dates that smell like the end of something.

The shopkeeper has no face. Not blank—just not important enough to remember. The shopkeeper pours tea without asking. It's colorless. The cup is warm.

Then the whisper comes, soft as silk in the spine: "You're tired, aren't you?"

Rufah doesn't answer. She opens the mirror instead.

The steam curls—and shifts.

The shopkeeper blinks, and for the first time, flinches.

The mirror shows a different stall. Velvet. Perfume. Coins like buttons on a closed mouth. It is Safa. Or was. The faceless one hisses. The walls of the shop ripple, and the tea goes cold in her hand. "You could stop," it says. "No one will blame you. No one will remember."

Rufah smiles. She pulls the thread. It burns white in her hand —but does not vanish. It glows brighter the longer she holds it. The Souk groans, just faintly.

She drops the salt onto the floor. It shatters like glass, and the sound is too loud.

The stall peels away like paper under rain. The faceless shop-keeper crumbles—no blood, no scream. Just...unwritten.

In its place: A staircase. Spiral. Stone. Wet with memory.

It was never meant to be found.

At the top of the stairs, there is a single word, carved into the lintel: Tariq.

Rufah's breath catches. She steps back. Not ready, not yet, but she's seen it now.

She carries the name back to the Lantern-Bearers, stitched into her pocket with ash-thread.

The first mission was not to destroy. It was to see, and now

Rufah sees more than she should, more than is safe, but less than what she's about to uncover.

꘎

THE NEXT NIGHT, THE STORY CONTINUES IN "THE STAIR BENEATH THE MAP":

Rafah returns to the unexplained stairs. She ascends. The air thickens. The stone beneath Rufah's sandals is slick—not with water, but with memory, old and curling like forgotten incense. Every step she takes up the staircase carved from the ruined tea shop is a step into a thread never meant to be rewoven.

She has her lantern, though, and the name: Tariq. The mapmaker. The thread-weaver. The one who disappeared.

The stairs turn seven times—an old number, used in bindings and bargains. At each turn, a flicker of something half-remembered whispers past Rufah's ear: A girl shouting in a language that's since turned to dust, coins being poured into an urn carved with flame, a boy—barefoot, laughing—dragging a thread through the market as if drawing the Souk into place behind him.

Rufah knows this is before. These are glimpses of the Souk becoming.

At the top of the stairs, a door waits. No handle or keyhole. Only a map, burned into the wood. A maze. A mark. A single glowing thread woven through.

She raises her lantern. The light bends. The thread shivers— and then parts, allowing her through. On the other side is... Silence. Not the stillness of night, or the hush of reverence—but suspended silence, like breath held by the world itself. A room, circular and domed, lit by stars that should not be visible underground. In its center: a loom.

Woven from glass bones and brass memory, the loom pulses faintly.

At its base lies a figure wrapped in layered robes, gold and ink stained.

Tariq. Or what remains.

He does not move, but his hand still clutches the final strand of the map—a thread that is not cloth, nor fiber, but choice.

When Rufah touches it, it twitches. Then she hears him, not aloud, but through the fabric itself. "They told me the gates would last forever, but the world does not traffic in 'forever.' Only trade. So, I made a loom to hold the price."

"The Unwoven offered silence. I offered story."

"But the thread frays. The flame dims. You...you are the first to come. Will you carry it now?" The map in his hand loosens, not because he dies—he already has, long ago—but because he trusts her.

Rufah kneels. She takes the thread. It wraps once around her fingers, then vanishes into her palm.

In that moment, she sees the Souk—not as it is, but as it could become again. Every trade. Every laugh. Every lie and blessing and fight and kiss. A place alive because it never stops moving.

She stands. Tariq's loom still hums. Now, she knows what it needs: a new weaver. Not to replace him—but to continue the thread.

She leaves the room with her lantern brighter than before, and the map not in her hand, but inside her.

The Lantern-Bearers wait below. Above them, the Souk stirs, sensing its next tale.

SCHEHEREZADE SAID, "LET US CONSIDER MAJDA IN THE CONTINUING story. Before the salt. Before the razor-laugh. Back when she was a priestess of trade, and the Souk still trusted its own tongue. So, here is the story of 'Majda of the Third Voice,'"

Majda once stood in the Singing Quarter, bare-footed and brilliant, her voice stitched with blessings. She was a haggle-priestess, trained in the Three Voices: The First - to tempt, The Second - to bind, The Third - to seal.

With those voices, she could bless a transaction so deeply that even forgotten gods would honor it. People came from as far as Samarkand to trade beneath her canopy of blue silk.

The Souk was vibrant then. Whole. The Unwoven was still a whisper outside the edges, watching, but it was clever. It found a weakness—not in greed, not in power.

In grief. Majda had a sister once, named Layal. Born of the same mother but sung in different octaves. Where Majda was fire and salt, Layal was twilight and snow.

She did not trade. She listened. She listened to patterns, to echoes, and to stories before they were spoken.

One night, she heard a story that shouldn't have been there. A tale of stillness, perfect and unearned. A tale that said: "Trade is suffering. What if you could let it all go?"

Majda was busy that night—blessing the union of a desert prince and a courtesan made of dust and dreams. She did not see Layal go, but she felt it. When her sister returned, she was quiet. Too quiet.

She spoke in echoes. She bargained for nothing. She said she had met a face with no eyes, and it had offered her peace.

Majda tried to bless her. The rites faltered. She tried to hug her.

Layal was cold, like paper sealed in wax. Then, she was gone.

Not dead, traded. To what, Majda never learned, but she heard the name: Safa.

Something inside her voice broke. She could no longer speak the First Voice—temptation. It soured in her throat. She could not bless. She could only salt.

So, she left the Singing Quarter. She vanished into the Hollow Quarter, where broken things go to rot or rise. There, she learned to speak without rites. She learned the silence between the trades. She learned to wield salt and thread and flame, and she watched.

She was the first to notice the missing stalls. The gaps in the crowd.

The hollow smiles of those who had traded too much of themselves and come back thinner in the soul.

She whispered to others. She found Rufah, and learned of the lanterns.

Now, they say she never laughs unless something important has died. That her salt can blind even the Unwoven for a moment. That if you ask her what she lost, she'll show you a strand of hair too white for her age, braided with silence.

Sometimes, though, when the Souk is very still...she hums the lullaby her sister used to sing, just loud enough that the wind might carry it past the veil.

In case Layal is still listening.

FOR 501 NIGHTS THE STORY CONTINUES, THE WAR BETWEEN CHOICE AND no choice goes on. There are triumphs and defeats for both sides because that is what life is. As the story continues, King Shahryar realizes slowly, oh so slowly, that he is part of the story as he has continued to make the choice of no choice. He has put himself on

the side of the Unwoven, but he knows he has never been happier, and he looks at his beautiful wife and realizes he has been a fool and decides.

The Norns smile at each other. They have saved a great weaver of tales.

THE BACON BUTLER

BY KR PAUL

I don't even remember rubbing the lamp. It's wild how we never see the most impactful moment in our life as it happens.

I stumbled out of a hookah bar into the sultry streets of the Marrakesh night markets. I stopped briefly to blearily take in the bright lights, mélange of exotic smells, and bustle of humanity. The heat of the day had evaporated while I was in the hookah bar and transformed into a vibrant scene. Despite my compromised state, I was conscious enough to know I needed to get back to my hostel. My feet took off without conscious thought, only vaguely pointed towards my place of rest.

Hawkers shouted their wares as I staggered through the souks. More to the point, I staggered from shop to shop, my shoulders brushing their wares, and I was fortunate not to bruise their goods. It may be the newest millennium, but punishments were still harsh to the unwary foreigner. Minutes or hours passed as I navigated the massive market, and I could feel my mental clarity slowly surfacing once again.

Even in my somewhat altered state of mind, I realized I must have turned down the wrong narrow alleyway. The shopkeepers here were odd and vaguely unhuman in a way that was too close to reality. Ears and noses only slightly too pointed. Eyes slitted vertically, not round human pupils. Every so often, a shopkeeper was a slight shade of green or blue, nothing that screamed mystical, but not human, either.

I staggered to a stop, my hand resting on the stone wall that framed the alley. I blinked hard to see if I could clear my vision and the lingering hookah haze. The shopkeeper of the stall beside me rose to approach me. With one blink, I could see a diminutive man, barely chest-high to me outlined against the riotous colors of his dangling mosaic lights. With another blink, his skin took on a greenish hue, his features sharpening, and his expression avid. At other stalls, more small, sharp-faced shopkeepers turned towards me, expressions showing they were keen to make a deal.

I had just enough sense left in my head to turn and flee before I could be ensnared.

Given my mental state, I suppose it isn't surprising that my shoulder must have brushed the lamp as I staggered out of the unhuman souk. It was equally unsurprising that I didn't notice the djinn that followed me for several city blocks back to my hostel. Or that the djinn stalked my every movement, even after I had staggered drunk and high into bed.

But when I awoke with a pounding head and sour taste in my mouth, he loomed over my bed. The djinn was big, blue, and lacking the friendliness a certain early 90s cartoon would have led me to expect. The djinn loomed in my tiny hostel room as I slowly sat up.

"Bro, what the actual?"

"*Salaam.*" The words were a deep rumble that seemed to shake my chest and the walls around me.

"Uhm, yeah, peace, bro," I mumbled as I clutched the worn sheets, so unlike my set at home. "But seriously, what are you doing in my room?" My head throbbed in time to my stomach's roiling from too many unfamiliar beverages last night.

"You summoned me," he stated plainly. No hint of expression on his face. And yet, somehow, I felt like I was being insulted for being so dense.

"Dude, what are you, even? Why are you blue?"

"I am a djinn. Djinn are blue."

I looked at him, waiting for further information or explanation, but he only stared at me with a suspiciously bland expression. Frustrated, I groaned and flopped back on the hostel's thin mattress.

"How did I summon you?" I asked as I pressing my aching head into the pillow and longing for my luxurious bed at home.

"You rubbed my lamp as you crossed the market."

"Wait, hold up," I said, and sat up fast. "Are you saying I rubbed a magic lamp and now I've summoned a genie?"

"Djinn."

"Whatever. So I can make wishes?"

"Wish. One. Use it wisely."

"Holy fuck." I bolted upright in excitement. "I mean, shit, man. I can make a wish? Damn. Yes. It needs to be good." Just then, my stomach lurched and grumbled. "Fuck. How long do I have to make the wish? Like, is there a time limit?" I rubbed my stomach. "I need food. I would love a piece of bacon for breakfast," I said to myself.

"As you wish," the djinn told me, and gave me an elaborate bow before disappearing.

"Fuck! Damn it, I wasted it."

In the djinn's place, a man appeared. He was short, but definitely human. He was dressed in an immaculate black suit with a black tie that was elegantly knotted and tucked into a perfectly pressed vest. Equally perfect black trousers ended over highly polished, black wingtip shoes. In his white gloved hand perched a domed silver tray.

"You bacon, sir," he said as he whisked the domed lid off the tray.

"This better be the best damn bacon in the world," I told him as I snatched the piece from its tiny white plate in the center of the silver tray. I took a bite and smiled. It was the perfect balance of chewy and crunchy.

"Hey, how did you get pork bacon in a Muslim country, anyway?" I asked around the last bite I stuffed in my mouth.

The butler merely bowed his head briefly and disappeared.

"Damn. Bacon for breakfast. It was good, but kind of a waste of my wish," I said to the empty hostel room.

I explored the city after a hasty shower in the hostel's communal restrooms and a moment to secure my watch. My vintage steel Rolex wasn't as flashy as several of the watches in my apartment's walk-in closet, but it was expensive enough for me not to risk leaving it in the hostel. The loose linen shirt I threw over my clothes covered it well enough and lent an aura of "shabby world traveler" to my look, allowing me to slip more easily from bar to bar, party to party.

My feet led me through the streets of Marrakesh, and I pondered the absolute absurdity of my encounter with the djinn. Had the encounter occurred the night before, I could have easily brushed it off as booze or bad green. But his appearance in the morning, when I was fully sober, led me to the conclusion that it had really happened. And I, an idiot, pissed away a shot at a real wish by thinking with my stomach.

Eventually, my feet found their way to the strange night market where I must have rubbed the lamp. The stalls were the same as I had seen before, a narrow stone alley lined with wooden stalls, bursting with sights, sounds, and smells to ensnare the senses. In the day's light, the assortment of non-human vendors had been replaced by very normal-looking men hawking their wares.

Maybe I could chalk some of this experience up to an altered state of mind. I swallowed down my disappointment and turned to head back to my hostel. The merchant in the strange little souk gave me a knowing nod and little wink. When he then smiled, I could see the same vertically slitted pupils I'd spotted the night before.

I choked down a laugh. I guess I wasn't so addled.

The rest of the day passed in a blur of street food, enticing smells, the scent of spices heaped in heavy canvas bags, and catching up with fellow travelers I had met in the hostel. I politely excused myself from joining their night of revelry after a humorous retelling of my stagger back the night before. I carefully left out any mentions of the strange inhuman souk vendors, the djinn, or my curious little butler as I was already starting to doubt I'd really seen him.

My evening passed as quietly as one can in a hostel filled to the brim with travelers, and by the time my head hit the thin pillow, I had fully convinced myself that the morning's strange interaction was nothing more than an extended dream and longed to return to my daily grind.

The scuff of a wingtip shoe on carpet woke me in the middle of the next morning. I groggily cracked open on eye to see the immaculately pressed trousers of the bacon butler at the edge of my bed.

I bolted upright in the bed with a shout of alarm, clutching the sheet to my bare chest, as if it would shield me from the diminutive butler.

"Your bacon, sir," the butler said, completely unfazed by my startled reaction. He leaned towards me slightly and doffed the silver domed lid from the tray. Once again, a single perfectly cooked slice of bacon sat atop a single white plate.

"I thought my wish was done? Spent?"

The bacon butler merely looked at me, holding his tray at my eye level. I took the slice and he recovered the tray.

"So, like, are you going to come every morning now?" I asked, stuffing the slice in my mouth.

"Yes." He watched me chew and swallow the slice, then disappeared.

"The heck?" I asked the empty air.

A single phone call garnered me an earlier return home, away from this stuffy little butler and his bacon, but not soon enough. Despite having one of the highest-priced travel agencies at my beck and call, I lacked the liquid assets to secure a private flight home and all the first class flights today were booked. Poor planning on my part once again, but that was the story of my life.

I spent my last day in Morocco going from souk to souk, looking for the inhuman market. No matter where I went or how I turned, it eluded me. With increasing desperation, I queried vendors, trying to get my questions across in a mix of English and Arabic. With each attempt, either our lack of common language was too great a barrier or, as I strongly suspected, they were unwilling to tell me about the odd little marketspace. Frustrated, I returned to my hostel to pack and idly wondered if a djinn's wish-granting abilities could follow me home to America.

I laid awake that night pondering what would happen tomorrow as I flew home. I laid awake possibly too long, getting only a few hours' sleep before having to be up for the trek from the hostel to the Marrakesh airport. The beautiful white-and-gold airport stood gently illuminated at the ungodly predawn hour. I wanted a full night's rest upon returning, which forced me into a horrible early morning flight from Morocco to France.

The early morning departure had afforded me the opportunity to drop my humble traveler persona, ditching my cargo shorts and sandals for well-tailored slacks and a polo shirt. I had learned the trick from friends of "dressing down" during foreign travel to make myself less of a target for thieves. I was able to leave the dingy hostel with none of my new travel friends seeing me and questioning the sudden change.

My first-class seat to Paris sadly lacked the fully reclining seat and suite my flight from Paris to Washington DC had, but it was only three hours of flying time. I had sunk gracelessly into my seat, accepting a quick glass of champagne from the flight attendant, before dropping back into a deep sleep.

I awoke a few hours later to my elbow being jostled. I expected to see some inconsiderate fellow passenger and was shocked to see my bacon butler. Still dressed in his immaculate uniform holding his domed silver tray, he stood in the aisle beside me.

I stared, mouth agape, wondering how on Earth he had gotten onto a moving aircraft. I quickly looked around at my fellow passengers to see if they had noticed a man suddenly appear in the aisle. To my great relief, it seemed most had followed my lead and were asleep.

"Your bacon, sir." His voice barely carried over the noise of the flight, but it was as crisp and polite as ever.

I snatched the bacon from its plate as soon as he doffed the silver dome. I stuffed the piece in my mouth, chewing and swallowing faster than was safe. He gave a polite nod and disappeared once more. I scanned the cabin again, looking to see if anyone had seen the brief bacon drop-off, but it seemed that it had transpired with none the wiser.

The rest of my flight to France was easy, but after the bacon butler scared me awake, I couldn't fall back asleep. My mind whirred as I jetted across the Atlantic. Was this my life now? To be woken up every single day by the mysterious bacon butler? I had no wife or even a girlfriend, but how would a one-night stand handle this strange little man appearing in my bedroom to feed me a single slice of bacon?

I laughed then at that thought. I was wealthy. Very wealthy. The kind of wealth that allowed for certain eccentricities, and the appearance of a little butler bearing bacon might be brushed off. As long as the butler afforded me my privacy, I supposed he wouldn't impact my life too much.

My last flight landed in Washington, DC in the late afternoon, and I stumbled through my door, exhausted from travel and jetlag, only two hours later. Customs had been delay after delay, and then my driver had been caught in the last of evening rush hour. I dropped my bags in the foyer, assuring myself I would unpack later, snagged a bottle of water and a sleep aid and fell into a deep sleep.

"Sir."

I felt a gentle push on my shoulder, but ignored it.

"Sir?" The voice was more insistent this time.

Another gentle push was ignored.

"Sir." The voice held a hint of annoyance under its professional calm.

The hand shoved my shoulder, and I slapped at it, annoyed. Annoyance shifted to fear when I found my wrist caught in a vice-like grip and yelped in pain.

"Hey, man, what the fu—"

"Your bacon, sir." He cut me off midswear, his hand still locked on my wrist.

There was a steely glint in his eyes that told me his professionalism only went so far.

"Jesus, man, give me a break. I'm not even awake yet."

"Your bacon, sir." This time it was said in a tone that brooked no arguments.

I twisted my wrist, trying to escape his grip, but he remained locked onto me.

"What time is it?"

"It is nearly nine o'clock in the morning for this location and the time for breakfast is nearly gone. Your bacon, sir." On the last repetition of his offer he dropped my wrist, flung the domed top off his tray and all but shoved the tray under my nose. The scent of orange, cloves and star anise wafted off his perfect black coat sleeve.

I locked glares with him, but took the bacon. Satisfied, he pulled the tray back from my face and replaced the dome.

"What happens if I don't eat this?" I asked, waving the slice.

"You will eat it, sir."

Feeling petulant and jetlagged, I responded, "I don't wanna."

His free hand shot out and grabbed my chin. The fingers of his white gloved hand curled just so and pried my jaw open.

"You will eat it, sir."

Horrified, I shoved the piece in my mouth and chewed. The bacon butler straightened as I chewed and the hand that had pried my unwilling jaw open smoothed his uniform.

"Every day?" I mumbled through the last crumbles.

"Yes, sir."

"No matter what?"

"Yes, sir."

"Crap," I said, and swallowed the last of the bacon.

He nodded politely, any hints of violence gone from his demeanor, and disappeared.

"Holy hell. Every day?" I asked my empty bedroom. I pondered my circumstances again. While no one would bat an eye at my assumed eccentricity, the little bacon butler had proven he was willing to use force to accomplish his daily duty. I worried what implications that had for my daily life.

The remainder of my week passed benignly. Each morning, no matter what time I rose, I woke to find my bacon butler waiting, tray in hand. Each time, I grudgingly ate the single slice before getting up and hurrying on with my day. The pause for bacon made me no later to work than usual.

I asked no more questions and didn't refuse his offer. He said nothing more than, "Your bacon, sir." And yet, there was an aura of expectation. Of waiting. From him or from me, I wasn't sure.

On Friday, my friends convinced me to try a new restaurant doing a soft opening. It was supposed to be a new, high-end French restaurant with a menu that caters to the very rich like ourselves. I knew it would be trouble when I walked in, because the odor of fish permeated even the seating area. I ignored my doubts about their quality and opted for a salad.

It was a terrible plan, because even the salad proved how little care they had for their food preparation and sanitation methods. By three in the morning, I was turning myself inside out with food poisoning.

My misery came in waves. First chills, then a stomach cramp, then sweating on my bathroom floor before the next round of nausea forced me to expel the tainted food. My misery compounded when I realized that in only a few hours, the fussy little bacon butler would be here insisting I consume his daily offering. Just the thought of eating bacon caused me to dry-heave.

As surely as the sun was rising outside the window of my bathroom, the bacon butler appeared. I gave him one miserable glance before the smell of his bacon had me gagging over the toilet.

"No, man. No. Not today," I said before he could doff the lid, one hand raised weakly as if to fend him off.

"Your bacon, sir." His tone was the same as always, but I caught the tiniest hint of sympathy in his face, the merest micro expression gone in a fleeting instance.

"No, please," I begged.

He raised his free hand in a gentle movement, but the threat he conveyed remained.

I took one ragged breath, choking down my nausea, and reached for the piece. As soon as my hand touched the bacon, my stomach quailed and I dry-heaved again. I looked up at the bacon butler. His expression remained unchanged.

Gagging, I stuffed the piece in my mouth. My stomach roiled and I dry-heaved as I chewed. I looked once more at the bacon butler, who simply nodded.

I swallowed, feeling each piece go down my raw throat, and my stomach started to cramp.

He nodded and disappeared as the slice came up again.

I'm sad to admit I laid on the cold tiles of my bathroom sobbing after that. But I had learned something valuable: as long as the slice went down, he would leave me alone, even if it came back up immediately.

Later that day, I laid in my bed recovering from my food poisoning and wanting to curse both the friends who had pulled me out and myself for ever having accepted a stupid wish from a stupid djinn. My mind worked through a week's worth of interactions, hoping for a loophole.

An hour and one more round of dry-heaving later, I came to three solid conclusions. First, the bacon butler always appeared in his uniform with the tray no matter where I was, including over the middle of the Mediterranean Sea on a passenger jet. Second, he always appeared at some sort of breakfast time and always before I ate anything else, so I quite literally broke my fast with the bacon. Third, I had to eat the whole piece of bacon, swallowing it all, even if it came back up immediately, and the butler seemed willing to use force to ensure I consumed his bacon.

Unfortunately, my conclusion led to more questions. What would happen if I stayed up late for a middle-of-the-night cheeseburger? Was there a time limit for how long between meals counted as a "fast"? What if I ate only half the bacon and refused the rest? Would he really use force or violence to ensure I ate the rest? The memory of his grip on my chin made me unwilling to test that question.

My final thought, if not really a conclusion, was that the little bacon butler rarely said anything other than, "Your bacon, sir." And if he did, it was only in response to a direct question or to wake me. The thought of this tiny but powerful little butler harming me to complete his task worried me, but perhaps I could engage him in conversation. I resolved to test his responses the next morning. I rarely set alarms for a Sunday morning, but before bed that night, I set the alarm for seven o'clock.

My alarm startled me awake right on time. I sat up and slapped it off, searching for my butler. To my shock, he wasn't there.

I scowled at my empty room. This prissy little man had been so deep into my personal space it was almost an affront for him not to be here now. I stomped to my bathroom to start my day. Twenty minutes later, showered and dressed, I found the bacon butler waiting in my kitchen, tray in hand.

"Where were you?" I asked before he could speak. I paused at the threshold.

"Your bacon, sir." He stood calmly in his perfectly polished uniform but something in his controlled expression hinted that he was annoyed by my question.

"You didn't wake me up this morning," I said. Then I realized I didn't ask a direct question. He also hadn't answered my first direct question. This plan wasn't working as I had hoped.

I walked to him, forcing myself to be calm, and took the bacon off his tray. Holding it without eating, I calmly asked, "Why didn't you wake me up today?"

"You seem imminently capable of rising with your alarm when not in an altered state of mind." He seemed to think this was enough of an answer.

"So," I tried to clarify, "you are not required to wake me?"

"No, sir."

"But if it looks like I won't eat before you 'breakfast' window ends, you will?"

"Yes, sir."

"What happens if I refuse?" I asked, and waved the piece I was holding.

He took a step towards me. It wasn't fast, but it was deliberate. He was so short that he didn't loom, but there was still an aura of menace in that single step.

"Okay, okay! I'm going to eat it, but you seem bound to stay until I do, so I'm getting my questions answered while I still hold you here."

That statement made him visibly agitated for the first time. He quivered and I couldn't tell if it was a shiver or him controlling his rage. The pungent smell of orange, cinnamon, and pepper wafted from him and stirred hazy memories of the souks.

"You don't like that." Damn it, not a question. "Are you bound to this service?"

"Yes, sir," he said through a clenched jaw.

I stepped back. This was the most emotion I had seen from him.

"Against your will?"

He frowned, but didn't answer.

I thought hard. The answer must be more complicated than a simple yes or no. His agitation made me decide to leave the rest of my questions for another day.

"Thank you, bacon butler," I said, and gave him a polite nod.

Once my piece was consumed, he gave me a polite nod in return and disappeared.

The next work week went smoothly as we seemed to settle into a routine. I set an alarm and he waited in my kitchen. I hadn't come up with any new ideas for loopholes, but I was at least satisfied that he would leave me alone as long as I was responsible and set my alarms.

I found that on top of avoiding having bacon shoved in my face, I enjoyed having time in the morning. I hadn't been late for work once and had a moment to savor my coffee before bolting out the door. On Friday, I even made the time to use my long-discarded French press. I sipped the coffee and smiled as I thought about the date I had planned that evening, the butler having departed my mind as soon as he left my kitchen.

My Friday night date went well. So well, in fact, I forgot to set an alarm and he appeared while I was engaged in the most harmonious of activities.

"Your bacon, sir."

My head whipped in his direction, and I swear I could detect a hint of a smirk on his prissy little face.

"Dude!" I yelled, but snatched the piece from the tray all the same.

I made no attempt to explain him to my date. I'm not sure I could have if I wanted to, and I got the distinct impression that she would not be returning for a second date. Fuming, I realized that like the plane, the bacon butler didn't seem to care where I was or who I was with. He would complete his daily task regardless.

I briefly contemplated living a celibate life to avoid this morning's embarrassment again. Ultimately, I decided that I would simply find a better way to handle this and dutifully set an alarm for Sunday morning. One might say I was finding personal growth and a sense of responsibility in my predicament.

On Sunday, I woke before my alarm and laid in bed, curious if he would remain in my kitchen. I lay waiting, scrolling through my phone, but didn't hear so much as the scuff of a wingtip shoe on my kitchen tile floor. A minute before my alarm was set to go off, I turned it off and padded to the kitchen in my pajamas. My bacon butler stood expectantly in the middle of the kitchen, as poised and polished as always.

"Bacon butler," I said by way of acknowledgement.

"Your bacon, sir," he said formally, and gave a little bow as he offered the silver tray. The little bow was, perhaps, a way to acknowledge me not only setting an alarm, but getting up before it went off and he had to force-feed me bacon in bed.

I took the piece and bit into it. As always, it was the perfect balance of crunchy and chewy, thick and meaty with a bit of salt.

"Excellent bacon, as always, bacon butler. Thank you."

"Thank you, sir," he said, and for the first time, he smiled.

I smiled in return. It was progress.

"I can't keep calling you 'bacon butler.' What should I call you?" I blurted out. "Do you have a name?"

"No, sir."

"You don't have a name? Wow." I held the last quarter of the slice of bacon in my hand.

He must not have felt the need to repeat himself and stayed silent, but I could see him eyeing the remaining bite of bacon.

"Sorry, I promise I'll finish. But you need a name. Bacon butler. Bee bee. Bob? How about Bob?"

"Very good, sir," he said reservedly, but I was rewarded with a second smile.

I smiled once more and popped the remaining bite in my mouth, dutifully chewing and gave him a thumbs-up. "Thanks, Bob!"

Bob gave a slight nod of acknowledgement and disappeared. The scent of cinnamon and honeyed lime hung in the air.

Progress.

I took personal responsibility for my alarms; Bob didn't force-feed me bacon. I act like a courteous person and thank him; he smiled in return. Damn, I had been kind of a dirtbag to Bob. I resolved to find ways to show my thanks and respect to the prissy and invasive little butler. I spent my week remembering to set my alarm so I could meet Bob in the kitchen rather than my bedroom. I even foreswore my evening drink or toke to ensure all my things were prepared for the morning. By Thursday, my CFO remarked on how focused I'd seemed this week.

"My trip to Morocco really helped, I guess," I told him with a little shrug.

On Friday night, I set my little breakfast nook for the next morning. My fridge was stocked with an assortment of prepared breakfast foods and I even remembered to set my coffee maker to start thirty minutes before my alarm. I planned to invite Bob to join me for breakfast. I couldn't imagine how frustrated he must be to cook a perfect slice of bacon and never eat it.

I gave the table one last glance before heading to bed. It was probably more effort than I had put into anticipating a date staying overnight. I realized I wasn't just being a dirtbag to Bob: I was more than a bit of a dirtbag to those around me. I gave my dates little thought beyond what I wanted from them. I was frequently late to work, frequently enough that family connections had saved me more than once. And I was being a dirtbag to myself. Clearly, I could do more than halfheartedly work, party, and screw around.

I decided to reach out to my date from the week prior, offer an apology, and beg for a redo. Perhaps a setup like the one I'd made tonight would encourage a third date. Once again, I was struck by how one silly wish gone awry had forced so much growth on me.

Nervous energy woke me well before my alarm, and I bounced out of bed to prepare the table. The coffeemaker hadn't started, and Bob had yet to appear. A swift glance at the clock on my stove told me I had a little time before I expected him to appear.

I snatched my prepared breakfast items and threw them haphazardly onto plates. My coffeemaker clicked on as I surveyed the sloppy effort and I decided to tidy it up while I waited on Bob and the coffee. A few minutes later, it wasn't a Michelin Star-level perfect plating, but it did show that I had put effort into the meal.

I poured the fresh coffee into the two coffee cups I'd set the night before. My cup was halfway to my lips when I wondered if drinking coffee would count as breaking my fast and put Bob in a bind. I set the cup back down.

"Your bacon, sir," Bob said quietly behind me.

"Good morning, Bob. May I offer you a cup of coffee?" It was a simple start, but perhaps I could entice him to stay for more.

"Your American coffee is very weak," he said bluntly.

Realization struck me hard.

The American accent is what had thrown me this whole time, I realized. Magic. Bound to service. Loved stronger coffee.

I smiled.

"Yes, Bob, I suppose a djinn would be more accustomed to Turkish-style coffee."

Bob gave me a very deep bow without so much as a wobble of his silver tray.

"Would you stay for breakfast?" I eyed him. "*Can* you stay for breakfast?"

"I'm afraid there is only so much I may accept from you, sir."

"And breakfast isn't one of those things?"

"No, sir." His smile was sad but accepting as he doffed the domed silver lid once more. "Your bacon, sir."

"You've really helped me, Bob," I told him as I reached for the bacon. "I've never had my life so on track."

Bob didn't say anything; only a small bow of his head acknowledged my statement.

I broke the piece in half. "I get that you can't accept breakfast, but can you have some of the bacon?"

Bob's face held no expression. "I do not think you understand what you are offering, sir."

I smiled at him, my hunch solidifying. "Bob, I think I do."

I held out half my slice of bacon.

Very slowly, his hand reached for the slice, as if he didn't believe I would let him have it.

"It has been a pleasure, Bob."

"Thank you, sir," Bob said, and ate his slice.

He gave me one final bow. The smell of sweet figs and cinnamon lingered as he disappeared for the last time, finally unbound from my silly wish.

A SOLDIER'S BARGAIN

BY STANLEY WHEELER

Francois Barbier pulled the black tricorn from his head. Leaning on his 1777 Charleville musket, he wiped his brow and looked toward the nearby desert hills studded with brush and briars.

"I see a dust cloud," said Andre Chauvin. "I'll wager it's more Ottoman warriors."

"Can we reach the hills before those devils catch us?" asked Jacques Wepierre.

"Only if our feet move faster than they have been," Andre said. "We must go before they see us. *Allons!*"

The three soldiers in blue coats with white collars and cuffs, lugging their muskets—the sixteen-inch bayonets of which slapped against their legs—ran across the barren ground toward the hope of sanctuary. They attained the slope and stopped to catch their breath.

"They've seen us," Andre said between gasps.

"Up there," Jacques said. "That may be a cave behind those bushes. We can get there before those devils reach us."

They scrambled up the hill, musket butts bouncing against the coarse ground and scraping through scattered briars and brambles. As heavy as the weapons were, the fugitives refused to abandon them; their lives might depend on the wood and metal burdens.

A dozen riders in billowing robes had broken from the main band and raced toward the fleeing French. They reached the slope as their prey dove behind a clump of brush. Their flintlock pistols barked and spat a flurry of lead into the bushes. Shouting with anticipation, they drew thin scimitars and urged their mounts up the hill.

The soldiers ducked into the darkness. Pistol balls ripped the brush and splatted against the rock.

"Fix bayonets and prepare for attack!" Andre commanded.

The three knelt with muskets extended from shoulders.

Shouts in a foreign tongue and the thump of hoofs mounting toward them preceded the view of sharpened steel crescents glittering in the late afternoon light.

"*Feu!*" Andre ordered.

The cave mouth belched flame and smoke.

Three Ottomans tumbled from their steeds. The other mounts trampled the brush as their riders developed a tremendous desire to be away from the hole bristling with steel. The Turks circled back for another try, slashing without effect at bayonets and stone cover. Realizing the futility of the effort, they withdrew, dismounted, and reloaded their pistols.

Francois dared to leave the cave and peer through the broken brush. "They're coming back," he said. "If they hold fire until they're upon us, we're dead men."

"The Ottomans never hold their fire. Every man shoots as soon as he has reloaded, whether he has a target or not. Reload," Andre said.

No sooner had he spoken than two shots ripped through the brush and smacked the stone above their heads.

"We'll hold our fire," Andre said. "They won't have any chance of hitting us from down there."

More shots spattered leaves and stone.

Francois pressed his back to the wall and stared into the darkness of the cave. The deep black became streaked like a wrinkled coat. The streaks shimmered like a distant mirage and became slits in the sable cloth.

"Jacques," Francois whispered, "look back there. What do you see?"

A ball zinged from the stone above the cave opening.

"The shadow—" Jacques stopped himself. "Light. There is light at the back of the cave."

"The battle is before us," Andre said. "Ready. They approach."

Francois glanced toward the enemy, but the wonder of the sudden light deep in the cave tugged at his mind and drew his eyes back. The slits of light expanded, and a shape beckoned him to the cave depths. *Is that a hand?*

A near report and movement of his tricorn startled him. He reacted by firing his musket at the shape rising from the trampled bush. The bright robes and the form they covered tumbled backward.

"Nice shot, Francois," Andre said. "He was hidden from my view until you shot him."

Francois dared another examination of the strange development within the cave. The slits had become one gauzy aperture extending nearly to the cave's walls. The bare shoulders of a beautiful girl with soft brown hair appeared for an instant before she was whisked away as though jerked by a cord.

Andre fired and another Turk fell beside the trampled bush. Jacques fired a moment later to drop another attacker.

Jacques said to Francois, "Did you see a girl? I saw a girl."

"*Oui*. I saw. She looked familiar."

"I thought so too."

"They will rush us now," Andre said. "Bayonets ready!"

"There's a light at the back of the cave. I saw a girl. I'm going to follow her," Francois said, retreating into the depths.

"I saw her too. I'm going with Francois."

"Wait! I need you," Andre said. "I can't fight them all!"

"Come with us. We'll die in this cave if we try to fight," Jacques said.

Francois was already advancing to the light.

Andre realized the futility of trying to face the enemies alone. He retreated behind Jacques, but his eyes never left the mouth of the cave. A few seconds later, three Ottomans rushed into the cave. They stood, wide-eyed and open mouthed at the entrance, stained teeth just visible through their black beards. They grabbed for one another as if in a drunken stupor and fell back from the opening.

Andre felt the strands of many spiderwebs clinging to his exposed skin. He passed into sunshine.

The hillside fell away. Barren of brush and grass, the coarse ground was marked by hoofs. On the valley floor below, a rider in black and white robes with a silver circlet about his black headscarf dragged a girl over the withers of an obsidian mare. The bare-shouldered girl fought the rider, but he heaved her aboard and sped up the brown valley on the glistening mount.

"Did you see that?" Francois asked. "He took the girl. She's French."

"How can you tell she's French?" Andre asked.

"I could tell too," Jacques said. "She looks familiar."

"*Oui!*" Francois said. "I'm certain that I know her."

"We must get away from here," Andre said. "If those Turks

find their way through the cave, we'll be killed. Let's follow the girl and the man in black."

"I concur," Francois said. "Follow the man in black, and don't get killed."

They descended rapidly to a dry streambed and hurried along the rutted path scattered with round pebbles and broken slabs of tawny stone.

"I miss the orange groves of Jaffa," Jacques said.

"And the plague house, as well?" Andre asked.

"Bonaparte took me by the hand and told me I would live. He said my case was not the plague. He was right. I live."

"I do not miss the executions," Francois said.

"Don't speak of it," Jacques whispered. "We had no choice. We had no food for the Jaffa garrison. They surrendered, but we fought the same soldiers before at El Arish. If we let them go again, we would have to fight them at Acre as well."

"Not us," Andre said. "I think we three shall never see Acre."

Each glance behind them revealed no sign of pursuing Ottomans. Ahead, a stream cascaded down a fall—a veil shrouded in mist—to flow into the valley. Green grass and a pool of clear water invited them forward.

"It's like the stream that flows through our farm," Francois said.

"I laid beside such a pool with a girl from Nancy not many years ago," Jacques added. "Her name was Muriel."

Andre felt himself drawn to the water by more than thirst.

A gauzy haze separated them from the pool and the greenery. An orange tree, its emerald boughs laden with fruit, stood near the pool. Francois and Jacques ran through the haze into the oasis. Jacques dropped his musket and raced into the pool. Francois' musket fell as he took an orange in both hands. Andre came behind. As he stepped onto the grass, the haze vanished, and the oasis shimmered in the caress of the setting sun.

They drank and ate, taking a little stale bread from their packs to accompany the juicy gifts of the tree.

"Now, we must find the girl," Francois said.

"Now, we must sleep," Jacques said.

They both yawned; Andre joined them.

They awoke to the rising of the sun. Dawn's pink fingers stroked the leaves and grass even as her lips kissed the pool. After eating the last of their bread with more oranges, the soldiers followed the stream through a rocky defile.

Jacques spotted hoofprints in a sandy bend.

"We're on the warrior's trail. There's no way out of this narrow canyon. We must come upon him soon."

"*Morbleu*, Jacques, you can't see beyond the next bend. There could be an entire city a quarter mile away and you wouldn't see it," Francois remarked.

"Well, we're on the right track," Jacques muttered.

"This girl. Of whom did she remind you?" Andre asked.

"Muriel, I suppose," Jacques said with a sigh.

"Sylvie, I think," Francois said. "We met in Compiegne at the Tour Jeanne d'Arc."

"For a moment, she made me think of my wife," Andre said. "I know it isn't her, yet the similarity whispers to me."

"We must rescue her," Francois said.

They hurried on with muskets loaded and bayonets fixed.

The defile walls retreated, and a gentle plain spread before them at the confluence of three streams. Francois peered ahead and wiped his eyes. Gray-brown walls rose from the plain. Orange and fig trees adorned the way to the town. Colorful cloth flashed within the broad gateway.

"They will kill us if we try to enter, *n'est-ce pas?*" Jacques said.

"I will go and find out," Francois said. "The girl, she must be there. If we are to save her, we must enter."

"*Attends*, Francois," Andre said. "We will wait and watch."

"While the girl is ravaged and killed?"

"Francois is right. We must do something now," Jacques said.

"*Bon, vas-y*, but remember Bonaparte's messengers to Jaffa. Their heads—"

"Spiked on the city gate and their bodies hurled from the walls," Jacques said softly.

Francois removed his pack, jacket, and hat. "Bring these with my musket if my body and head maintain their happy union."

"They could impale you whole before the gate," Jacques warned.

"You have my permission to do as you think best in that case."

Francois marched toward the gate, and a light breeze laced with the fragrance of oranges and figs beckoned him onward until a woman with dark hair streaming from beneath her scarf stepped from the gate to approach him.

Her almond eyes flickered with light. The thin veil failed to hide her lovely mouth and fine lips.

"*Bienvenu, voyageur*," she said with hands lowered and palms open. "Bid your friends welcome as well. All are invited to Lutin and its market," she said in voice that touched the ear like oranges to the tongue and roses to the nose.

Francois stepped back. "You speak French?"

"Of course. We receive all nations here. I know many tongues. Come inside. You will find refreshment and rest."

"We will not be hanged? Beheaded? Impaled?"

She provided a negative to each of his inquiries.

"We may keep our possessions, even our muskets?"

"You may bring all that you possess. Nothing will be taken from you against your will."

Francois waved his comrades forward and waited for them to hurry up beside him. Andre and Jacques stared at the girl until she moved through the gateway, motioning them into the avenue. She pushed them forward between walls of mud and stone.

Alleys broke left and right, but the way led to a great square filled with many booths shaded beneath strips of brightly colored cloth staggered at different heights overhead to allow light and air into the busy market. The stone walls of a fortress within the town rose on their left. Several openings broke the sides of the square.

"I forgot to ask her about the French girl," Francois said.

"Ask about the rider in black. He must be someone well-known in this place," Andre said.

"I'll wager he took her there." Jacques pointed to the fortress.

"No. I see her," Francois said.

He jerked his head toward a fluttering veil of fabric, behind which the feet, shoulders, and heads of four women were visible. The French girl stood at the end of the line with her head bowed and eyes cast down. The other three maids, all enchanting, failed to rival her loveliness.

"Some emir will add to his harem today," Andre said.

Francois marched, blind to the many booths, vivid colors, and buzzing voices about him. When he and his comrades were nearly to the fabric barrier, the man in black robes stepped in front of them.

"Back, Infidels! None may approach my goods but those with the gold to make a purchase. Deserters like yourselves have neither honor nor gold." He drew a scimitar, punctuating his statement with the flash of steel.

"*Morbleu*, that girl is French. She's not your property. We're taking her with us." Francois brought his musket to bear on the Arab.

From behind a rack of grilled goat heads stepped a barrel of a man with two pistols cocked. He spoke in Arabic. A bearded figure in a knee-length hauberk turned from a booth selling fruit, bearing a longsword in his hands.

"He bids thee lower thy weapon and sweeten thy tone, my friends," the bearded man translated. "This is the Lutin Souk. Nothing may be taken by force, but all is for sale or barter. If it is one of Rashid's maidens thou seekest, thou mayest present an offer, but all bargains are voluntary at the Lutin Souk."

"He has no right to that girl. She's not to be bought and sold like a goat," Jacques said.

"Thirty goats or a steed of best quality," Rashid said. "Have you goats, steed, or gold?"

Francois lowered his weapon. "We have these fine jackets and our packs," Francois said. "We offer these in trade."

Rashid gave a hollow, derisive laugh. "The former are ill-suited to this climate, and the latter are of inferior quality. They may be worth two goats—a dozen if you add your muskets to the bargain. Well short of the price she's worth. I thought about keeping her for myself, but the fair ones never last long. Her best hope is that the emir takes her. She may survive for years in his care if he doesn't weary of her. If Ibn Badr takes her, I give her two months, maybe less."

"Won't you consider releasing her to us?" Andre asked. "She is one of our people."

The hollow laugh returned. It ended when Rashid leaned close and spoke softly.

"You have neither gold nor goods that I desire. However, there is a horse for which I would trade your pale maiden along with any one of these other beauties. A beautiful woman may enchant a man for a time, but she eventually becomes a burden to him which he cannot abandon. An extraordinary horse remains a blessing and boon to a warrior every day of its life until it falls in battle. I would not hesitate to give two of these maidens-beyond-price for the remarkable bay stallion at the far corner of the souk. You can't see him from here, but you will know him when you see him. He, too, is destined for the emir if some fortunate warrior does not obtain him first."

"Thirty goats would be far easier to obtain," the man in the hauberk said.

"I will exchange her to you for that bay and on no other terms. Not even a hundred goats and thirty other horses would I take from you."

"By what right do you sell her at all?" Andre asked. "How did she become your property?"

Rashid stood with his hands on his hips. The light breeze tugged at the edges of his headscarf, and his dark eyes blazed above his neat mustache and beard. "By the right of conquest. By my cunning, my sharp sword, and my fast horse have I brought her here. Here she may only be taken from me according to my terms. Remember that, Infidels. *Allahu Akbar*."

The French knight stepped between them, gathering the French soldiers with his outstretched arms.

"*Mes amis*, thou thinkest, I deem it, to rescue yon damsel by cunning art or strength of steel applied with deft skill. Thou dost deceive thyselves with such notions. Thou wist not that such endeavors be forbidden and do yield the whirlwind to all who do sow thereof. If thou art earnest in thy quest to obtain her liberty, the way lies in obtaining Le Bayard for Rashid. For indeed, the noble steed seemeth me to be Rinaldo's fabled mount. Sheath thy steel. Naught may prosper in Lutin Souk save for transactions forged in free will. Beware and mark ye well, all such pacts be rigorously upheld without regard for aftereffects."

"Who are you, and why are you so attired?" Andre asked.

"*Henri* have I been called since before I came to the Holy Land. We all remain clad in the garments in which we didst arrive hither. Get thee to yon corner and make bargain for Le Bayard with Conrad, if indeed ye would court success in thine endeavor, lest the emir doth descend from his fortress and deprive thee of thy bargain."

Henri pushed them off before moving to a booth of dried herbs.

"He talks funny," Jacques said.

"He has a peculiar way, like everything about this place," Andre said.

"Let's find the horse. It sounds like this marketplace recognizes commerce and nothing but commerce," Francois said.

"Old Henri never did say what the problem with just taking her would be," Jacques noted.

"The whirlwind. He said it would bring the whirlwind," Francois snapped.

The soldiers moved through the lanes, passing among the booths, oblivious to the chatter in multiple tongues and the wafting fragrances of food, herbs, and spices, to reach the livestock area of the souk.

Sheep, goats, cattle, and horses spread across the entire end of the square. Near the corner, a great bay stallion stood apart from the other pens and stalls. A handsome, well-built man with a short dark beard and clad in chainmail with a small iron crown upon his head held the charger by a rope and halter. His green eyes evaluated the soldiers in silence.

"Are you Conrad, and will you part with the horse?" Francois inquired.

The green eyes continued to examine them.

"Are you some kind of king?" Jacques asked.

"I wear the crown for which I bargained but never received."

"You've got it now, haven't you? What are you king of?"

"I do wear it, and yet I have no kingdom. The emir will wish to possess this extraordinary horse. Me thinks ye cannot compete with him."

"Perhaps there's something you would like that the emir can't give you," Andre said. "Maybe we could obtain it for you in exchange for the horse."

The green eyes completed a quick interrogation of Andre. "The dust of thine arrival remaineth fresh upon thee, and yet thou thinkest to procure something beyond even the emir himself?"

"There's a French girl the emir's going to purchase if we don't get her first. Doesn't your oath of chivalry obligate you to help her?" Francois asked.

"Nothing bindeth me in this realm but the bargains I undertake. Only the emir may release me, and he would not do so even for this steed. It will mean nothing to him except to deprive other men of the ownership. He taketh no joy in the having, but findeth pleasure in the preventing of others. The maiden is lost to you."

"But what if she wasn't?" Andre asked. "What if we could deprive him of this horse and the maiden. Wouldn't that provide you with some measure of satisfaction?"

The steed raised its head and stamped one foot. Conrad stepped back and conferred with the beast.

"Thy words hold a promise I would not ignore. Nevertheless, I must demand a price commensurate with the animal's value. Thine appearance belies the fact that gold be a stranger to thee. Thou hast naught else of worth. Thy words hold promise, and yet the vessel that beareth them be barren."

"How do we fill it up?" Francois asked. "How can we get something to match the steed's value?"

"The Hall of Wagers." Conrad pointed to a low opening and a

stairway. "The old city upon which all ye see hath been constructed. Seek there for wherewith to bargain."

"How much?" Francois said. "How much for the horse?"

"Everything."

"Is that fifty gold coins, a hundred, five hundred?" Francois asked.

"Aught that thou may'st acquire."

"What if we don't acquire anything?"

"Welcome to the Lutin Souk," Conrad said.

They walked to the stairs. Torches splashed light within the darkness, and they descended to the lower marketplace of brown walls and flickering shadows.

"We'll need to know when the emir comes," Jacques said. "Shall I keep watch and return to warn you before he takes the girl?"

Neither soldier answered.

"Someone must do it," he said. "If he comes and takes the maid, our efforts are wasted, and she is lost."

"Go," Andre said.

Jacques mounted the stairs back to the vivid hues of the souk.

Francois and Andre passed through a short hall to a T, where an aged man with a lengthy gray beard sat at a table between two torches with two silver coins before him.

"Welcome to the Hall of Wagers. There are two silver dirhams before you. I take one and you take one." He paused his thickly accented speech to pick up a coin. "On this face is Saladin, seated on his throne. On the opposite side is written in Arabic script, 'The victorious king, righteousness of faith, Yusuf Ibn Ayyub.' I place my coin upon the table with my hand hiding the face. You take the other coin and do the same. Then we wager whether the hidden faces match."

"For what do we wager?" Francois asked.

"What have you to wager?"

"Our clothes and our muskets."

"Rubbish. I offer you one gold coin against each month of your life that you wager."

"What would you do with a month of our lives?" Andre asked.

"If you lose the wager, you must reside in Lutin, bargaining each day in the souk."

"You mean to say that if I wager a year of my life here at the souk, and win, I get 12 gold coins?" Francois asked.

"Verily, you understand."

"How long may we continue this game of coins and months?" Andre asked.

"Three times you may wager today at this table. Then you may leave or go to the left or right to wager at other tables."

"Can't we go left or right instead of wagering at this table?"

"You must wager here before you can proceed. If you come away from this table with coins, you proceed to the right. If you have no coins, proceed to the left."

"And what is to the left and right?" Andre asked.

"To the right, you may make more wagers with your coins. To your left, you will find wagers for something other than coins."

"I don't like it," Andre said. "We came to save a girl, not to pledge our lives in games of chance."

"Isn't that what soldiers do? We gamble our lives on the skill of our generals and the quality of our arms."

"We've left the ranks. We're no longer pieces on the gaming tables of kings."

"You may always leave without a wager," the old man said.

"I'll wager a year," Francois said, snatching a dirham.

"*Quelle folie!*" Andre warned.

"The coin has been taken up and the wager stated." The old

man took the other coin. He concealed it within his palms and placed it on the table.

Francois slapped the coin down, keeping his fingers over the face.

"The choice is yours."

"I say they match," Francois said.

"You owe twelve months in the Lutin Souk," the man said as the coins were revealed.

"Can he wager back the twelve months?" Andre asked.

"All wagers are final. Years may not be wagered for years. He may wager more years for more coins, but he owes one year at the souk."

A cacophony of voices and the report of a musket echoed from above.

Andre and Francois rushed up the stairs. The commotion came from the slave market, and they raced to find Rashid bathing the ground with his blood. Jacques' musket lay at his feet; the rotund man and the old knight held him by the arms.

"He refused to part with the girl," Jacques said. "It isn't right that he should sell her like a goat or a bolt of cloth."

"Thy friend and Rashid did possess a grave dissention of thought," Henri said. "Their words found utterance most vehement, even unto the passage of arms."

"He pulled his pistol, and I shot him," Jacques said.

"Would that I couldst have interceded to hinder thy friend's hasty deeds. I do lament my tardiness to action."

Rashid rose on both arms. He laughed, and blood spilled over his lips. He coughed and collapsed.

"That one has found release," Henri whispered.

A flurry of hoofs on the square and a stern voice broke the silence. Henri and the rotund man released Jacques.

"Rashid had five years remaining of his bargain. He honored

his word and his contracts. This one—" he pointed at Jacques "—has prevented him from completing his agreement. He shall serve the remainder of Rashid's bargained time."

"The emir," Henri whispered.

"Five years?" Andre said. "Can we buy him back?"

The emir, dressed in gold and white robes, sat atop his white Arabian. His dark eyes looked down a straight nose at the French soldiers. He stroked a gray and black beard with finger and thumb. A breeze played with the corner of his keffiyeh.

"You are already indebted for a year," he said to Francois.

"I'm not indebted," Andre countered.

"And you have no reason to be," Henri whispered.

The white steed shifted, and the emir nudged him forward to stand over Andre. "What could you offer for your friend?"

"I have nothing but the glory of my arms and the courage in my heart."

The emir laughed. "What glory and courage has a deserter?"

"We defeated a dozen Turks only yesterday. We didn't desert by choice. Circumstances forced us to flee when we were cut off from our comrades."

"You would return and win glory with your courageous heart?"

"We would. As would Jacques."

"If I'm to fulfill Rashid's time, I give my friends this girl," Jacques said.

He moved to the girl and pulled her toward his comrades. Tears tracked the dust on her cheeks. She glanced at the emir and bowed her head.

"Speak and be glad," Jacques said. "I give you your freedom."

She raised her bound hands to her throat, opened her mouth, and shook her head.

"She cannot be given," the emir said. "Perhaps she has

bargained away her voice in the Hall of Wagers. All bargains are for fair value. No gifts are given in the Lutin Souk."

"If she was Rashid's, she's mine, and I'll do with her as I please."

"You have not understood. You will take Rashid's place, but not yet. You have no authority. Even if you did, all bargains must be for fair value given."

"Then whose is she?" Jacques asked.

"I'll take her," a new voice said.

A tall man in dusty boots, a French hussar's blue breeches, a white blouse, and a light blue pelisse draped over one shoulder, along with a bicorne hat angled over his black locks, jingled the contents of a leather bag in one hand while the other stroked the butt of one of the pistols in his belt. Tarnished bracers covered his forearms.

"Ibn Badr," Henri whispered.

"I have fair value." He emphasized the words with the jingling of the bag's contents.

"We were to purchase the girl," Francois said. "We'll pay a fair price."

"But can you match my price?" Ibn Badr inquired.

"What's your bid?" the rotund man asked. "I am Hajib, the successor of Rashid."

He tossed the bag to Hajib, but Rashid's successor missed it. The bag clinked against the ground, silver coins spilling from the open mouth.

"Is that your final bid?" the emir asked.

"It's more than enough for a pale wench who can't speak."

"Some would say that makes her even more valuable," the emir said.

Hajib scooped up the bag and coins. He dumped it into his hand.

"Thirty pieces of silver. It is more than enough."

"I bid twelve pieces of gold," Francois said.

"Nearly thrice Ibn Badr's bid, but you have it not," Hajib said.

"I can yet get it."

"I have my money now. I'm ready to make the purchase."

"Ibn Badr," the emir said.

"O Most Noble Emir," the hussaresque bandit answered, "*Assalaamu alaikum.*"

"*Wa alaikum salaam.* Your vendor wishes to entertain a higher price. It is his right. I may consider entering the bidding. Let the newcomer seek his means in the Hall of Wagers while I consider my own interest in the matter."

Ibn Badr made a slight bow, bringing fingertips to his forehead as he did so. "As you wish, Emir."

"When the trump sounds, I shall return," the emir said, nodding to Hajib.

The rotund one grabbed an hourglass and turned it on the table. "All bidding is paused for the space of one hour."

"You have one hour," the emir said to the French soldiers.

"Go, if thou must," Henri said. "Wager nothing thou art not willing to lose. Once lost, it cannot be regained."

Francois and Andre hurried back to the stairway and down to the old man at the table.

"I can't believe she has no voice," Francois said. "I know her voice must be like sweet music."

"Perhaps it was. I wonder how long it is lost to her. Perhaps you can hear it when the time wagered has expired."

"You have returned," said the old man at the table. "I am sorry. I can make no more wagers today."

"What?" Francois said. "I need twelve gold coins. I would wager another year."

"So sorry. This wagering table is closed for the day. You may come back tomorrow."

"How do I get twelve gold pieces?"

"To the right or to the left. As you have no gold pieces, you must go to the left. Make such wagers as you will."

Francois and Andre looked toward the opening at the left. When they looked back, man and table were gone.

"We seem to be out of options," Francois said.

"You do not need to do this."

"What choice do I have? I've already given a year for nothing. I may as well redeem my loss somehow. The girl needs our help— my help. Your wife needs you to return to her. You must remain free and unindebted to this place. Promise me you'll not wager anything."

"I was going to wager at the table for a year. What is a year when one is a soldier?"

Francois leaned his musket against the ancient stone wall. He removed his jacket and tricorn, stripping down to his breeches and blouse. "You must not. I am indebted. You must remain free. Someone must take her away from here if I cannot leave after paying the price."

They passed through the opening and via a short passage into another torchlit chamber. Two tables with standing attendants faced each other.

"You have come on a long journey, and you have no money," said a small bald man from the far east. "Come, let us wager together." He tumbled a gold coin across his fingers.

"This way, my friends," said a tall, bald black man at the opposite wall. "Wager at my table. Every wager wins."

"Every wager wins?" Francois said.

"You may win; I may win. Someone always wins."

"What do you wager? Where is your coin?" Andre asked.

A coin appeared in his hand. He held the glistening coin against his dark cheek, next to his bright white teeth. "One day of your life for one gold coin is the wager."

"This is much better than the man at the stairs. He required a whole month for a coin."

"He required the wager of a month at the Lutin Souk for each coin. I require one day from your lifespan."

"If I lose the wager, I die a day earlier?"

"It is as you say."

"Let's see what the other table offers," Andre whispered.

"Honorable wagerers, I do not ask for any time. At this table, you wager something small, insignificant. Should you lose, you won't even miss it."

"I think this is better," Francois said. "What is so small that I won't miss it?"

"The most trifling and inconsequential of things, I assure you. I am Feng."

They waited, expecting the man to name the trifling thing. When he did not, they approached the table. Two white cubes cast tiny shadows in the torchlight.

"Take up the dice and make a throw. If the dice total seven, you win the wager. If the dice total something else, you lose."

"What do I lose?"

"That's only a one in six chance to win," Andre whispered.

"What do I lose?" Francois repeated.

"A memory. A trifling thing."

"Can I wager for more than one coin at a time?"

"A fearless bettor," Feng said. "I may offer you three coins for three memories."

"Which memories?"

"That is for you to choose. State the memories and roll the dice. It is that simple."

Francois took the dice in hand, shaking them as he spoke. "The slaughter of the Jaffa garrison, the plague deaths at Jaffa, and the wound I received at the pyramids."

He rolled the dice, bouncing the stone cubes over the dark wood. Five and Two.

"Seven. Well done." Feng stacked three coins beside the dice.

Francois took up the dice again. "The same." He shook his hand, the dice clicking with the motion.

"Not so," Feng said. "You have already wagered those memories. To wager again, you must select new memories."

"But he won," Andre said. "He still has those memories to wager."

"Memories, once wagered, pass from the reach of chance at this table. He retains those memories, but they cannot be offered again."

"*Morbleu*! I don't like this," Andre said. "There's something unfair in all these wagers."

"*Ca va.*" He waved off Andre's concern. "I have three gold coins already. The death of Robert before Mount Tabor, Lucien's sickness and death in Cairo, and the time the goat butted me in the face when I was four."

Feng nodded, and Francois cast the dice. Four and Three.

"Fortune favors you." Feng added another stack of three coins. "You may cast the dice one last time at this table."

"The odds are against you." Andre said.

"I've already won twice. I have half the coins needed. I'll throw again." He took up the dice. "The drowning death of my sister, Patrice; the death of my father when the horse kicked him, and the death of my mother in her bed. No. Wait. Not the death of my mother. I cherish it."

"The wager has been spoken and may not be recalled. Cast the dice."

Francois sighed and released the stone cubes. Five and four.

"Nine. A valiant attempt." Feng took the dice and backed away from the table

Francois swayed in place. After a moment, he asked, "Is there another room?"

"There is," the black man answered. "After you wager at my table, you may try your luck at the next room."

Feng nodded.

"I must wager a day of my life before I can go beyond?"

"Come. I am Koloda. Take up the dice," he gestured to four pyramid-shaped pieces. Each piece had two black corners and two white corners. "Cast the dice. If more white corners show at the peak of each pyramid than black corners, you get a gold coin. If more black peaks show than white, I win one day of your life. If the black and white peaks are equal, the bet is doubled, and you must cast them again."

"That looks dangerous. The doubling could lead to the loss of many days," Andre warned.

"Or the gain of many gold pieces," Koloda countered.

"I'm committed now. I have no choice." Francois shook the pointed pieces and cast them on the table.

"Two white and two black. The wager is doubled," Koloda smiled. "Two days or two coins."

Francois repeated the roll with the same result.

"The wager is doubled. Four days against four dinars."

Francois shook the four pyramids vigorously. The objects rattled until he gripped and then released them in a toss.

"The wager is doubled. Eight days against eight dinars. You bring me joy. You are a true gambler."

"I knew it," Andre said. "These games aren't—"

"*Ca suffit!*" Francois snapped. "I'm committed."

He gathered the dice. Shaking them with both hands, he expelled them to the table.

"Such luck. Three white tips to one black." Koloda presented eight gold coins. "Fortune hides its face from me, but embraces you like a son."

Francois gave all the coins to Andre. "Hold these for me."

Andre wrapped twelve coins in a cloth he had inside his jacket, shoving the other two into his cartridge pouch. "Well done. My fears were unfounded." He paused. "Tell me, how did your mother die?"

"What makes you think she's dead? She was ill. She's probably recovered now. My father and sister will see after her needs. You should meet my sister. You would like her."

"Of course. Let's get to the market. You have a fortune here. You will use it to buy the girl?"

"That's what I came for. I owe a year to the market, and I've risked several days of my life. I will see it through."

Francois gathered his clothing and equipment, and the two soldiers moved to the stairs. Ibn Badr stood at the top, pistols drawn.

"I'll take those gold coins."

"Nothing can be taken by force in the Lutin Souk," Andre said.

"You wish to serve my time in the souk?" Francois asked.

"You're not in the souk. You're in the Hall of Wagers. I'll wager all your gold that you can't dodge my pistol balls."

The soldiers lifted their muskets. Ibn Badr extended his pistols. Two shadows surged into the light above. The pistols fired as Ibn Badr tumbled down the stairs. The pistol balls smacked the stone floor and ricocheted to the wall behind. Ibn Badr rolled to find himself facing the deadly end of two bayonets.

"I prithee, accept my humble incriminations," Conrad said.

"Le Bayard did startle and caught me unaware. Did the fall bring thee injury?"

"He's fine," Andre said. "He's lucky."

Ibn Badr snatched his fallen bicorne and raced up the stairs. The Frenchmen followed after.

"We only have enough for the girl," Francois told Conrad.

"How much—"

The Frenchmen didn't hear the question as a trump sounded in the market.

"The bidding reopens for the girl," Francois said, racing to the souk with Andre at his heels.

The emir stood in his white and gold robes, scimitar resting on his shoulder. His eyes examined the girl Hajib held by bound wrists. Her eyes were dry, but the tear tracks remained. Ibn Badr stood with arms folded and chin high. Jacques remained nearby but without any weapons. Henri stepped next to Francois. Conrad and Le Bayard approached to within a few yards.

"Have you the substance of your bid?" Hajib asked Francois.

Andre handed Francois the wrapped coins, which Francois revealed and held in his palm.

"I have twelve gold dinars offered for this maid. Are there any other bidders?" Hajib asked.

All eyes looked to the emir.

He placed the point of his sword near the toe of his boot. "She is a remarkable beauty who would bring a grace I find lacking in my palace at present. I bid twenty gold dinars."

"Emir—" Francois started.

"No argument. It is gold that speaks here, unless you have something more to bid?"

"O Emir," Conrad said, "I have here the greatest horse in all Christendom. I have struck a bargain with this man for Le Bayard.

72

Perhaps he would trade you this horse for the girl and three fair horses from your stables with pistols and saddles."

"What—" Francois began.

"Silence. I beseech thee," Henri said, clutching Francois' elbow.

Ibn Badr fumed. His hands formed fists at his sides.

The emir brought the scimitar to his shoulder and approached the girl. He scrutinized her before moving to Conrad and Le Bayard.

"This is the finest animal I have ever seen. You have a bargain with this one for it? For fair value?" The emir waved toward Francois.

"Indeed, Most Noble Emir. We were concluding the bargain when the trump sounded."

"You would make the trade of this horse for the girl with horses, equipment, and pistols?"

Francois swallowed. "It is as the noble Conrad says."

"So be it. First, let me see the bargain made for this finest of all horses."

"Wilt thou bring the horses and equipment immediately?" Conrad asked.

The emir clapped his hands twice and a servant boy a few paces to his rear dashed away. "It happens as we speak."

"All thou hast, as set forth previously in the terms of our bargain," Conrad said to Francois.

Francois handed him the twelve dinars. He passed over his musket and cartridge pouch, and stripped off his coat and tricorn.

"Don't forget these," Andre said, passing over the two other coins from his cartridge box.

Conrad passed Le Bayard's rope to Francois.

"This is a mockery!" Ibn Badr shouted. "This is not a bargain for value."

"It be aught that he hath of value. We struck this bargain for aught that he could perchance obtain in the Hall of Wagers. He hath added thereto as surplusage of his goodwill certain of his accoutrements. Pursuant to the rules of the souk, this be a bargain fair and seemly."

Everyone turned to the emir, who held his blade horizontally across his midsection with the blade away from him. "A bargain, unlike my scimitar, is a sword of two edges. It cuts both ways with unforeseen swiftness. Sometimes one gets the better result, and sometimes one does not. I am satisfied with my bargain."

THEY RODE PAST THE OASIS AND THROUGH THE STRANGE HAZE. THEY reached Bonaparte's army before Manon regained her voice. She had simply lost her voice and had never been to the Hall of Wagers. She went to France with Francois, living on his family farm, which a cousin had occupied in his absence. Francois never understood why his parents and sister were not waiting at the farm.

Jacques perished in the snows of Russia. Francois and Andre marched to Moscow and back to Paris again. They fought at Waterloo as lieutenant and captain, respectively. Andre rode to share the sad news of Francois' death on the field with Manon and her children.

"He has gone to serve his year in the Lutin Souk," she said between sobs. "I owe my life and all my happiness to him and to you."

Francois stepped into the souk, removing his shako with the officer's gold braid. He was without a musket, but he had his pistol and sword.

"Welcome, Francois," said the veiled maid at the gate. "We've been expecting you. Everything is as you remember."

"*Bonjour*, Francois," Jacques cried at his approach. "You must visit the Hall of Wagers. Guard your coins and make good bargains, and you will extend your time but little. Conrad and Henri will want to greet you as well. I am a slow learner, and have added two years to my time here. You will do better. Tell me—I must know—did the Emperor escape Russia? In what battle did you fall?"

"That's a long story, my friend, and it appears we shall have plenty of time to discuss it."

A THIEF'S LUCK

BY DEAN STONE

Raen had never gotten used to the Other Market. He could accept the existence of the Many Worlds, in an abstract sense. When the trade caravans passed by his estate in Aelun, bearing strange goods and stranger people, it made no difference to him whether they came from another continent or another world. He would ride into the capital every so often to see what the traders had brought in. When he bought a trinket for his wife, Sella, he only cared whether she would like it, not from which world it came or how it had finally reached him.

The Other Market was something different. It was all of the Many Worlds, all at once, their richest and their poorest smashed together like a madman's idea of a marketplace. He had lived here for two years now, and it still bewildered him. The streets had no pattern he could discern, and they seemed to twist as he walked them, yet sooner or later he wound up where he wanted to go. The streets thronged with people, all clamoring for attention. The poor searched endlessly for the one opportunity that would reverse their fortunes. The rich worked just as hard to outstrip their peers in money, power, and prestige. Beings from a thousand worlds flocked to the Other Market, united by the one universal emotion: greed.

It made Raen's skin crawl.

He longed for his estate on Aelun. He missed the rows and rows of grapevines that his family had grown for generations. He longed to take his favorite slateback out for a ride, then return the lizard to the sunning stables for some well-earned rest. He wanted to see Sella in her emerald evening gown one more time, the gown he had given her when she agreed to marry him. He had been happy on Aelun.

All of that was gone now, sold at a discount. No matter how much he mourned the loss of his old life, he would sell it all again in a heartbeat; some things were worth more than money.

The tenement he lived in now wasn't so bad. True, the room he rented was smaller and shabbier than even the lowliest of servants' quarters back on Aelun, but he couldn't bring himself to hate it. Not when he passed urchins without a roof over their heads every day in the street.

The remnants of his old life were almost gone. Even after selling his estate at a loss, he still had been rich. Two years later, he was down to four chests of belongings. Still a small fortune, but much smaller than it once was. The rest had gone to his search.

Raen felt his heart quicken as he stared at Sella lying in bed. How fragile she looked, like a crushed flower. The illness had eaten her bit by bit: the color of her cheeks, the glint of her eye, the fat and muscle under her skin. She was little more than a corpse. These days, she slept more than she was awake. Raen would have hired someone to watch her while he was out searching, but he had to be frugal. Every coin counted. When he ran out of money, he ran out of hope.

Not after today. Two years of trawling every corner of the market until, at last, he had found it.

A knock came at the door. *That would be the porters.*

Raen limped to the door and let them in. "Keep quiet. My wife is sleeping."

Jorin grunted noncommittally and pushed past Raen. He was a short, gristly man—human or a close relative—and almost as laconic as his crew. They pushed into the room after him, crouching to fit through the doorway. Each one was a towering, hairless sculpture of muscle, with four arms and a ridge of horns down his spine. Raen did not know where they came from or what their true name was, but everyone in the Other Market called them brutes. The brutes didn't seem to mind. In fact, Raen had never seen them exhibit any trace of personality. He suspected they were constructs of some sort, bred or created to serve, but he had no knowledge of such things and no desire to ask.

Jorin held out a palm. Raen didn't need to be told twice. He handed over a purse of coins. "The other half on delivery, as agreed."

The short man gave another grunt. Not that it would have been hard for Jorin and the brutes to simply rob Raen, now that they were past the cheap wards he had purchased, but he had heard from half a dozen people that Jorin was trustworthy.

"Those four chests," Raen said, pointing to the last of his worldly belongings.

Jorin snapped his fingers, and two brutes went to pick them up, each one hefting two chests as if they were made of paper. The other brutes carried cudgels. They were here for security.

Raen limped over to his sleeping wife and leaned down to kiss her one last time. Her thin lips curved in a slight smile, but she did not wake. He grabbed his cane, the one his father had bought him after his accident so many years ago, and led Jorin and the brutes out of his meager apartment and onto the streets of Otherside.

No one had ever given Raen a straight answer about what the Other Market was. The people trying to make a living on its streets did not care, and the merchants and magi who might know had no reason to tell him. He had pieced together what he could, but there were still frustrating gaps in his understanding.

Raen knew the Other Market was a constructed place. Long ago, some gods or magi had worked powerful magic to sculpt a new world and place it at the crossroads of the Many Worlds, a world devoted to trade. The Other Market had direct gates to hundreds of worlds at least, and Raen privately suspected the true number was in the thousands. Even more could be reached by passing through the gates on other worlds, so that goods and people from the farthest reaches of the Many Worlds washed up here.

The magic that built this place still governed it, enshrined as the Thirteen Laws of the Market. Within the boundaries of the Other Market, certain rules applied to allow fair trade. Many types of magic did not work, placing the magi on an even footing with mere mortals. Theft and violence were next to impossible. The Market preferred its inhabitants mete out their own justice, but Raen had heard countless tales, each more unbelievable than the last, about the ill luck that would befall a thief. The milder ones involved the thief trapped in a labyrinth, wandering the empty back streets of the Market forever. Others were more graphic. All Raen knew for sure was that even the starving urchins were well-behaved.

That only applied to the Market proper, though. Otherside was lawless. It had started as a neighborhood, a place for magi to practice their magic while maintaining close access to the Market. Then the merchants had moved in, building lavish villas where the land was cheaper. Then it was only a matter of time before gangs followed, robbing those who were not rich or savvy enough to hire their own security. Now Otherside was a city in its own right, holding the overflow of the Market. Raen had quickly found it was the only place he could afford to live, at least if he didn't want to waste all of his fortune on lodging.

Hence the brutes' cudgels. Once inside the Market, Raen and his belongings would be safe. Until then, the brutes would discourage thieves.

Raen led the odd procession through the streets of Otherside. No one gave them any trouble, but he could feel eyes on him wherever he went. Gang lookouts stared hungrily and exchanged glances. Children came to beg but were scared off by a glare from Jorin or the stature of the brutes. Despite the protection, Raen felt vulnerable.

He breathed a sigh of relief when he crossed the invisible boundary of the Market proper. The uncomfortable slums of Otherside gave way to the bustling streets of the Market. Hawkers fought for the attention of passing shoppers. Vendor stalls packed with exotic goods spilled out into the streets. Here, poor farmers from across the Many Worlds could sell their wares next to the richest merchants, and no one would bat an eye. Here, the richest king or the wisest magus could brush up against a man who had come to spend his life's savings on a single spell.

Not so different from what Raen was doing, now that he thought about it.

Jorin seemed to relax as well as the familiar sounds of the Market engulfed him. His sunken eyes ceased their endless searching, and he shifted his attention to elbowing his way through the crowd. Behind him, the crowd parted naturally for the brutes.

"This way," Raen said, more to reassure himself than for

Jorin's benefit. He had been to this merchant twice, once for information and once to negotiate the deal. Today would be his final visit.

At long last, the stalls of Pyata the Merchant emerged from the chaos of the Market. Pyata had taken over an entire block and turned it into a private empire. Every stall in his domain sold something different, and each one had a crowd of people waiting in line to buy from it. A man in bone armor tested the heft of a blade. A magus wearing the anonymous Mask of the Traveler pored over a stack of books. A nobleman haggled with a blue-skinned demi-human woman over the price of elixirs, her rapid speech carrying over the din.

Jorin took point and shoved his way through the mass of people until he had reached one of the stalls, the one where the nobleman was failing to negotiate a discount for an elixir. The blue-skinned woman was tearing into him, her red eyes gleaming as she insulted the nobleman, his mother, his father, the stars under which he was born, and every miserable ancestor who had made him so stupid as to think she would accept such a pittance for such a prize of a potion. The whole time she was grinning from ear to ear, as though she lived to tear her impudent customers down to size.

Next to her, sweeping behind the table, was a plain human girl still a few years from adulthood. Raen called out to her. She looked around slowly, as if hoping he had been calling to someone else, then walked up to him. She curtsied.

"How can I help you, sir?"

"My name is Raen. I have an appointment with Pyata."

The girl thought for a moment, then tugged the sleeve of the blue-skinned woman.

"Excuse me, Chay?"

The woman paused in her tirade. "What-is-it-Teak?" Raen could barely make out the words, she talked so fast.

"There's a man here to see Pyata."

"Well-go-on-an'-take-him-then. Can't-you-see-I'm-helpin'-a-customer?"

The girl, Teak, bowed her head and gestured for Raen to follow her. Chay went back to cursing the pond scum whence the nobleman had spawned.

Teak led Raen around the side of the stall, to a narrow alley that gave access to the interior of Pyata's domain. Jorin and the brutes trailing behind, Raen followed her back into the maze of tents, buildings, and piles of goods that kept the stalls supplied and bustling. In the center of it all was a white tent as large and lavish as a king's bedroom. This was the heart of Pyata's operation, the place where he ran his business and met his most valuable customers.

The tent flap was open so Pyata could look out over his empire. Teak led them in and gave another curtsy.

"Raen to see you, sir."

Pyata lounged on a mound of cushions in the center of the tent, a pipe dangling from his lips. The cushions had been red during Raen's last visit. Now they were blue with gold trim. The carpets had been changed out as well. Raen had never seen finer furnishings in his entire life, and Pyata had enough of them to rotate through. Wealth beyond compare. It made Raen's four measly chests seem like nothing in comparison.

Pyata waved a hand at the girl. "Thank you, Teak. You may go."

She bowed her head and left.

"My daughter," Pyata said, although Raen did not see the resemblance. "I will make a fine merchant of her one day, but for now she works with her hands. I have always found labor to be the best teacher."

"Yes," Raen said without really meaning it. Pyata made him nervous. The man had a way of using his smile as a weapon. The merchant's green skin unnerved Raen as well. He had seen a handful of others with the same skin, all of them rich, powerful, and otherwise human. Raen did not know whether it was an illness or the mark of some shared origin, but none of the people he had met had any trace of kindness.

"You have brought what I asked?"

"All of it." Raen took out the second purse and handed it to Jorin. "Thank you for your service. That will be all." The short man hefted the purse and seemed satisfied by the contents. He tucked it away in a pocket, then snapped at his porters and pointed at a spot on the ground. The brutes set down the chests, then filed out of the tent with their master not far behind.

Raen and Pyata were alone.

"Show me," the merchant said.

Raen walked over to the chests and unlocked them one by one. Piles of gold coins, rare jewels, and a few other items of worth. The last of his savings. The dregs of his old life.

The merchant nodded. "Now strip."

"I beg your pardon?"

"Take your clothes off," Pyata said, as if talking to a horse. "Our agreed price was everything you own, save for one coin. That includes the clothes you are wearing."

"I want to see it first."

"After." Pyata met his gaze. "I haven't spent all this time just to cheat you. But I expect what is mine. All of it."

Raen sighed and began to disrobe. Two years ago, he would have found this an unacceptable humiliation. Now it barely mattered to him. He had meant it when he said he would give Pyata everything he owned.

"Put your clothes on the chests. There we go."

Raen did as he was asked. The cool air of the tent prickled his bare skin.

"The cane too."

Raen almost argued. The cane, with its wolf's head handle, was the last keepsake he had of his father. But at the end of the day, it was just a stick: nothing compared to what he was gaining.

He set the cane on the chests.

Pyata gave a slow clap and rose to his feet. "Well done. You are an honest man, Raen. That is a rarity in the Market. As a reward for your sacrifice, I have prepared new clothes for you. They are perhaps not as lavish as you are accustomed to, but I can hardly have one of my customers walking home naked."

Pyata handed Raen a set of brown, threadbare robes, handling them as delicately as the robes of a king. Raen eyed them with distaste. Back home, he would never have been caught dead in anything so pitiful. But he wasn't home, and he would endure worse for his prize.

He did not take them, however. If he'd learned one thing in the Market, it was never to take something without knowing its price.

"Free of charge," Pyata clarified. "Consider them a sweetener."

That was good enough for Raen. He took the robes and slipped them on. They were woven of something coarse, but Pyata was right: they were better than walking back naked.

"Now that the pleasantries are out of the way, let's get down to business."

Pyata turned to a small chest sitting on a low table near the mound of cushions. He fished a key out of his robes and unlocked the chest. Then he pricked his thumb on a needle and smeared the blood over a glyph carved on the side. The glyph began to glow a dull red. Finally, Pyata leaned down to a glyph on the other side and whispered a few words. The second glyph glowed green. At last, Pyata opened the lid and reached inside.

He pulled out the most beautiful object Raen had ever seen.

It was a small statue made of ivory, standing just over a foot tall and carved into the shape of a woman. She had the bearing of a goddess and probably was meant to be one. Pyata himself did not know the statue's origins, only what it could do. The name of the goddess was lost to the eons, but a fragment of her power still lingered on.

The goddess had four faces, one on each side of her head and each carved with a different expression. The one facing front wore a greedy sneer. The others were a joyful grin, a contented smile, and an expression that Raen could only describe as wrathful. She held a tablet in her hands.

The words carved into the tablet were familiar from Raen's last visit:

> *Luck if given,*
> *Health if bought,*
> *Wealth if stolen,*
> *Death if caught.*

Somehow, they were written in the script of his native Aelun, even though the statue looked like nothing he had ever seen there. Raen suspected it was magic, but whether it was the Market or the statue he could not say. The magic of the Market translated all spoken words, enabling the people of a thousand worlds to conduct their business, but Raen had never known the enchantment to extend to written ones.

"Is it all you hoped for?" Pyata asked, already knowing Raen's answer."

"It is beautiful. Does it work?"

"Exactly how I explained. I swear on the Laws. Now do we have a deal?"

Raen licked his lips. There was no turning back after this. If the statue worked, all of the pain, the suffering, and the loss would be worth it. If it failed, he would be out of options.

"Deal."

Pyata's smile could peel paint. "Excellent. Then take these, with my blessing." Pyata went to Raen's chests and fished out the coin he had promised to leave him. He handed it to Raen, then the statue itself.

Raen grasped the statue carefully. He felt the change right away.

For all of his adult life, Raen had walked with a limp. It had been the result of a stupid accident when he was a young man, racing his slateback lizard with his friends. Ever since, he had lived with the dull pain of a leg that had never set quite right. He had grown to ignore the pain, and even without a cane, he could hobble along well enough.

Now the pain was gone.

Raen smiled and took a few experimental steps around the tent. No limp. No pain. He was healed.

He looked down at the statue in his hands. She was smiling too; the greedy sneer of one face swapped with the tranquil smile of another. Raen laughed with joy. Its magic had cured him.

"I trust you are happy with your purchase?" Pyata purred.

"Ecstatic."

"It was a pleasure doing business with you. Travel home safely and give my regards to your wife."

❧

BEHIND THE TENT OF PYATA THE MERCHANT, NEXT TO THE PEEPHOLE HE had cut in the white fabric, Vigo turned to Misha and grinned. "She was right," he whispered. "Lyna was right."

Misha glanced around nervously. There was not a soul in sight, but he couldn't bring himself to relax like Vigo. Merchants did not take kindly to trespassers.

"Not so loud. The guards will hear."

Vigo got the look he always got when Misha said something stupid: one part anger and one part pity. "I know what I'm doing, Mish. I've been at this longer than you have."

Vigo was two years older than Misha, and he lorded it over him every chance he got. True, surviving to the age of fifteen was an accomplishment in Otherside, especially without the protection of a gang, but those two extra years didn't make Vigo a king.

Misha decided not to argue the point. This was the wrong place for it. Instead, he said, "So are we going through with it?"

Vigo blinked. "Of course. Lyna was right. Some rich bastard just bought something from Pyata for a fortune. Whatever it is, it's worth more than all the money he just paid for it, and it's small enough to carry. We'll follow him back to Otherside and take it there."

The younger boy chose his words carefully. This was a sore subject, and the last thing he wanted was to start an argument. "Are you sure you don't trust Lyna too much? How did she even know all this?"

Vigo scowled but kept his voice low. "What do you care? She has sources. She was right about everything. That's all that matters. Besides, she offered to take it off our hands for a fair price. All we have to do is snatch it and deliver it to her tonight, and then we'll be rich."

"If you say so." Lyna was too pretty a girl and too smooth a liar for Misha to trust her the way his companion did. He saw the way they looked at each other. Vigo was convinced he could have her someday; Lyna knew he was already hers.

Vigo turned back to the peephole in the tent. "Come on. He's leaving."

The duo crept around the tent, both of them looking in every direction for guards. Sneaking in here had been surprisingly easy. Lyna had suggested a route to take, a narrow passage between two stalls that hadn't been sealed off properly, and they had gotten in with no fuss. The trip out was almost as simple. Pyata's domain was almost a city unto itself, but the route Lyna had suggested was all but empty. If not for the Laws of the Market, Vigo and Misha could have walked away with whatever they liked. As it was, they left empty-handed.

For now.

Once they were out on the street, they hurried around the stalls until they spotted the rich man. He had changed clothes and hidden the statue in a small bag he held close to his body, but he was easy to pick out in the crowd. Instinctively, Vigo and Misha spread out, maintaining a fixed distance from each other and from their quarry.

Following people without being noticed was a skill one acquired quickly on the streets of Otherside. Vigo trailed the man on one side while Misha followed farther behind on the other. Every few blocks, they would change positions, always keeping each other in sight and never letting the man get too far ahead. Having two people helped avoid recognition, but the rich man never even looked back. Misha could almost hear what Vigo was thinking: "A man like that is too stupid to deserve such a treasure."

The bustle of the Other Market was too much to take in

consciously, so Misha let his instincts take over. He kept one eye out for threats and the other on the rich man. He did not worry about where he was going or how long it would take. That was a sure way to get lost on these streets. Instead, he let himself drift, feeling his way through the crowd and pausing when it felt right. The rich man was an easy target, but it never paid to get sloppy.

Before Misha knew it, they had crossed over to the streets of Otherside. The border was hard to pin down, but anyone who had crossed it enough times could feel the moment the Laws released their hold. There were more mundane cues: the abrupt cutoff of the nicer merchant stalls, the ramshackle housing that had sprung up over countless years, the wary looks among the pedestrians. But Misha always felt it in his spine.

Otherside was home, with all the danger and opportunity that entailed.

Vigo paused long enough to catch Misha's eye, then nodded. Both of the boys knew what to do. Now they were in a race against time. The longer they waited, the more likely one of the gang lookouts would notice their prize. Even if the rich man managed to avoid scrutiny, they couldn't afford to let him reach home, where he might have guards or wards that would complicate things. The thieves had to act as soon as an opportunity presented itself.

Misha focused on the layout of Otherside. The slums were not as fickle as the Market proper, and a little bit of planning here could give them exactly what they wanted. Misha settled on the closest spot for an ambush and broke off down a side street, picking up his pace as much as he could without drawing attention. He trusted Vigo to keep following their target. No doubt he had the same plan in mind.

Knowing these streets opened up routes unknown to outsiders. Misha cut through the rubble of a collapsed building, through its unoccupied neighbor, and out past a food stall where a brute was standing guard. He ducked down an alley, took a right turn—

—and came face-to-face with the rich man as he was walking down a narrow side street. For a moment, the man's eyes widened in surprise, and then he regained his composure. "Excuse me," he muttered with a polite bob of his head and tried to walk past Misha.

He stopped when he saw Misha's knife.

"Now wait a minute—" the rich man began.

Misha didn't bother with threats. He took a step towards his prey. The rich man clutched the bundle he was carrying even tighter and took a step backwards.

He screamed as Vigo's blade sliced into his side.

It wasn't a deep cut. Misha disliked violence, and even Vigo didn't like killing if he could help it. It was enough to startle the rich man, though, and that was enough of a distraction for Misha to snatch his bundle.

It was all over before the man could react. Misha yanked the bundle out of his hands and sprinted back the way he had come. Behind the man, Vigo raced to the opposite end of the street. The man shouted and chased after Misha, but he was too slow to catch him. The poor fool was running with a heavy limp.

Misha kept up his sprint for two blocks, just to put some distance between him and the man. Once he had broken line of sight, he slowed to a casual walk. Running was a good way to attract attention in Otherside. If he was lucky, he hadn't passed any of the lookouts. He caught a few people looking at him, but all of them turned back to their own business.

After a few more minutes, Misha was convinced no one was following him. He picked his way towards the rally point he had chosen with Vigo: a secluded spot that had once been the garden of a merchant's estate. The merchant died long ago, and squatters had taken over the mansion, but nobody had bothered to claim the garden. Out in an abandoned maze of dead, dry bushes, Vigo was waiting for him.

The older boy grinned as soon as he saw Misha. "You got it?"

Misha returned his grin. "Yup. Easy as sweets."

"So, open it up, and let's have a look." Vigo urged.

Misha reached into the bag and pulled out the ivory statue. He had only caught a glimpse of it back at Pyata's tent. Now he finally got a good look at the four-faced goddess. Her front face wore a sneering grin. In her hands was a tablet carved with a piece of verse.

Vigo jostled Misha for a better look. "What does it say?"

Misha read the inscription out loud. *"Luck if given, health if bought, wealth if stolen, death if caught."*

"Huh. I wonder what it means."

"I don't have the slightest idea." Misha frowned at the statue. "I swear it just got heavier."

"Your arms are just weak."

"No, I mean it. Feel this."

He handed the statue to Vigo. The older boy hefted it a few times, then frowned as well. "Something's rattling in there." He shook the statue, and now Misha heard it too, like a rock caught in a jar.

"Careful. You'll break it."

Vigo scowled. "You were the one running around with it. Imagine if you'd tripped."

Misha opened his mouth to argue, then thought better of it. "It wasn't doing that before. Do you think we broke it?"

Vigo felt around the base of the statue. "Wait, there's an opening here." He felt around inside for a moment, then pulled something out of the statue: a golden sphere two inches in diameter.

"What is that?" Misha asked.

Vigo stared at the sphere in wonder. "I think it might be solid gold. Feel that. It's heavy."

He handed it to Misha. Sure enough, it had the heft of gold. Misha took out his knife and pressed it into the metal. "Soft, too."

Vigo laughed out loud. "How's that for a thief's luck?"

Misha frowned. "Don't tempt the Market like that."

"You know the rules. Anything is fair game in Otherside."

"All the same, I wish you wouldn't." Misha looked at the bauble in his hand. "Besides, that can't be it, can it? That man paid Pyata way more than this for the statue."

"Maybe it's enchanted gold."

Misha rolled the sphere in his palm. Perfectly smooth, except where he had marked it. "No, I don't think so."

"Wait a minute." Vigo reached inside the base of the statue again and pulled out a second sphere, identical to the first. His eyes widened. "I think there's more." He reached in again and again, until between the two of them they were holding five perfect gold balls.

"It's not getting any lighter," Vigo said. "There's still something in there."

"Is it making these?"

"There's no way all of them fit inside the statue. It has to be magic."

"I wonder if it can make anything else."

As if the statue had heard him, Vigo reached inside and pulled out an emerald ring.

The boys shared a look.

"Magic, then," Vigo said.

"'*Wealth if stolen.*' Maybe it has to do with the rhyme."

"You think it's making us rich because we stole it? That doesn't make sense. Who would make a statue like that?"

Misha didn't think he wanted to know the answer to that question. "It creeps me out. Let's just get this thing to Lyna and go."

Vigo grinned. "Come on, don't you want to make some more money first?"

"If it's magic, I don't want anything to do with it. You said Lyna will give us a good price for it, right? So, let's just take that and not get greedy."

"You're never going to get rich with that attitude."

"But maybe I'll live to be old. Come *on*, Vigo."

Vigo opened his mouth to say something, but he never got a chance. From behind him came a feral roar, and something lunged at him through the bushes. Two arms wrapped around him and tried to wrestle the statue away.

Misha just had time to recognize the face of the rich man they had robbed before the man and Vigo fell to the ground in a tangle of limbs.

"Ow!" Vigo screamed as the man wrestled with him.

That snapped Misha out of his paralysis. He reared back and kicked Vigo's attacker hard in the head. Stunned, the man fell limp to the ground. Vigo scrambled to his feet, the statue in his hands, and stared down at the man.

"Where did he come from?" Vigo asked.

"I don't know. Are you hurt?"

"Just a little rattled. Except—" Vigo looked down at his hand. He was bleeding. "The statue bit me."

Misha felt a chill run down his spine, as if he knew what he would see before looking. The statue had changed faces. The wrathful one was facing front. Vigo's blood dribbled from its clenched teeth.

"Mish—" Vigo began. Then he started to convulse. He fell to the ground, the statue dropping to the dirt next to him, and shook like a doll in the hands of an angry child. His limbs bent in ways that pained Misha to look at. Bloody froth spilled from his mouth. His eyes rolled back into his head. Then he was still.

"Vig?" Misha asked, already knowing that it was too late. "Say something, Vigo." He knelt down next to his friend, but there was no breath on his lips and no pulse at his neck.

Vigo, his friend and protector, the boy who had been his sole companion for as long as he could remember, was dead.

Misha was alone in the world.

There was nothing he could do but cry.

It wasn't supposed to go like this.

That was the only thought that would fit in Raen's addled head. His head hurt from where he had been kicked. His side was still bleeding from the thief's knife. His limp had come back with a vengeance as soon as the statue left his hands. He hurt worse than he ever had before, and all that he could think was that he was supposed to be home by now.

Raen had found it. After two years of searching, he had finally found it, and he was going to cure Sella.

Slowly he came around. One of the thieves was lying on the ground, still. The other was kneeling over him, sobbing. Without their knives, they looked so young. Deadly, if they wanted to be, but they could have killed him easily if they had wanted to. So foolish of him to walk back alone. He should have kept Jorin's brutes with him a while longer.

Pyata had warned him that people would want to steal the

statue. That was why he had dismissed Jorin. That was why he had tried to sneak the statue home on his own.

How foolish.

Raen pushed himself upright. Everything hurt. He could still feel the pull that had drawn him here. It had guided him down one street after another until he had at last found the thieves in this dead garden. Even now, it drew his gaze to the statue where it rested in the dirt, its face angry and bloody. He wanted nothing more than to reach out and take it.

But that would be a risk. He was in no shape for another fight.

The surviving boy noticed him staring. Grief turned to anger on his face.

"What did you do?" he screamed.

"Please, you have to listen to me," Raen said. The words came out slurred, but the boy wasn't attacking him yet, so they must have been comprehensible. "I didn't mean for this to happen. It was the statue. It punished him."

Pyata had mentioned the statue would protect itself against thieves, but he had been vague on the details. Raen was beginning to understand. The statue only killed the thief when Raen caught him.

"He's dead!"

"I know. I'm sorry."

The surviving boy stared at him, and for a second Raen thought he was about to die. It would only take a few heartbeats for the thief to draw his knife and cut his throat. In the state Raen was in, he could not put up much of a fight.

Then the anger drained from the boy, replaced with a weary grief Raen knew all too well from the hours he had spent keeping watch over Sella's sickbed. Whether out of mercy or morality or plain exhaustion, the boy chose to spare his life.

"Thank you."

"Leave before I change my mind."

The voice was too young for such heavy words, but Raen could not leave just yet.

"Please, I need the statue back. My wife is dying. It's the only thing that can save her."

Raen could see the wheels turning in the boy's head. "How?"

"It gives health to its owner, but only if it is bought. I bought it from Pyata for my wife. I gave him everything I had, but he let me keep one coin to give to her, so she can buy the statue from me. As long as the money changes hands, it should work. And then she will be healthy again."

The boy was looking at his friend's body. "Then Vigo—"

"It's too late to save your friend. The dead can't buy from the living."

Despair washed over the boy again, but he choked it down. "You really gave away everything you had to save her?"

"Yes."

"Vigo was the only one who cared about me. He kept me from starving when I was too young to look out for myself. We shared everything we had. You can't trust anyone on these streets, but I could always count on Vigo."

The boy looked up at Raen. Fresh tears glistened in his eyes. "Take the statue."

"You mean it?"

"I never want to look at that cursed thing again. Go heal your wife."

"Thank you."

As Raen reached down to pick up the statue, he noticed that its face had changed again. This time it wore a smile of pure joy.

"They're late."

Lyna leaned back in her chair and drummed her heels against the floor. She had rented out the back room of this tavern for a bit of privacy, but now it looked like she had wasted her money.

From the shadows beside her, a voice said, "They are not coming."

Her companion dropped his veil. Lyna did not know what kind of enchantment he was using, but one moment she was sitting next to a blob of darkness, and the next, she saw the familiar features of Pyata the Merchant. Green fingers adorned with priceless rings reached into his robes and pulled out a pipe. He lit it and puffed something foul into the air.

With what he was paying her, he could smoke whatever he wanted.

"What makes you say that? I told them exactly what you said, and I know Vigo. He would never say no to an opportunity like this. They should have been here an hour ago."

"Vigo's dead."

"Oh." Lyna felt a pang of something close to regret. She had liked Vigo, in a way. In a world of schemers and planners, he had been refreshingly predictable. "He always had a thief's luck. And the others?"

Pyata shook his head. "Gone. My spies lost track of them in Otherside. I don't know where the other boy went. Raen returned home, took his wife, and disappeared."

"Lucky for them."

"Yes, I expect so."

Lyna eyed her companion. "Were you going to kill them? Vigo and Misha."

"Of course. No loose ends."

"Except me."

"Except you."

Lyna grinned lazily to mask the fear churning in the pit of her stomach. She knew she was too useful to throw away, but Pyata was a dangerous man. A schemer and a planner. She needed to stay on his good side for as long as possible. Once she had enough money saved up, she'd disappear. Preferably before she became a loose end to tie up.

"And the statue?" she asked.

"It will turn up again sooner or later. It never leaves the Market for long. When it surfaces again, I'll be ready for it." Pyata turned to look at her. His eyes glowed in the dim light.

"I never let go of something useful."

Lyna smiled, and her blood ran cold.

Need something for the mother-in-law this Christmas?

Consider **KELLY KADABRA'S SECOND HAND BROOMSTICKS!** Kelly's has everything from traditional besom style cobweb brooms, to more modern ergonomic nylon! Is she a country hag? How about a nice corn broom? Get mom something as bristly as she is and tell her where to park it! Right here at **KELLY KADABRA'S SECOND HAND BROOMSTICKS!**

THE UNEXPECTED GIFT

BY TED BEGLEY

There was a chill in the air as the old woman made her way through the crowded streets of Istanbul. She was attempting to get to the Kapalıçarşı, the souk in the Fatih district, without drawing unwanted attention. It was early in the day and she hoped to make her purchases and leave before the tourists from the various cruise ships arrived en masse. There would be thousands of them haggling with the merchants trying to buy authentic Middle Eastern souvenirs made in China, and boxes of Turkish delights from the candy stores that were so numerous they seemed to be spaced out every third shop.

The marketplace was ancient, originally constructed in 1455, making it over half a millennium old. The structure had been rebuilt many times over the centuries, mostly due to fires and earthquakes that had ravaged it, but it had survived. The latest renovation was finished in 1959, giving the more than three thousand shops within the unique status of being in the largest souk in the world under one roof. While most bazaars were open-air affairs, housed under awnings in narrow alleyways throughout the ancient cities of the Middle East, this one sported modern tile floors and white stucco ceilings, which reminded the visiting tourists of onion-domed minarets stenciled in ink blue patterns. The Grand Bazaar provided a shopping experience like none other in the entire world. Or at least, not in this world.

The crone made her way to the market's oldest entrance. It was a stone archway which had somehow survived all the disasters that had befallen the building over the centuries, and had even outlasted the Ottoman Empire. She ducked past the security guard and through the metal detector that guarded the entrance. But as she passed through the six-foot-thick arch, she made a sudden turn to her left and instead of bumping into a solid stone wall, she vanished through it, and by doing so pierced the veil between realms.

When she stepped into the Fae Kingdom, she was standing just inside the Ethereal Souk. Álfheimr, the Fae Realm, touched the human world at a number of points around the globe. At those locations, various marketplaces had emerged over time. This particular one was at an energy midpoint along a ley line between Carlisle, England and Mumbai, India. The market itself was located in the ancient city of Constantinople, the Fae king not being of a mind to change the city's name on his side of the barrier to conform to human sensibilities. If the city on the human side of the veil was still called Istanbul in five or six centuries, he might revisit the topic.

The old woman pulled back the hood of her cloak and reached behind her head to undo a silver chain which held an amulet around her neck. Once the clasp was open, the illusion spell broke and the visage of the old woman disappeared. In her place stood a somewhat shorter creature with the countenance of a gargoyle. The goblin put the amulet in his pocket, shook his hairy pointed ears, then scratched himself in a way which would have been unbecoming of an elderly woman. Snarlak was finally free to be himself again.

The goblin made his way through the maze of tents and kiosks to the booth of an Elven cobbler. The man sat on a padded stool in the center of his booth, surrounded by stacks of boxes which contained an assortment of shoes, boots, and slippers. He was currently re-soling a pair of English riding boots designed for a Fae dragon rider. As Snarlak approached, he looked up from his work and spit a mouthful of tacks into his hand. "Can I help you?"

Snarlak nodded. "My master..." he almost choked on the word, "has sent me to retrieve a pair of slippers that he has ordered for his granddaughter."

"And who is your master?" the cobbler inquired, as he stood up and put his hammer and tacks down on the counter.

"I am in the service of His Majesty, King Darach the Second, Ruler of All of Álfheimr." Then, with a sour expression on his face, Snarlak added, "And my personal benefactor."

"Oh! You're *that* goblin. The one who turned the King's grand-daughter into a rabbit." The cobbler chuckled to himself. "His Majesty has you serving as his personal valet for the next hundred years, doesn't he?"

Snarlak snarled. "It's only fifty years, and I've been in jail longer before. Now, do you have the shoes or don't you?"

The cobbler retrieved a box from a set of shelves at the side of his tent and placed it on the counter in front of the goblin. He removed the lid, exposing a pair of pink gossamer silk dancing slippers which shimmered iridescently. "You may tell His Majesty they were constructed just as he asked. They will always fit, they will give the wearer enhanced dancing ability, and as long as she leaves the shoes resting upon her dress for at least ten minutes before putting them on, they will match the color of the garment in question until midnight. But warn her not to put these slippers on paisley—we don't want to have one of *those* incidents again."

The cobbler laid the lid back on the box and tied it closed with a matching pink ribbon. Snarlak muttered a halfhearted thanks and picked up the package, tucked it under his left arm, then began trudging back toward the portal to Istanbul.

As he walked by the booths, a metallic object caught his attention out of the corner of his eye. Leaning against a stack of boxes toward the back of a booth of odd antiques—junk, really—was a solid brass hookah. Snarlak gawked at it, wide-eyed, when he realized how it was made. Whether by accident or intent, the water basin at the bottom of the hookah had been fashioned out of a brass bottle which had been used to trap a powerful djinn more than two thousand years ago. The only question was, did it still contain the genie?

Snarlak caught the eye of the proprietor and pointed to the hookah. "How much?"

The kobold who was running the little kiosk looked over its shoulder and furled its brow in thought. "Five drachma."

"I'll give you three," Snarlak told him while rummaging through his pockets.

The kobold shook its head. "Five."

Snarlak counted through his money. "Only if you can ship it."

The kobold scratched its knobby chin, then kicked the dirt with one of its bare feet. "Ship it where?"

Snarlak got half of a twisted grin on his face. "Carlisle, England, in the human world." He paused, then asked, "Can you ship there?"

The kobold thought for a moment, nodded, and shoved a pad and pencil over to the goblin. "Write down the address. The post office has a pickup on this side of the portal now."

Snarlak took the pencil and began writing: Peri Turner, 119 Castlerigg Drive, Carlisle, United Kingdom.

§❧

"It's a hookah." Peri Turner looked at the object which unexpectedly occupied the center of her coffee table, and was completely baffled as to why her father thought this was an appropriate gift. While it was true they hadn't spoken to each other for sixteen years, she thought he should know his own daughter better than that.

"I know what it is, dear," Beatrice told her daughter-in-law in a gentle tone. "I just don't know why it's here."

"That makes two of us." Peri crossed her arms and huffed.

"Maybe it's a mistake," Beatrice suggested. "What did the note say?"

Peri took out a little scroll that she had placed in the top bowl of the hookah and unfurled it. "I've missed far too many of Morgan's birthdays. Please give her this token of my affection. I had it picked out especially for her. Your mother and I look forward to seeing our granddaughter and your husband again tonight at dinner. Love, your father."

Beatrice looked at the note and then back at the brass monstrosity on the coffee table. "This has to be a mistake," she said decisively. "Maybe he intended it as a gift for Jacob."

Peri shook her head. "I don't know. Father has only met his son-in-law twice now and they barely spoke to each other. I would think it's a stretch to assume that someone you hardly know is a smoker. Especially since my father doesn't smoke, either."

"Well, Jacob did smoke a pipe in college, dear," Beatrice offered.

"He chewed on a pipe in college," Peri corrected. "I don't think I ever saw him light it. Considering how young he was when he began teaching, he thought the pipe made him look older and more intellectual. Some of his students were only two or three years younger than him."

"I see," Beatrice nodded. "Sort of in the same way that he thinks the beard he wears now makes him look more distinguished as a professor. Anyway, we can ask your parents tonight when they come for dinner."

"That's another thing," Peri said with exasperation. "Why do they think I invited them to dinner?"

"Well, you did give them an open invitation, dear," Beatrice reminded her. "It's been more than a month since he invited us to the palace to watch the Winter Guardian hand over the mantle of duty to the Summer Guardian on the equinox. By the way, that was such a lovely ceremony," Beatrice enthused, "but you did invite your parents to drop in any time, and today is a holiday."

"I realize it's a holiday," Peri replied. "But Saint George's Day just isn't something that we celebrate in Álfheimr. There must be something more to all of this."

Peri thought Beatrice was going to say something more on the topic, but it was then that the back door slammed. "Morgan? Is that you?" Peri called out to the kitchen.

"Yes." The single word reply came back practically dripping with sarcasm.

"Your grandmother is here. Come say hello," Peri prodded.

A very audible groan came from the other room.

Peri rolled her eyes and looked to the ceiling. Beatrice covered her mouth with her hand in an attempt to not laugh. Once she got her smile under control, Beatrice asked, "Are sullen teenagers something the Fae doesn't have to deal with?"

Peri turned and looked at Beatrice. What she saw in the

woman's face was a combination of concern, amusement, and affection. Peri couldn't help but give her a tired smile. Sixteen years earlier, when Peri Shikana, daughter to His Royal Highness King Darach the Second, had wandered through the stone arch from the Fae realm to the human world, Beatrice Turner was the first person she met. Rather than being surprised or shocked at seeing a six-foot-tall Fae with large, steel gray wings, Beatrice had looked at her kindly and said, "Dear, your wings are showing. Most people around here might not understand that." Then she had smiled that warm, friendly smile.

Peri had struck up a friendship with this kind woman, who always saw a new friend in everyone she met. It would be many years before she learned that Beatrice had often visited the faery market in her youth. The way Bea saw the world as a whole meant the Fae world had never been concealed from her in the first place. It was much later when Peri learned that Beatrice could see behind the hidden veils of individuals as easily as she could between worlds.

"Bea, what am I going to do with that child?" Peri lamented.

"Just give her time, dear," Beatrice said soothingly. "She will be fourteen years old in a few weeks. Morgan's going through a lot of changes right now. It's been a big year for her, after all. It's hard enough just going through puberty, let alone finding out you're half-mythical being at the same time." Beatrice followed up the last statement with a wink.

"I should have told her sooner," Peri admitted. "At least she's finally gotten to meet her other grandparents, and my father seems more accepting of the life choices I've made."

Her last declaration was punctuated by the sound of a door slamming further down the hallway. This time, it was Beatrice who sighed. "Why don't you find a suitable place to put your father's gift, and I'll go talk to Morgan?"

"Thank you, Bea." Peri smiled gratefully at her, then picked up the hookah to take it into the kitchen.

Beatrice walked down the hallway and knocked on Morgan's door. "Can I come in, sweetheart?"

"Whatever," came the muffled response from behind the door.

Beatrice opened the door to Morgan's room and walked in. She looked around the bedroom, which was decorated in typical teenage fashion: mismatched furniture, posters of popular heart-throbs, and clothes strewn around the room. What was not typical was Morgan standing next to her dresser, furiously working a wooden backscratcher down the collar of her jumper. "Are you okay, sweetheart?"

"No, I'm not okay," Morgan practically whimpered. "My back has been itching for a week and I can't get it to stop."

"Let's take a look and see."

Beatrice had her granddaughter turn around and lift up her jumper so she could examine her back. There was a palm-sized rash in the center, right between her shoulder blades. "Well, no wonder you've been prickly. That's a nasty-looking rash."

"Oh, I was afraid of something like that," Morgan whined. "What am I going to do?"

"The first thing we are going to do," Beatrice told her, "is get you out of that itchy jumper and into a nice, soft, cotton t-shirt. Then I'm going to rub calamine lotion on your rash and see if we can get that itching to stop."

A short time later, Morgan was facedown on her bed and sighing in relief. "Thank you, Grandmother. That feels so much better."

"You're welcome, dear. It's no wonder you've been in a bad mood lately."

"I have not been in a bad mood," she snapped. Then Morgan

turned to see the reproving look on her grandmother's face, and thoughtfully added, "Well, maybe I have been. Just a touch."

"Just a touch," Beatrice agreed. "Now, help me gather up all of your clothes." She gestured at the piles on the floor. "And we will wash them with hypoallergenic detergent just in case you're allergic to something. But if that rash doesn't get any better in a day or two, we are going to take you to the doctor."

"Yes, Nana." Morgan relented.

PERI SPENT THE REST OF THE AFTERNOON PREPARING THE HOUSE TO receive her parents. Morgan had even emerged from her room to help her mother with the task. Bea's conversation with her granddaughter had obviously mellowed the teen's mood. In the meantime, Beatrice had gone next door to cook for the evening's feast. It had been extremely convenient over the years that Peri's in-laws lived right next door. She had been worried at first about them living so close, but when they had offered to sell the newlyweds the other half of their semi-detached house—what the Americans and an increasing number of Brits called a duplex—they couldn't refuse the offer. While their family lived comfortably, you don't get rich on a professor's salary.

Peri needn't have worried; Beatrice and George had given the newlyweds their privacy. They had been so kind about it that eventually Peri and Jacob finally suggested taking down the fence that had divided their backyard gardens. This had become their family gathering space, complete with a large outdoor dining table, and it was where Peri planned on hosting tonight's dinner. To her amusement, George had hung several strands of fairy lights over the table. He had just smiled at her and told her it seemed appropriate for the occasion.

George was putting the last of the place settings around the table when Jacob came outside, lugging the big brass hookah, and placed it in the middle of the table as a centerpiece. He had detached the hoses so it looked more like a Persian urn than a hookah. Jacob ducked back inside and quickly returned with a piece of wax paper and a pair of scissors. He trimmed the paper to size and used it to cover the wide brass collar near the top of the hookah, then stacked a variety of Turkish delights on top of the wax paper. As a final touch, he placed three red carnations in the very center, where hot coals would normally go. He stepped back to admire his handiwork. "Voilà. Middle Eastern candy dish."

Beatrice emerged from her house carrying a tray of appetizers, looked at her son's handiwork, and shook her head in amusement. Peri, on the other hand, grimaced upon seeing it. "That thing is hideous. I still don't know what my father was thinking."

"It doesn't matter why he chose this gift." Jacob reached out and put his arm around his wife's shoulders. "The fact that he is opening up enough to even send a present is a positive step. Hopefully, this will lead to a better relationship with your family."

Peri turned her head to look into her husband's eyes. "My family is here, in this house."

Everyone continued with the final preparations, getting the garden ready to accept visitors. Peri performed a minor piece of magic that kept the patio at a pleasant room temperature, and the chill of the otherwise clear spring evening at bay. Now that Morgan knew about the other side of her family, Peri had begun using her magic again.

Everything was in place and ready for guests when the hall clock chimed six and the doorbell rang. Morgan rushed to the entry and opened the front door to see her grandparents, King Darach and Queen Faylinn. She curtseyed to them. "Welcome, Grandfather, Grandmother," she said, nodding to each in turn.

Queen Faylinn smiled brightly and opened her arms. "None of that. Come here, child," and embraced her granddaughter in a warm hug.

King Darach reached around and hugged both of them, placing his arm across Morgan's shoulder blades. The girl winced. "Is there something wrong, my child?" The king withdrew his hand.

"It's nothing," Morgan replied offhandedly. "Just a rash."

The king looked to his wife and smiled brightly, then down at Morgan. "I'm sure it will go away shortly. Try not to scratch."

Jacob and Peri watched the interaction from the living room. When King Darach looked up to meet his son-in-law's gaze, Jacob greeted them with, "Welcome to our home, Your Majesties. Please come in."

"Thank you, young man," the king replied approvingly, while the queen merely nodded and smiled warmly. As they cleared the threshold, they were followed by two others—a younger Fae woman with pale skin and raven hair who walked a few steps behind the queen, and bringing up the rear, the goblin Snarlak.

"Let me introduce you to my lady-in-waiting," Queen Faylinn said to Jacob and Peri. "This is Sabia." Then, looking down and further back, she added, "You already know Darach's valet."

"We've met." Peri's words came out as cold and sharp as icicles, causing Snarlak to shrink behind the women.

"So you have, daughter." Queen Faylinn smiled approvingly. "Sending Snarlak to your father as a rabbit was a nice touch. We decided to keep the creature where we could keep an eye on him. We expect that fifty years of service to the Crown will instill some manners."

Peri heard the capital "W" in that last statement. Queen Faylinn rarely spoke in her "Royal Voice," but when she did, it was significant. Whatever differences Peri might have with her parents, they were accepting of their granddaughter and were willing to extend their protection. For the first time in a very long time, Peri felt as if there may be a glimmer of hope that her husband and his family might be accepted by hers.

Peri escorted her parents into the garden where Beatrice and George were just setting out the last of the food. The table looked exquisite. Peri's mother-in-law had outdone herself with this meal. The dishes ranged from fish and chips to Lancashire hotpot, and many of Beatrice's specialties in between. She had even baked a Victoria sponge, complete with buttercream and strawberry jam filling. A royal feast, indeed.

Everyone took their assigned seats around the table. Beatrice had made the extra effort earlier in the day of inscribing hand-made place cards, showing off her beautiful calligraphy skills. Sabia and Snarlak were seated at a small bistro table off to the side, which Peri had set up in anticipation of her parents bringing at least one attendant each, even to a family dinner. If there was one thing to say about the king and queen, it was that they were consistent.

Once everyone was seated, King Darach cleared his throat. "I would like to thank you for inviting us to dinner." Peri raised an eyebrow, but did not interrupt as her father continued. "Faylinn and I hope this is the first of many such dinners."

"You're always welcome in our home, Your Majesties," Jacob told his in-laws. Turning to Peri, he added, "I think this calls for a toast."

She nodded in agreement, and Jacob stood up and went into the house. Moments later, he returned carrying a bottle of wine and a corkscrew. He uncorked the bottle and poured some of the white wine into everyone's glass, except for Morgan's, of course. Jacob then raised his glass and stated, "May our differences never be so great that we lose sight of the fact that we are family."

Everyone raised their glass to toast. Queen Faylinn poured a splash of her wine into the empty glass sitting next to Morgan.

"Mother," Peri said with mild reproach, "we don't give Morgan alcohol. You really should have asked."

Seeing the hurt expression on his wife's face, Darach interjected. "You mean like the way your husband asked me for your hand in marriage?"

"Daddy," Peri explained, "that's not fair."

"It's perfectly fair. He did not ask me for your hand in marriage. You were already married to this...this..." Darach extended his arm and gestured at Jacob with his hand palm up, "ephemeral...before I even knew of his existence."

Morgan leaned over and whispered to her Nana Bea, "What's an ephemeral?"

Bea put her lips close to Morgan's ear. "It means that your mother and her side of the family live a very long time, compared to your father's family."

"Sir, it was not my intention to offend you," Jacob offered.

"I don't know how it is with royalty on this side of the barrier, but in Álfheimr, it is customary for a suitor to ask the king's permission before proposing to the crown princess. And one simply does not elope with her." King Darach's words were loud and pointed. He drained the rest of the wine from his glass, then continued. "We didn't even get a birth announcement."

Snarlak jumped from his chair and rushed to refill the king's wine glass.

"Daddy, please," Peri started. "It's not Jacob's fault. He didn't know that I had parents."

"Do you mean to tell me that this simpleton thought you were hatched under a cabbage leaf?"

"Daddy, don't call Jacob names. I meant he didn't even know

you and mother were alive," Peri told her father as her face reddened.

"What do you mean he didn't know we were alive?" Faylinn interjected.

Peri sighed. "When we first started dating, Jacob didn't know I was Fae. When he asked about my parents, I told him I was all alone in *this* world. He assumed I meant that the two of you were dead. He didn't know what I was until after he proposed, when I told him everything. It would be wrong of me to accept his proposal unless he understood exactly what he was getting himself into. I didn't hold anything back, and I showed him my wings as proof. I told Jacob to ask me again once he'd had time to consider all of it, and what my being Fae might mean for our future. He thanked me for trusting him, gave me a kiss, then dropped down on one knee and asked me again right there. And I said yes." Peri looked over at Jacob, who smiled at her lovingly, and took her hand gently in his. She turned her attention back to her father. "So if you think it wasn't proper for Jacob to ask me without talking to you first, then I'm sorry, because I think it was the sweetest and most proper proposal ever."

"It sounds very romantic, dear," Faylinn admitted, "but it was definitely not a proper proposal for a royal. There are protocols to be followed, and your elopement was an embarrassment that we still deal with."

"We wouldn't have eloped if father had treated Jacob better," Peri retorted, the ire in her voice palpable. "He kept calling him 'that human,' as if a human were something terrible. Jacob is the kindest, sweetest, most thoughtful person I have ever known. He deserves to be treated better by my own parents."

Faylinn looked from her daughter to her husband with a pained expression. It was obvious she sympathized with both of them. "Maybe we shouldn't have come tonight, Darach. We seem to be opening old wounds."

"Nonsense," the king replied. "We've missed far too many of our grandchild's birthdays. We are not about to miss this one."

"Today isn't my birthday," Morgan told her grandfather. "It's two weeks from now."

"That's right," Darach agreed. "But it is the first day of the Fortnight of Festivities held as an annual celebration for a member of the royal family."

"We don't do the Fortnight of Festivities, Father." Peri was genuinely confused by her father's assumption. "We will have a party for Morgan on her birthday."

"Well, if this isn't for her birthday, what's the occasion?"

"This is the Feast of St. George, Your Majesty," Jacob told his father-in-law from the other end of the table. "It's an occasion my family has always observed."

"Saint George?" Darach stood abruptly and pounded his fist on the table, causing the wine glasses to jump slightly. "This is a celebration for that maniac?"

"Father, what are you talking about?" Peri was thoroughly confused.

Queen Faylinn sighed. "You were traveling with your grandmother at the time, Peri. While you were away, Dadianus got out of the castle and crossed the barrier into the human realm. He started eating goats, getting into mischief, and frightening the herdsmen. One thing led to another, and the villagers called upon this Saint George person to do something about him. We still aren't exactly certain how it happened, but he managed to kill Dadianus."

Peri turned to her father. "You told me Dadianus got loose in the mountains, and you couldn't find him to bring him home! You might as well have told me he went away to live on a farm."

"I don't understand," George said to the group as a whole. "You raise dragons?"

"Just the one—my pet! And that assassin killed him!" Darach hissed through gritted teeth. "Dadianus was no bigger than one of your Great Danes and this...this...knight errant comes along and slays him. And you invited us to a party in his honor? Come, Faylinn, we're leaving." Darach moved to help his wife out of her chair.

"Now just one minute." This time Jacob stood. "You may be the King of Álfheimr, but this is my home and I'm King of this castle."

All eyes turned to Jacob. He was normally a quiet and retiring individual who spent most of his time poring over ancient history texts. Generally, he avoided conflict, and preferred to wait for cooler heads to prevail. But the academician was taking matters into his own hands this evening, which meant he thought the situation was only going to deteriorate further.

"We need to get a few things straight," Jacob began. "First, we didn't send an invitation for you to come here tonight. We sent you one for two weeks from now, for Morgan's birthday. Second, you've managed to climb atop your Royal high horse and insult your daughter repeatedly for her life choices. Third, you've done this in front of your granddaughter, my child, and caused stress during what should be a time of fellowship with your family."

Jacob took a deep, calming breath before he continued. "I'm sorry for the embarrassment you felt because of our elopement. But know this: I will never feel sorry for my decision to propose to Peri, or for our life together since. The choice to be part of this family is yours, not ours. We haven't been keeping you from Morgan and I haven't been keeping Peri from you. Please understand: you are welcome in our home, but you need to decide what is more important to you—your family or your pride."

"I don't need lessons in manners from the likes of you," Darach stormed, "and we were indeed invited here tonight." He snapped his fingers in the direction of Sabia, without taking his eyes off Jacob. The young Fae produced an envelope, seemingly out of nowhere, curtseyed, and handed it to the king. Darach opened it and read: "You are cordially invited to attend the beginning of the Fortnight of Festivities for your granddaughter, Princess Morgan, to commence promptly at six o'clock in the evening of April twenty-third."

Darach tossed the card into the center of the table, causing it to land in front of Beatrice. She picked up the invitation, turned it over and looked at it, then shook her head. "This isn't the card I sent. The invitations for Morgan's birthday party, which is on May seventh, had a picture of a clown holding balloons on it." She took the place card from in front of her plate, and held it up next to the open invitation. "And this definitely isn't my handwriting."

"Clowns with balloons?" Darach practically sneered. "How positively hideous."

"You're one to talk about hideous," Peri stated, and gestured at the hookah in the center of the table. "Did you think *that* was an appropriate gift for a teenage girl?"

Darach blinked twice in surprise. "I did not send that monstrosity." His tone was one of confusion. "I thought that was one of your husband's relics from his research. I sent Morgan a pair of Elven dancing slippers."

It was at that point everyone around the table began trying to speak at once. The chatter, confusion, and recriminations were becoming louder and louder. King Darach was about to say something rude and inappropriate about his son-in-law, when Beatrice shouted, "You!"

Everyone turned to stare at the matron of the family, who was pointing directly in front of her. All eyes followed her finger to the figure of Snarlak, who was sitting at the little bistro table, absent-mindedly rubbing his hands together like a housefly grooming itself.

"You," Beatrice repeated. "You are behind this. You've been sitting there watching everything happen with a look of absolute glee on your face."

"Your Majesty, I don't know what this crazy woman is talking about." Snarlak made his plea directly to the king. "I was just sitting here quietly, awaiting your orders."

"Snarlak," Darach began slowly, "where are the dancing slippers I sent you to retrieve?"

"A mistake in shipping, Sire. I assure you the slippers will arrive by her birthday. The hookah is a present from my cousin." Snarlak gestured to the centerpiece on the table. "I thought he would enjoy it, since he collects antiques. This one is even inscribed by the metalsmith."

Morgan, who was sitting directly opposite the centerpiece in question, looked at the hookah more intently. "There does seem to be something inscribed on it," she offered, "but I can't quite make it out." She picked up her napkin and attempted to wipe away the layers of grime which had worked its way into the brass inscription.

A low rumble began to emanate from the chamber at the base of the hookah. The intensity slowly rose as the centerpiece began to shake. Suddenly, the seam where the top of the ancient brass bottle met the stem of the hookah split, sending the top half into the air, and raining Turkish delights and carnations across the table. The bowl of the hookah arced out of sight, across the fence and into the neighbor's garden.

Everyone watched as a wisp of red smoke began to swirl from the newly exposed opening at the top of the bottle. Slowly, the spiral continued upward over the table, becoming more and more substantial as it rose. As the smoke became denser, it coalesced into the shape of a muscular man from the waist up. When the details were fully formed, the visage of the giant, with bright red skin, soot-black hair, a single gold earring in his left ear and thick gold cuffs on his wrists, raised his powerful arms skyward. He grabbed the strands of fairy lights which had gotten tangled around him, and easily pulled them asunder, destroying them. He spoke in a booming voice. *"AZADI!"*

"What did he say?" George asked, more curious than afraid.

"I don't recognize this language," Darach admitted, the previous argument temporarily forgotten.

"He said 'Freedom.'" This time, all eyes were on Jacob. He shrugged. "I read and speak Persian."

The giant figure waved his hand around the table and mumbled softly to himself. Then he spoke again. "Is this the barbaric tongue which you speak?"

"If you mean English, then yes," Jacob replied.

"I am the *Gharmaz* Djinn," he replied with a slight nod. "Who among you rubbed the bottle and released me from my prison?"

"I did." Morgan waved up at the djinn as she spoke.

The giant red figure bowed to Morgan in midair, then with a sweeping gesture of his right hand, told her, "For releasing me, I grant thee three wishes."

"That's very kind of you, Mr. Djinn, but I don't need a reward for releasing you from the bottle."

"The three wishes must be granted," the djinn said flatly.

"Don't do it, Morgan." Darach moved to stand next to his granddaughter. "It's a trick. Wishes from a djinn always come with a price."

"No one asked you, Mortal." The djinn leaned toward King Darach and sniffed the air. "No...not mortal! I smell the stench of Fae!"

"Hey, that's my grandfather you're talking to!" Morgan was indignant.

The djinn sniffed the air again. *"Dorgeh,"* he snarled, and rose to his full height.

"Now wait just one damned minute." Jacob moved to stand beside Morgan, opposite of Darach. "That's my daughter you're speaking to, and this is my house."

Peri stood and flanked Morgan. "Our house," she chimed in. Then as an aside to Jacob, she whispered, "What did he say?"

Jacob whispered back. "He called her a half-breed."

Peri's face reddened, and hints of golden flame flared in her eyes and danced around her irises. Peri knew Morgan had heard what her father said. She put her hands on Morgan's shoulders and squeezed gently.

"Ignore these swine and make your wishes, child," the djinn ordered, irritation rising in his voice.

"Yes, Morgan, make your wishes." Snarlak approached the table from the opposite side. "Three little wishes and he goes away. Poof!"

The djinn turned and sneered at the goblin. "Go away, you insignificant piece of camel dung. I do not require help from the likes of you."

"I was only trying to aid my master." Snarlak bowed to the djinn, sweeping his arms wide as he did so. "I meant no offense."

The djinn threw back his head and laughed. "Aid your master? If you wanted to aid your master, as you say, then why did you purchase my cursed vessel and have it sent here?"

"I did no such thing." Snarlak's eyes darted from the djinn to King Darach.

"The bottle may have been my prison, but it did not prevent me from perceiving the outside world," the djinn replied boldly. "I remained aware of everything. From the moment you purchased the hookah from the Kobold in Constantinople, through my journey across the waters in the belly of that giant metal bird, to the moment this child rubbed the lamp. I even know of the deception that you told your master about the slippers. They were never sent here. Even now, you carry them in your pack."

Darach looked sharply at Sabia. "Check it."

Sabia placed the goblin's pack on the dining table and unbuckled it. Before she could open the flap, Snarlak moved to stop her, but he was no match for the speed of the young Fae. Sabia grabbed the side of his head with her left hand and smashed his cheek onto the table in a pile of sticky Turkish delights, holding it there firmly. With her other hand, she opened the pack and reached in. "Dead space, Your Majesty."

"Dead space?" Jacob asked Peri.

"It's a magically contained dead universe. You can store unlimited quantities of practically anything in it, and the items will be held unchanging in what you would call stasis. Like those bags in that roleplaying game you enjoy."

Sabia reached into the pack until her arm disappeared all the way to her shoulder. "I've got something," she said, and extracted her arm. She held a box wrapped with a pink ribbon.

"You little thief," Darach exclaimed. "Those are Morgan's shoes, aren't they?"

"There's a lot more in the bag than that, Sire," Sabia replied.

"Enough of this," bellowed the djinn. He leaned forward, placing his bearded face right in front of Morgan's. "Make your three wishes NOW."

"Why are you in such a hurry for me to make these wishes?" Morgan asked, taking a step backwards, further into her mother's grasp.

The djinn straightened, raised his face to the sky, and screamed as if he were in agony. His red skin practically glowed with power. With gritted teeth, he stated, "As soon as you make your third wish, my curse will be broken and I will be free of my prison forever. I'll finally be able to take my revenge on those who placed this curse upon me."

"Let me see that bottle." Darach grabbed it from where it laid on the table and turned it over in his hands. The red djinn, who was still tethered to the bottle by the trail of smoke emanating from it, was dragged along.

"Stop that, you impudent creature," the djinn bellowed.

Darach ignored him and examined the bottle more closely. "The bottle is definitely cursed. Several curses were laid upon it, as a matter of fact. Imprisonment and compulsion to tell the truth, amongst others. It seems to be from the reign of Xerxes the Second."

"Xerxes the First," Jacob corrected.

"Don't presume to tell me what era this is from, mortal. I lived through it."

"Well, then," Jacob replied, "you should know that Xerxes the Second's reign was only forty-five days long. You should also know that the decorative artwork on the side of the bottle is the seal of his grandfather, Xerxes the First."

"I don't need condescending lectures like I'm some sort of schoolboy," Darach snapped.

"Obviously you do, if you believe that is from the reign of Xerxes the Second," Jacob countered, absentmindedly adjusting his glasses.

Morgan placed her hands over her ears as her father and grandfather continued to argue about the origins of the bottle.

"Daddy, put that bottle down," Peri told her father as she moved to take the object from his hands.

Darach jerked back, holding the bottle out of her reach. The djinn was whipped around like a giant party balloon. "Don't you give your father orders," he said, glaring at his daughter.

"Daddy, the truth curse isn't limited to the bottle. It's affecting everyone around it."

While everyone's attention was now on the bottle and the exchange between Darach and Peri, Morgan began to sob softly. The stress of her family fighting, the frightening countenance of the djinn, and the persistent itch from the center of her back, was more than she could bear. Finally, she balled up her hands into fists and yelled. "Enough!"

Everyone stopped talking immediately and focused their attention on Morgan. Her brunette hair began swirling around her head as if it were being blown in a breeze. The flickering light of emerald fire seemed to burn around her irises. "I can't take any more of this! You want three wishes, I'll give you three wishes! Wish number one: you're my family. Don't you understand you're supposed to love and care for each other? You're not supposed to fight. I wish you would realize how important you all are to me, and how important you are to each other." Morgan paused and took a breath.

"Wish number two—" Morgan pointed across the table at Snarlak. "I wish you would stop being so conniving, and understand that being good and decent and honest can get you further ahead, and stop being such a little sneak thief and do something productive. Your cousin runs a shop—he understands what hard work and determination can do. Why can't you?"

"And wish number three." This time, Morgan looked directly at the djinn. "I wish you would realize your enemies don't exist anymore. No one knows who their descendants are. The Kingdom of Persia no longer exists. You should use your power to help people, not bring your wrath down upon the innocent people who just happen to live there now. Above all, I really wish this itching would stop!"

Morgan screamed in pain, and a wave of green energy discharged in a sphere around her, sweeping out and over the entire dinner party. Those gathered just stared in shock. Peri was about to say something to her daughter when she heard a tearing sound and watched as a set of iridescent wings ripped through the back of Morgan's jumper. Morgan looked over her right shoulder to see the edge of one of her wings, which seemed to contain all the colors of a peacock.

Embarrassed at this unexpected event, Morgan turned and ran into the house, down the hall, and into her bedroom. Everyone heard a distant door slam shut. After a moment or two of silence, George cleared his throat and spoke up.

"I don't think any of us saw that coming..."

"I had better go talk to her," Peri told Jacob.

"No, let me," Faylinn interrupted. She laid her hand on Peri's shoulder. "I have more experience dealing with a teenage girl who has just gotten her wings." Faylinn stepped inside and disappeared down the hallway.

Everyone around the table was uncertain what to do next. George reached for his wine glass when a clanging sound got his attention. The two gold cuffs around the djinn's wrists had fallen to the table. More smoke began billowing out of the brass bottle, and soon the djinn had solid legs, clad in loose-fitting black pants. He was staring at his hands when his skin started morphing from red to blue. The new color soon spread evenly across his entire form.

"This is...unexpected," the djinn said to no one in particular.

"If you don't mind, could you get off of my table, please?" Jacob slid a chair out, offering the djinn a step down to the ground.

Once off the table, the djinn—who was an impressive eight feet tall at this point—placed both hands on Jacob's shoulders and grinned. "That is a remarkable child you have, sir. Quite remarkable, indeed."

"I've always thought so," Jacob replied. "But what makes you say that?"

"She had an opportunity for riches and powers beyond her wildest dreams, and chose instead to give us the gift of her perspective. I see she was right, and I have no need for revenge. And how about you? How do you see your father-in-law now?"

Jacob looked at the ground, contemplating, and then looked at Darach. "I can see that our youth and impetuousness hurt him, and he still loves his daughter."

"And what of you?" the djinn asked the king. "What do you see in your son-in-law now?"

King Darach cleared his throat. "I see someone who deeply loves his family. Someone who has cared for my daughter as much as I do."

"I think she got her wishes, then."

"It would seem so," the king agreed. "But let's test it. What of you, Snarlak?"

The goblin, whose cheek was still firmly held in the Turkish delight by Sabia, raised his eyes to look at the king. "I want to help my cousin run his shop. Nothing else I do seems to work out for me."

Jacob nodded. "That would be three for three."

"Release him, Sabia," King Darach instructed. "We've all had a change of heart today. It seems we've created quite a mess here," he added, looking at the dinner table, littered with broken pieces of hookah, remnants of candy and carnations, the spilled glasses and toppled plates. Darach faced Beatrice, and bowed. "My sincere apologies. My behavior tonight was uncalled for, and unseemly for the ruler of the Realm. I am truly sorry."

Beatrice reached over and gently patted the king on his cheek. "Apology accepted, dear. We are family. Getting on each other's nerves is part of it."

She turned her attention back to the table and sighed. "Let's get this mess cleaned up before Morgan and the queen get back."

"Allow me," the djinn said. With a flourish of his arm, the table was restored to the condition it was in at the beginning of the evening, including the Turkish delight-laden brass hookah centerpiece, and with the addition of an eighth place setting. The djinn looked at his handiwork, then turned to Peri. "I hope you don't mind if I join your dinner? I haven't eaten in twenty-five hundred years and am a bit famished."

After about fifteen minutes, Morgan and Faylinn returned to the outdoor dining area. Morgan's wings were no longer visible and she had a different jumper on. Everyone was once again seated, but not where they had been originally. Jacob was to the right of the king, and the two were engaged in an animated conversation, both of them smiling and laughing. Peri and Beatrice were seated on either side of the djinn, who was now for some reason blue. George was at the foot of the table, trying to listen to both sets of conversations at the same time.

"The tone of the party has definitely changed since we've been gone," Faylinn observed.

Darach looked at his wife and smiled. "Quite. Our son-in-law here was informing me about a project he has coming up in Giza, and I was telling him how the desert looked before they scattered all those pyramids around it. More importantly, we've discussed Morgan spending a month in Álfheimr with us this summer. It will give us quality time with our granddaughter, while Peri accompanies Jacob to Giza on a bit of a second honeymoon."

Morgan smiled and nodded. "I would enjoy that."

"Things really did change while we were away," Faylinn remarked, as she and Morgan took the remaining two seats at the table. "And for the better, in my opinion. Shall we resume the festivities?" the queen suggested.

"What a splendid idea," Darach said, "although I'm still not thrilled about celebrating the man who killed my Dadianus."

"This pet dragon of yours," the djinn inquired, "is it anything like the one which slumbers within the goblin's pack?"

Darach bolted upright in his chair. "How do you know there is a dragon in the pack?"

"My magic allows me to see everything contained within. There are quite a number of items in that pack, but most of them are junk. The dragon is slumbering within arm's reach."

The king looked to Sabia, who shrugged. "I did not find a dragon inside, Sire."

The djinn stood and walked over to the pack. "Allow me." He opened the flap and reached in. Seconds later, the djinn extracted a miniature winged black dragon, which was the size of a large dog. The dragon yawned, raised its head, and looked around. Upon spotting Darach, the dragon leapt from the djinn's arms, rushed to the king, and began excitedly licking Darach's face.

The king laughed as he stroked the dragon's head, and murmured, "Who's a good Dadianus? Who's a good Dadianus?"

Faylinn turned to face Snarlak. "Where did you get that pack?"

"I found it in the Treasury Room," Snarlak admitted. "I've been stuffing things from the treasury in it for weeks now. I was planning on putting everything back when we return to the castle. I've had a change of heart."

"Oh, keep whatever trinkets you've put in the bag," Darach told the goblin as the dragon curled up at the king's feet. "Getting Dadianus back is well worth it. He must have crawled into the pack and got trapped. I just assumed the stories about the drag-onslayer involved my Dadianus because he disappeared at the same time." Looking directly at Jacob, the king added, "I should know better than to make assumptions."

"Speaking of assumptions," the djinn said quietly to Peri, "I would like you to give this to your daughter when she turns of age, whatever that is in this century." The djinn surreptitiously handed her a gold coin. On one side was a profile of the djinn; on the reverse, the number three.

"What is this for?" Peri inquired.

"That," the djinn said with a touch of mischief in his voice, "holds the three wishes I granted to your daughter. The magic she used tonight—including that which broke my curse—was her own. Your daughter is wise beyond her years, and has a kindness which is far more rare than it should be. I will always cherish having met her."

The djinn reached over and picked up his wineglass. "I would like to make a toast. Until tonight, I have never known the peace and contentment that comes with a loving family. And while you had your differences, those have finally been put aside. It is my fondest wish for each of you that no matter how different you think you are as individuals, you are all alike as family."

As the djinn took a sip from his glass, and the others followed suit, a feeling of togetherness permeated the small gathering. Each and every one of them felt a sense of serenity, but George, Jacob, and Beatrice began to feel something else, as well—an unmistakable itch in the center of their backs.

Tomorrow was going to be a different kind of day.

THE BEST BARBECUE IN TOWN

BY CHRISTOPHER MARKMAN

Skeeter, not his real name, reflected that he should be called Bubba. But Bubba was already taken, which was a problem. Really, Bubba was the problem. Always had been and always would be. Skeeter and Bubba were cousins, born the same week. They competed in everything. But Bubba had gone too far. Worse, he'd gone too far down at the Possum Palace.

"Skeeter," he said, "the only thing you know about it is you have to wait in line for your turn to buy Barbie." Skeeter had to have Delores, the waitress, explain it to him. Bubba was making a pun. It was Barbie-queue instead of barbecue. Bubba must have surfed the web for a week looking for that insult! Bubba had won the Plump Pig Cookoff for the last five years. Skeeter had come in second place for the last five years. This year, Skeeter vowed he would win. It didn't matter the cost. Bubba was going down.

BUBBA LIKED TO CLAIM THAT APPRECIATION FOR PUNS SHOWED A SUPERIOR intellect. Skeeter disagreed. Skeeter was a welder, and stupid welders don't stay employed. Bubba worked down at the Co-op and sold tractors. He got some nice commissions, but Skeeter made more money. Better yet, Skeeter could control when he worked and when he didn't. Skeeter had more time to work on perfecting his sauce.

Darlene, like all good wives, put up with her husband's insanity. Some husbands hated fish, some hated deer, and some chased little balls all over a pasture. Darlene felt fortunate that she only had to put up with the endless creation of barbecue, which she and the kids all enjoyed. Darlene was a teacher, and she took Skeeter's sauce into school and had the staff critique it. Skeeter placed second for the sixth year in a row. After a week, he found his sobriety, but his mind was still lost.

SKEETER BOUGHT A COMPUTER. HE HAD AN ACCOUNTANT AT THE PLANT teach him Excel. Skeeter tried every recipe on the internet. Each sauce was an experiment. He tracked different ingredients, grills, temperatures, and times. Anything he thought could make a difference, he tracked. He was popular at the plant; he brought in free barbecue every day.

One day, he noticed the wife and kids were gone. Not gone, as in gone to the store, but clothes and toys were missing. Despite that, he continued his experiments for the perfect sauce.

Bubba won year seven. Skeeter turned to the Dark Web.

COOKING IS COMPETITIVE. BARBECUE IS ONE OF THE BIGGEST competitions outside of chocolates, and competition can sometimes bring out the less savory side of people. Tips that Skeeter would consider ethical and useful were few and far between on the Dark Web. However, he regularly posted in hopes that he would draw the attention of someone who could help him. Then, one night—

Goda123: "You are most knowledgeable."

Skeeter: "Thank you. I don't remember seeing you before."

Goda123: "Longtime reader, first-time writer."

Skeeter: "How can I help you?"

Goda123: "I help you maybe. You say you try everything, willing to do anything. Would you meet my cousin? He tell you what is in Bubba's sauce and how to beat him."

Skeeter had gotten good at deciphering sauces. He'd seen a show on TV once when he was little. They would give a chef different things, and he would identify all the ingredients. Skeeter was good, but not that good. But it was possible.

Skeeter: "I would love to meet your cousin!"

Goda123: "Is not simple. You must start in Scherwiller, Germany. He is close to Giessen River."

Skeeter still had his passport from when he and Darlene had been talking about a family vacation overseas.

Skeeter: "I can do that. I can go in four weeks, if that is good?"

Goda123: "My cousin is very strange. You must walk a long way to *das Haus*. He will help you only if you pay him in gold. He does not speak English."

Skeeter: "Can you come to interpret?"

Goda123: "No. Family is mad at me. I can meet you at hotel and take you halfway. He will see only you, no interpreter."

Skeeter: "Your cousin makes this hard."

Goda123: "Is more difficult. No cell or internet. You cannot use translation device. You must learn fourteenth-century German."

Skeeter got bright red. This was some grade-A moo mud. This was a bigger pile than a whole dairy barn. This sick jerk had gotten his hopes up only to play games with him. Skeeter stabbed the off button to his computer and went to get some of his cooking bourbon, only without the cooking.

Skeeter looked at Bubba's picture in the paper. Bubba had won first place for the eighth year in a row. Skeeter hadn't won anything. He hadn't even entered. Skeeter thought it couldn't get any worse, except it had. Bubba had a deal to make his sauce for a popular supermarket chain. He was going to call it Bubba-Q. Skeeter had hit rock bottom.

Skeeter: "Goda123, are you there?" He had been trying for two months to contact Goda.

Skeeter: "Goda123. I apologize. I am ready to listen."

Goda123: "You were most rude."

Skeeter: "Yes, I'm sorry. I have started learning German."

Goda123: "It must be fourteenth century. You must speak and read."

Skeeter: "I have done research. I have started learning modern German and I have Wright's primer. Oxford, Berkeley, and Cambridge all have formal programs. I can't attend any of them, but I have found a student at Berkeley who is willing to tutor me."

Goda123: "Good, you will need two marcs of gold, two more of silver, and one marc of copper. A marc is close enough to eight ounces, so use that."

Skeeter: "One minute." He googled and saw the price of gold at $2,921 per ounce. Figure $3,000 to be safe multiplied by sixteen is forty-eight thousand dollars! "That is $48,000 of gold! Do I need to buy old German coins, too?" He meant the last facetiously.

Goda123: "No, bullion is best. Krugerrands are good, too."

Skeeter: "It will take me longer to save the money than to learn the German."

Goda123: "My cousin is hermit. He does not go anywhere."

ELEVEN LONG MONTHS PASSED BEFORE SKEETER WAS READY. HE TOOK AN extra job welding on offshore oil rigs. He moved into a shack on his grandpa's hunting property. His wife had filed for separation and claimed the house. He worked at saving the money he needed for the trip. He even sold his bass boat.

SKEETER FLEW INTO ZURICH, SWITZERLAND. GODA HAD TOLD HIM THIS would be the cheapest way for him to buy gold and silver. He bought the precious metals at a variety of dealers so he wouldn't attract any government attention. He didn't want to have to pay taxes or fees on gold he wasn't bringing home. Since he could only buy small amounts, this was time-consuming, but after two days, he had his necessary sum.

Skeeter had brought the copper marc from home. Goda had originally suggested copper coins, but when Skeeter saw the price of a penny from 1850, he went looking for an alternative. Through more discussion with Goda, he found an acceptable alternative. He bought copper chop from Amazon. One of his buddies made half-ounce molds and converted two pounds into sixty-four copper medallions with a picture of a barbecue grill on one side and a pig on the other. Further discussion with Goda had him bring the whole two pounds

Next, he took a train to Basel and walked across the border into Germany. Just another tourist on a walking vacation. He took a German train to Scherwiller. The fact that he spoke German surprised people, and they were glad to talk with him, allowing him to practice. Before long, he had found the house recommended by Goda. A widow woman had a room to rent, and he had followed Goda's advice to book the room for a week. He told her he was going to meet some friends, so he might be away a couple of nights. He rented a car and returned to the house. After a good dinner of sausage, potatoes, and beer, he fell into a deep sleep.

SKEETER WAITED IN THE PARKING AREA NEAR THE CHÂTEAU DE RAMSTEIN. It was six a.m., the time he was to meet Goda.

"Are you Skeeter?" asked a peculiar voice from out of the shadows. The voice was both nasal and raspy. The speaker spoke in German—in fact, the accent was High Middle German.

"Hello, Goda, nice to meet you," said Skeeter.

"Are you ready? What did you bring?"

Skeeter had been given directions by Goda to bring his own food and water. "I have three days of food and water, a change of clothes, the gold, silver, copper, my sauce, and Bubba's sauce."

"I am physically disabled," said Goda. "Do not be alarmed. My appearance is not a joke."

"All right."

A short, hunchbacked figure slid out of the shadows. He wore a cloak of all things and had a walking stick. As the figure came into the light, Skeeter saw long hair hanging out of the cloak's cowl. Then the face came into view, led by a long nose, none too straight, with nostrils that looked like twin caterpillars. The eyes were deepset. Skeeter got the impression of beady little eyes, but it could have been that the eyes were deep in shadow.

"Let me see a farthing," said Goda. Skeeter dug into his pocket and pulled out one of the copper medallions his buddy had made. Goda bit into it, then licked it, then put it in his mouth and sucked on it. He spit it back out and handed the wet token back to Skeeter.

"Acceptable," said Goda. Next, he produced a worn leather belt with a large knife. "Take this and wear it. It will rain. Are you ready for rain?"

"Yes," said Skeeter, who had a poncho and a big floppy hat. He took the belt and looked at the knife. It was even bigger than the camp knife Skeeter's brother had for hunting. The blade was roughly twenty inches long, and when he pulled it partway from the sheath, Skeeter saw that it was edged and sharp on both sides. Skeeter had heard all sorts of things about Europe's laws, so he didn't even bring a pocketknife. He put the belt on and felt more like he was wearing a sword than a knife. He felt foolish.

"Here!" Goda handed over a staff. Skeeter hadn't noticed, but Goda had a staff for each of them. "Follow me." Goda didn't head towards the Château but southwest instead. Skeeter had spent a fair time in the woods as a boy. He'd thought hunting was his passion until he found barbecue. Still, he couldn't see any trail that Goda was following.

Eventually, they came to a river. *"Der Giessen,"* said Goda, his first words in over an hour. "We rest here." Skeeter drank some water and used his water filter to refill his water bladder. After about ten minutes, Goda said, "Come."

Now they went slower. Goda was hunting around, looking for landmarks. Eventually, they came to a huge oak tree on the river-bank. The roots were exposed from the water washing the dirt away during flooding. Goda got down on his hands and knees and crawled under the roots.

"Wait a minute!" yelled Skeeter.

"Trust me or trust me not. If you want to meet my cousin, you must follow." Feet disappeared into the dark.

Skeeter got out a flashlight; he never left home without two. He eventually managed to follow, but he had to drag his backpack behind him using some paracord. A tunnel under the roots of the tree was revealed by his light. He'd gone about thirty feet when his light quit. Two is one, and one is none. Except his second light was in his backpack, where he couldn't get it right now. As he laid there thinking about what to do, he noticed a light ahead.

"Come, come," prodded Goda. Skeeter crawled and exited from the other side of the tree. Now there was a path, and Goda began to walk it. The path was to the northeast, back the way they had come.

After an hour, they took a break. Skeeter swapped out his flashlight, but his second one didn't work, either. He wanted to check his map app, but his phone was off, and it wouldn't start back up. They walked for four more hours until the sun was high in the sky. Skeeter had a good sense of direction. The path continued northeast. They hadn't seen a road, powerline, or house. He hadn't heard traffic or seen any planes in the air.

Goda stopped by a creek, sat down, and said, "Eat now." He pulled a bag out from under his cloak and pulled out some bread, cheese, and sausage. Goda made a fair bit of noise chewing, and when he was done, he drank water directly from the creek.

Skeeter had some protein bars and drank filtered water. Skeeter refilled his water bladder, and they resumed their walk. When they finally saw a wall, the sun was getting close to the horizon.

"That is the south gate," said Goda. "I am not welcome. I will wait here for you for three days. Do not eat any of their food or drink, or they will not let you leave. Take no insult, or they will think you weak and rob you. Vendors will try to hand you things. If you grab it, they will claim you steal it. You will have to pay too much money to the bailiff to be free. It is a trick; do not fall for it. You seek Fridwald on Kochsosse Strasse. If he asks who sent you, answer, 'His lost cousin.' He will know it is me. My name here is not Goda. You should wait till morning, but if you want, you can enter now."

Skeeter thought. This whole thing was weird. He'd looked over the map of the area while at the widow's. The area around Scherwiller was pretty densely populated by Alabama standards. Yet they'd walked a whole day without seeing anyone or anything. Now Goda was telling him some truly weird stuff and giving him the choice of sleeping on the ground or going into town. "What's the problem with getting a hotel in town?"

Goda made a noise of frustration. "More chance you are robbed. These people very greedy."

A thought occurred to Skeeter. "If this is where you came from, why did you leave?"

"Reasons," was the cryptic reply.

Skeeter looked at the gate, trying to decide if he should go in when the gate closed. Decision made.

Skeeter was back at the same spot as the sun came up. He'd spent a very uncomfortable night sleeping in his poncho. Goda wouldn't start a fire. He said the bailiff would tax them and fine them if they got caught. When Skeeter asked how much the fine would be, the answer was twice whatever you had on you. That was the most Skeeter learned all night. Goda found a spot he pronounced as good, ate a little more bread and cheese from his bag, and fell asleep.

Skeeter didn't sleep well. He figured Goda's snoring kept the lions, tigers, and bears away. There had been a heavy dew, so he was wet. He'd had to drink his instant coffee cold, and a second day of protein bars was already one day too many. They were off the path, waiting for the gate to open. When it finally did, Goda stopped him. "If you seem anxious, they will charge you more to enter."

"What?"

Goda said, "The guards must collect five farthings for you to enter." Goda held up the largest coin. "They will try to get more. If they try to search you, walk away and tell them you will go to a different gate. The north gate only charges three farthings. Tell them you would rather walk than give them any more than five."

"What happens if they still want more?"

"Walk around. They will accept five when they see you are serious. Do not be surprised if one of them chases you down."

"Okay, why don't I see any guards?"

"They want you to enter to claim you entered without permission, so they can search you and take all your money. Stop outside the gate and request to enter."

"When were you going to tell me all this?" Skeeter was exasperated.

"Before you walk to the gate," was the smug reply.

"I can see why you left!"

"I did not leave. I was exiled."

"Why?"

"Not your concern." Goda gave him specific directions for the gate. "Remember, everyone will know you are a stranger, and they will all want whatever you have. Visitors have left naked. Do not eat or drink. Do not touch any merchandise. Pay for everything you receive. And never appear anxious, or the price goes up!"

"Why are you helping me?"

"Not your concern. Sooner you start, sooner you can go home and beat your cousin. Go. Go." Goda gave a shooing motion. Skeeter hitched up his pants, put on his backpack, and walked to the gate. As he got close, he could see through the gate down a straight street to what was presumably the north gate. It couldn't be much farther than a quarter mile. He looked left, then right. The wall he was at was maybe a quarter mile wide, with his gate in the center.

Remembering what he'd been told, he stopped ten feet away from the gate and yelled, "Request permission to enter."

"Come ahead!"

Skeeter didn't move. "What is the price of entry?"

"One gold marc!"

Skeeter guffawed. "No, really."

"One silver marc!"

"No. No, it's not. For the last time, how much to enter?"

"One copper marc!"

Skeet knew a marc was sixteen farthings. "I'm going to walk to the north gate. I hear their prices are much more reasonable." Skeeter turned left and started walking along the wall.

A huffing sound came up behind him. He turned to see a shorter, fatter, uglier version of Goda in chainmail. The guard skidded to a halt, bent over, and began gasping for breath. Skeeter waited. After half a minute, "Ten farthings," the guard wheezed out.

Skeeter turned and started walking away. "Seven!" Skeeter

didn't even slow. "Five! It's five! I can't go any lower!" Skeeter stopped. He knew from Goda that was indeed the true amount, but Goda had also told him to always appear reluctant.

Finally, Skeeter turned and said, "Fine. I'll give you five at the gate. I get a receipt."

"What? You don't trust me?" came the indignant reply.

"I do not," replied Skeeter.

He walked back to the gate with the guard. "Corporal, this human does not trust us!" exclaimed his escort.

Skeeter, in his studies, had read about goblins. Early writers treated them 0matter-of-factly. Goda had thought they were just talking smack about foreign merchants. Scholars were divided as to whether the legendary creatures originated in France or Germany. The appearance of Goda and the guards made sense if goblins weren't legendary at all. Skeeter remembered something from one of his texts and repeated it. "Goblins don't trust goblins; humans should not, either."

"Hmmm, that is insulting. The last five humans who have visited all ended up in the slave pits. Perhaps I will go rent you to clean out my chamber pots."

"Do you want five copper farthings or do you want to trade insults?" asked Skeeter. Eventually, he got his receipt, but only after he had caught errors and had the receipt rewritten twice. He handed over five of his medallions immediately after the corporal handed him the corrected receipt. As he walked through the gate into a tunnel, he heard one guard say to the other, "The big ugly brute is smarter than he looks."

Goda had warned Skeeter that he would have to pay for directions. He had given Skeeter general directions to get him close. Skeeter was to exit the gate tunnel and turn right. Go three streets and turn left. Skeeter exited the tunnel and stopped. What met his eye was a medieval town straight out of the woodcuts shown in the books he had studied. The streets were cobblestones. Houses lined each street. They were covered in stucco or plaster and were two or even three stories high, with each story extending beyond the one beneath. The homes had peaked roofs ornamented by gables. Some of the houses had balconies. It reminded him of the time he had visited Helen, Georgia. The only difference was the height. The goblins were four feet tall, and their buildings were correspondingly short. At almost six feet, Skeeter had to watch his head so he didn't bump into the balconies that overhung the street.

The goblins wore simple clothing that was probably wool. Everyone's hair was long and stringy, although the women wore a kind of headscarf. Their complexions were at best unhealthy, ranging from pale yellow to motley green. Moles and warts were in abundance. Their chins were narrow, and their noses were long. Skeeter thought some of the men had funny-looking mustaches until he realized it was actually untrimmed nose hair.

Stopping was a mistake. The next thing he knew, goblins started yelling at him about things they had to sell. Skeeter started walking according to his directions. The goblins would get in front of him and hold out fruits or things. Some things he could recognize, like a spoon, but others were definitely mysterious to Skeeter. He just kept slowly moving in the direction he needed to go, endlessly repeating, "I do not want to buy that. I do not want to buy that."

Finally, he got to the end of Goda's directions. He was in a small square with a water fountain. He repeated his mantra until he was left alone. He looked around and spotted a kid.

"Hey, kid, how would you like to earn a farthing?"

"Hey, ugly, how would you like to give me ten farthings?"

"Tell you what, you take me directly to where I want to go and I'll give you two. Try any tricks or lead me anywhere else, and you'll get nothing. But if you do right by me, I'll give you the chance to earn another five. All you have to do is stay with me until I get what I want and then take me to the South Gate."

"Deal!" said the kid so fast that Skeeter knew he had offered way too much. But a short time later, he found himself at a door. The kid knocked. After a wait, the kid knocked again. It took several attempts before a little window in the door opened.

"What!"

"Fridwald, you old sot! You have a visitor!" said the boy.

"Your lost cousin recommended you to me," added Skeeter quickly. An eye peered out the little door, and he heard some mumbling.

The door proper opened, and the voice said, "Come in." Skeeter stooped and entered. The ground floor of the house appeared to be just one large room. There was a ladder going up into the ceiling on the left-hand side of the back wall and stairs going down on the right-hand side. The left wall had a fireplace made of brick and clay, the kind with an oven built into it for cooking bread. There was also a small kettle stove, and the exhaust was patched into the wall and presumably the chimney. There were several tables. There were pots, pans, knives, ladles, and other cooking parapher-nalia all about. Fridwald gestured to a table, the only one with chairs, and there were only two, and said, "Sit. Coffee or tea?"

"Neither, thank you," said Skeeter. He remembered Goda's injunction not to accept any food or drink.

"Politeness is a form of weakness. Why are you here?"

"I have spent the last ten years of my life trying to make the best barbecue sauce in the world, but my cousin Bubba always wins. I want to beat him." Skeeter reached into his backpack and pulled out a bottle of Bubba's sauce from the last competition and a bottle of Skeeter's best sauce. He pulled out small tasting dishes and put a bit of sauce on each.

Fridwald tasted each and pointed to Bubba's sauce. "Much better."

"There's very little difference," said Skeeter.

"Then you are not a good saucier. Find another line of work."

"I want to win. I have to win," said Skeeter.

"I am a master chef, and I cannot help you. You are beyond help. You cannot taste the difference between the sauces. But there is one thing I can do."

"Yes?" said Skeeter anxiously.

"I will take you to where you can buy the ALLSPICE."

Skeeter could hear the capital letters. Fridwald obviously thought allspice was special. "I've tried allspice in my mix; it doesn't do anything good."

"Ohhh, not your spice. Our spice. Every person is a bit different. The best sauce for one is not the best for another. ALLSPICE is an herb that makes whatever is being eaten perfect for the person eating it. Very expensive. Very expensive."

"How much are you going to charge me for it?" asked Skeeter suspiciously.

"Oh, I do not use it. I am a master—I do not need it. We must go to the souk."

"I'm ready whenever you are," said Skeeter.

"Hmmm. First, you must pay me to guide you. I want one silver marc."

"Ummm, Deal."

THE BOY, WALDHAR, WAS WAITING OUTSIDE THE DOOR WHEN THEY exited the house. He would go with them and then guide Skeeter to the South Gate. It would be up to Skeeter to buy as much ALLSPICE as he could bargain for.

As they walked, no one tried to sell him anything. When Skeeter remarked on it, Waldhar said, "Everyone has already heard about the tall pale fat human who doesn't fall for the 'do you want this' trick, so they do not try."

Three turns and maybe a hundred yards later, they came to a gate in the middle of the street. The street dipped down below a brick arch and disappeared below ground. "This is the only entrance to the souk," said Fridwald. "If we get separated, just stay on the cobblestone road and always turn left when you have a choice, and you will come to this exit. If you go right, you will find the slave pit. They will make you a slave, and you will never leave." He went through the gate. Skeeter bent his head to duck under the arch and followed.

Once inside, Skeeter was able to straighten up. There was a roof overhead, made mostly of cloth and wooden slats. Skeeter looked around and saw stalls lining both sides of the road. Most were a rough-cut wooden table with a vendor sitting behind it. Some had a cloth hanging to separate them from their neighbor, but some didn't. Each table had a sign highlighting what was being sold and a sample sitting on the tabletop.

Fridwald began walking rapidly, and Skeeter had to walk quickly to keep up. He looked ahead and saw the street extending as far as he could see. The street was packed with shoppers of every shape and size.

Fridwald took a right turn. Skeeter followed and looked at the stalls more closely. Each stall on both sides of the path was selling wooden spoons. He read the signs, somewhat limited by his vocabulary. Teaspoons-Ash, Teaspoons-Oak, Teaspoons-Mesquite. After wood ran out came lead, pewter, bronze, aluminum, stainless steel, titanium, gold, silver, platinum, rhodium, ruby, emerald, diamond, fossilized wood, scallop shell, and Tyrannosaurus Rex Shin Bone. And those were just the signs Skeeter could read and remember. Then came two tables with one spoon. One table had what appeared to be a silver spoon, and the sign said, *"Spoon of Poison."* The other table had a small wooden spoon with the sign, *"Spoon of Smiting."* Behind each table was an old woman. They could have been twins.

Fridwald took a turn, and now the stalls on either side had forks. Again, Skeeter observed the same pattern in the forks. They went from cheap to more expensive. This time, there was only one table that held one fork with its own placard. It read, *"Fork of Mending."* The old woman behind the table smiled at him and gestured for him to come over. She could have been the twin or triplet of the two previous old women.

Fridwald kept moving, and Skeeter hurried along to keep up. They turned onto a street of knives

"What is with the tables with only one item and the odd name like Fork of Mending?" asked Skeeter.

Fridwald ignored him, but the boy answered, "Those have magic."

"Okay, but what kind of magic?"

"The kind you need," answered the boy, which told Skeeter nothing.

They walked past knives for at least a mile, as there seemed to be endless variations. The style of knife changed along with the material it was made from. Finally, they came to a table with *"Knife of Choosing."* Skeeter stopped to talk to the vendor. She was the twin, or triplet, or quadruplet of the old women with the spoons.

"What does the knife do?" asked Skeeter.

The old woman answered, "It chooses who lives and who dies."

Skeeter said the first thing that popped into his mind. "All knives do that."

"*Nein*," drawled the old woman. "The person with a knife decides when he uses the knife to stab or cut someone. This knife, all you must do is touch it."

"How does it decide?"

"No one knows. I have had it many days and it does not sell. For you, handsome boy, I make very special deal." She batted her eyes at him.

"That is crazy," said Skeeter, resisting her charms.

"Special deal for you. Just touch the knife!"

"No." Skeeter almost thanked her, but remembered politeness would be seen as weakness, but he also remembered he needed to pay for anything he received. He passed over one of his coppers, "For your time." The old lady grinned at him.

After knives came ladles. Something began to wiggle its way into Skeeter's mind. He started looking at the vendors. He thought some of them looked alike, but it was hard to tell. They all seemed to wear the same style and color of clothing. Most wore hats that hid some part of their face. He could always see the eyes, yellow and rheumy with a light glow. Every set of eyes tracked him as he passed. Tables in front of him that had customers would be customer-free when he was even with them. The closer he looked at the vendor's clothes, the more generic they became. The harder he looked at faces, the more he saw only the eyes that looked back at him.

His guide unexpectedly took a turn, and now they were on Egg Street. The first vendor had white chicken eggs, the next brown, then spotted. The eggs changed size and color. He was pretty sure he recognized an ostrich egg, but what egg is the size of a small boulder? Then he saw a normal-sized egg, but it was as if the shell was made of fire. He read, *"Egg of"* on the placard, but couldn't decipher the rest of the words. The next vendor had one egg that was coal black and emitted a bit of smoke. The next vendor had an egg that was a brilliant lapis lazuli blue. He couldn't decipher any of the signs. All of them appeared to be staffed by the same old woman who had been selling the Knife of Choosing.

"What kind of eggs are those?" asked Skeeter.

"I am not a tour guide," came the testy reply from Fridwald.

They made another turn. Now, Skeeter saw the pattern. Two vendors selling roughly the same thing would be on opposite sides of a street. That street contained whatever was being sold in great variety and ended with one-of-a-kind magical items sold by an identical old woman. But the streets weren't arranged in any logical order to Skeeter. Egg Street was connected to Chair Street. Chair Street was connected to Drinking Mug Street. Drinking Mug Street was connected to Fireplace Street.

As they walked, Skeeter's attention turned to the customers. The booths ahead were full of customers, but somehow, every booth to his left and right was customer-free. Looking behind, he saw customers at the various tables. Try as he might, he couldn't see the customers disappear or reappear. Somehow, every table next to him was free of customers and presumably ready for him.

Skeeter's lack of progress in school hadn't been due to a lack of brains, but due to competing priorities. In learning Fourteenth-Century German, he'd picked up a good bit of history: the interesting stuff, the stories of how people lived. When he looked ahead, he was pretty sure he saw Egyptians dressed the way they were pictured inside the pyramids. There were Babylonians, Phoenicians, Greek Hoplites, Mayans, and many he didn't recognize. He saw chainmail and boiled leather armor. Men with stone and bronze weapons, with clothing made only from leather. The latter were often short, but very broad with thick muscles. Then he noticed a very tall, very thin man with pointed ears. He even observed a taller man who appeared to be covered all in fur, and a centaur. Skeeter realized he couldn't see faces, no matter how hard he stared.

"The Souk protects the anonymity of its customers," said his guide. Skeeter tried again to see faces, but in return he got a headache. His guide continued to take different turns, and Skeeter was thoroughly lost.

Finally, they turned onto Spice Street. Skeeter noticed other streets branching to the sides, but Fridwald continued straight. Skeeter tried counting paces to gauge the distance, but he couldn't keep the count in his head. He tried counting Mississippis to try to track the time, but he couldn't keep track of that, either.

After an unknown time and distance, the street ended with a booth going across it and blocking the road. There, an old female goblin sat in the stall. She looked to be the same old woman who had offered to let him touch the *Knife of Choosing*.

"Granny, this is a human who calls himself Skeeter. He wants to buy some of your ALLSPICE." Fridwald looked at Skeeter. "I have brought you here and kept our bargain. Do you agree?"

"Yes," said Skeeter. He handed over one little bag containing eight ounces of silver.

Fridwald poured the coins out, counted them, appeared to weigh them, and then put them back in the bag. "Our bargain is concluded," he said and walked away.

Skeeter looked at Granny, who looked back at him. "Did you offer to let me touch the Knife of Choosing?" he asked.

"You are a chef?" she asked, completely ignoring his question.

"Yes," replied Skeeter.

"And your cousin is better than you, but you still want to win at any cost. Yes? Am I right?"

"Yes." At one point, Skeeter might have answered grudgingly

through gritted teeth. But now, he had spent all this effort and had come to terms with himself.

"Tell me, human. How many chefs beat you?"

"I only lose to Bubba. I beat everyone else."

"So, second best. You are the first-place loser. How many years?" The old thing had a wicked grin. She was enjoying needling Skeeter.

"Eight years."

"Eight years. Eight long years, yes?" She chuckled. "Because you cannot admit your cousin is better, you must cheat. Yes?"

"No!" exclaimed Skeeter. He was getting flustered. The old crone was getting under his skin. He knew she was trying to get to him, so he should ignore her. But he couldn't.

"Don't get upset, boy." This, of course, irritated Skeeter more. "Makes no never mind to me. You chefs all be the same. You ignore all the other lovely items in the market. You only want the ALLSPICE, yes? You want to win, yes? Well, I'll give you enough spice to win one contest. My price is all you own."

And Skeeter teetered on the edge of the trap. He almost said, "Deal!" but he didn't. He realized the hag was trying to get him so upset he wouldn't think. What was it she didn't want him to think about, and why? He remembered Goda's admonition to pay for everything, and then Skeeter realized what was going on.

"Granny, you have given me something more precious than the ALLSPICE: you have given me wisdom. If I cannot win without cheating, then I am not the best chef. I realize now I should have accepted this and spent my time with my family. In payment..." Skeeter paused, reached into his backpack, and pulled out the four little bags that contained all his gold coins. "Here is all the gold I have. Please accept this as a token of my thanks for helping me to become a wiser man." He poured out all four bags onto her table. She immediately scooped the gold off the table.

"Well done, human." Skeeter turned and saw a goblin behind him, who was dressed much like the guards at the tower. "I don't have to take you to the slave pits for stealing wisdom from an old lady. You have trod the Bailiff's streets and disturbed his citizens. I would suggest a gift for the Bailiff is in order."

Skeeter nodded and handed over his last bag of silver.

The guard, deputy, or whatever he was, looked in the bag. "An acceptable gift. Waldhar, take this." A small baton was passed over to the boy. "This is a pass for the human; everyone is to leave him alone while you take him to the South Gate. Then you are to bring that to me straight away. If I find out you used it for anything special, it's to the slave pit with you."

"Yes, Deputy," said Waldhar. "Follow me, human."

The boy was in a hurry, but Skeeter quickly figured out he didn't have to hurry. Waldhar was to show him out, so Skeeter was free to set the pace. Skeeter slowed his pace, looking at each stall to take it all in. He saw mundane spices like black pepper, paprika, and cumin. Then came newt's eyes, and powdered frog liver. Dried sunshine looked like sparkling dust. Moonbeams were like cinnamon sticks if cinnamon could be a pale white powder that glowed faintly.

They took a left-hand turn and saw candles, lamps, lanterns, and, strangely enough, multiple tables that had LED flashlights for sale. The vendors ignored him, even when he stopped and looked.

"This stick means you're broke." Waldhar waved the baton. "No one will waste their time on you."

"I could always come back if I see something I like," replied Skeeter. Waldhar just started moving again.

The next aisle was pets, maybe. There were all sorts of creatures in terrariums and cages. There were snakes, lizards, toads, and different birds, unlike any Skeeter knew. He saw a bird whose feathers shimmered like fire, and a little humanoid with wings in a cage saying, "Help me, help me!" in a high-pitched voice. Skeeter made what he hoped was an apologetic gesture and kept moving.

They turned left again and were on the main thoroughfare of the souk. Skeeter continued to gawk. He saw cloth, coats, blankets, rugs, jewelry, candy, and other items. He slowed at the candy because he'd never seen a gummy toad. Then it blinked, opened its mouth, and stomped its feet. Confused, Skeeter moved hurriedly to catch up with Waldhar.

They exited the souk and were ten feet away from a tunnel.

"South Gate," said the boy.

"Can't be," said Skeeter, who turned around. The entrance to the souk was nowhere to be seen.

"If the souk is happy with you, it makes your journey home short," said Waldhar.

"Oh." said Skeeter, who dug out all the copper coins he had left and gave them to the boy. "A tip for good service."

The boy grinned big enough for Skeeter to make out his sharp pointed teeth that went in every direction, and then he took off back into the crowd. Skeeter turned, walked through the tunnel, and out the gate.

Skeeter walked down the path for about five minutes and came to the oak with the tunnel between its roots. Goda was waiting.

"So not a slave and you have clothes. Did you get what you came for?"

"I got what I needed," replied Skeeter.

"Of course you did. Come." Goda dove under the tree. On impulse, Skeeter pulled out his flashlight, then rigged a pullcord to his pack and followed. Sure enough, about halfway, Skeeter's light came on. As soon as he was back in daylight, his phone chimed, letting him know he had notifications.

They started walking. Skeeter decided he wanted to visit the souk again. He was pretty sure he saw a fairy, and he hoped for a magic carpet. He started to look around to get his bearings. The huge oak tree was missing, even though they hadn't walked any more than twenty feet.

Goda noticed and said, "A once-in-a-lifetime trip. You will never find the tree again."

SKEETER RETIRED FROM COMPETITION. BUBBA, NOW CONSIDERED A professional, couldn't compete.

"Are you sure you don't want to enter?" asked his wife. In the few months since he had returned home, Skeeter had reconciled with his wife and kids and moved back in.

Skeeter replied, "Darlin', there's things more important than barbecue."

She smiled and sat down on his lap, hugging him. At just that moment, Skeeter Jr. came around the corner and said, "Dad, there's this chili cookoff. Do you want to enter it with me?"

THE UNFULFILLED WISH OF ALI ZA'HAD

BY J BENJAMIN SANDERS JR

On the shore of the Arabian Sea lay the great Caliphate of Qua' Nar.

It was known far and wide as the true jewel of the land, a lovely and peaceful place where the much beloved Caliph ruled with a gentle hand. It was also where a young man known as Ali Za'had lived, who, with no other family, had survived on the tough streets long enough to have reached that most awkward point in his life: when he was no longer a boy and not yet a man. But Ali was unlike most of the other boys who had been abandoned to the streets as young children to survive as best they could, in that they had no memory of a mother or father, but he did.

He had dim memories of a young dark-haired woman with large eyes and wearing a look of utter sadness. He could vaguely recall how she would often sing soft songs to a restless babe, and there was a stern-faced father who showed him little patience or love. All because Ali Za'had had been born with an unforgivable flaw that marked him as unworthy to be loved: he had been born a mute, unable to talk and express himself to those around him.

Ali could still recall the day his father had taken him by the hand and led him away from their home and sad-eyed mother, only to abandon him on the street. He had been left to steal or beg until he grew old enough to do small jobs for some of the merchants, earning a brass penny, a meal, or a place to sleep away from the elements.

One day, while on an errand for Master Ben'Haman, the iron-smith, he stumbled across something that would change his life forever.

The orphan boy had been on his way to deliver a set of fire-dogs to the home of Azwa' Sudan, a local merchant. He decided he could save time by walking across an abandoned farm field. There, he spied an object with a dull shine sticking out of the fallow ground.

Ali's curiosity roused, he dropped to his knees and dug through the hard soil with nothing more than his bare hands until he exposed a simple brass lamp.

Ali rolled it over in his dirty palms and inspected it closely. The tarnish and verdigris had etched into and covered the aged surface that was marked with a series of swirling symbols that made little sense to the boy. He determined it might still be worth a penny or two to a junk dealer or metalsmith. If he cleaned it up, it might be worth more.

He stuck it into his pouch next to the firedogs and went on to deliver his goods to the merchant's house. He left the firedogs with the man's servant and received a penny and a pair of ripe pomegranates in return for his efforts.

With his last errand done for the day; Ali went home a little richer than he had been that morning. With several new pennies in his pocket and two pomegranates for his evening meal, he reached the hovel where he lived atop a low hill on the outskirts of the city, situated where he could enjoy the cool breeze coming in from the sea.

After eating the ripe fruit to ease the gnawing in his belly, Ali pulled out the lamp and set about scrubbing away the dirt and the accumulated tarnish with a rag and spit. As he worked it, the lamp quickly grew warm in his hands. Then it began to shake and shiver before a vaporous cloud spewed from the narrow spout. Ali dropped it as the cloud coalesced into a fierce-looking creature with flesh the color of stone, a being so large that the low roof of Ali's hovel forced it to crouch on all fours.

Scrabbling back, the mute boy stared fearfully at the scowling creature, whose protruding canines jutted from its upper and lower jaws. Twin slits where a nose should be, and a pair of oval eyes glowed a sulfurous yellow that seemed to stare through the young man with a look that left him shivering. Its bald head gleamed, with a scalp lock hanging down his back that twisted and writhed like a serpent when he shifted his body. Blunt fingers on his large hands ended in hawk-like talons that pierced the hard-packed dirt floor of the boy's hovel.

Raking the boy with a cunning look, the strange creature's voice came out deep as a lion's growl. "Thank you, Master, for my freedom. I am the Jinn of the lamp, and as a reward for releasing me, I will grant you a single wish. Whatever your heart desires, be it power, riches, or fame, all you need do is speak it and it shall be given."

A fearful Ali studied the self-named Jinn, reading the hungry anticipation in his eyes. The boy then pointed to the door and crawled outside. Under the vault of the clear sky, Ali stood and looked out over the grand and imposing city spread out before him, buildings shining golden in the sun, towers covered with colorful mosaics, and bustling shops of all kinds. His eyes swept all around, to drink in what could be his if he could but speak.

The Jinn appeared at his side, towering at least ten feet high. He wore nothing more than a pair of silky pantaloons held up by a wide sash, velvet slippers, and golden bangles around his wrists and ankles. Large golden hoops hung from the elongated lobes of his pointed ears and glittered in the evening sun.

"Fear me not, young Master. Tell me your heart's desire and it shall be yours, so I swear." The Jinn's grin exposed row upon row of needle-like teeth. Like a shark's, it was a smile intended to sow fear in an ignorant young man's heart. But despite his affliction, Ali was not an ignorant young man. He was wise in the way of the streets, having survived them for many years, and how the many merchants he dealt all his life with reminded him of the Jinn's avarice.

Gathering up his courage, and after a moment of perceived contemplation, Ali stretched out his arm to point toward the city, then looked up at the arrogant Jinn.

"What's this? Did I not say you must speak your wish before it can be granted? Do you seek to make a fool of me?" the Jinn growled. But Ali shook his head and pointed to his throat and made a grunting sound.

"You cannot speak?" The Jinn looked perplexed, as if unsure of his next step.

Ali shook his head.

He stared down at the boy from his great height and studied him for a moment while he considered his options. He had been freed from the lamp, and by all known customs and beliefs, he owed the boy. He would not be free to leave until he had discharged his debt. For now, he realized, custom must be subverted.

"Very well—show me what you want and it will be yours.

Then I will be free to leave and roam the world for the next ten years. Then I will be forced to return to the lamp, where I must wait for another to find it and free me once more. So has it always been, and so it must always be. But know this: if you play me false, I will know it and will rip your liver from your belly and eat it before your very eyes."

Ali nodded to show he understood. Then he turned and pointed once again and waited. The Jinn followed his finger and spied the Caliph's palace in the middle of the city. Built of pure white stone, with high walls, towering minarets, and lush gardens filled with flowing fountains. Rows of fig trees and vines laden with grapes. Towering palms with clusters of dates ready for plucking, stables filled with fine horses, and warehouses filled with many goods. These are what the Jinn saw, and more. He turned to look at the hovel the boy called home and believed he understood. He made several quick passes through the air with his nimble fingers. Around them, the hovel transformed into an identical copy of the Caliph's palace with its high walls and sprawling buildings, down to the cracks in the garden stones.

"Here is your wish fulfilled, boy, so you and I are done." The Jinn showed Ali a hungry grin, but it faded when the boy shook his head from side to side.

"Is this not what you wanted?" the Jinn demanded, and Ali shook his head once again.

The Jinn roared in anger, for he knew the boy spoke true. He raged against the clear heavens until the sky darkened, and then the ground beneath him shook and split, filling the air with a cloud of dust. Regaining control, the Jinn looked down at the boy once more.

"What has been given cannot be taken away. I must be given time to renew my strength, so I will return tomorrow to grant you your wish. Then you and I will be done." The Jinn vanished in a fiery flash of light and a puff of smoke.

Ali went inside his new home and cautiously explored it with wonder in his eyes, fearing it might all be a dream. Ali found his private quarters on the second floor and took a long bath in one of the deep pools. Then he dressed in the rich clothes he found in the closet and slept through the night in a soft bed for the first time in his young life.

The next day, late in the afternoon, the Jinn appeared once again and glowered at Ali. "I've wasted enough time; it is time for you to make your wish."

Ali stepped out on the balcony outside his bedroom and looked toward the city spread out below him once again, to spy his heart's desire so the Jinn could give it to him. He pointed toward his simple want. The scowling Jinn searched the area, his eyes shifting from side to side, until he spied the Caliph's beautiful daughter strolling through the souk. Dark-haired and doe-eyed, slender as a river reed. She was accompanied by her maids and a small contingent of her father's guards. Dressed in black silk and armor, faces hidden behind opaque veils, they were the dreaded Black Scorpions.

Grinning with satisfaction, the Jinn used his magic to bring her forth and cast a spell of devotion over her. When she laid eyes on the young Ali Za'had, she instantly fell in love. Nothing else would do for her but to wed the handsome young man. The Jinn then sent her back to her father's palace to make arrangements for the forthcoming wedding.

"I have fulfilled my duty and granted you your wish, so now we are done." But before the last word had passed through the Jinn's lips, Ali violently shook his head from side to side, telling the Jinn he had failed once more. In disbelief, the Jinn howled in anger. He used his needle-like talons to rake his flesh in frustration and splattered greenish blood all about, until he finally calmed and was in control once more.

Breathing hard, he said, "What has been given cannot be taken away. The fair princess is yours, but I must renew my strength before I can grant your heart's desire. I will return in seven days to grant your wish and be done with you."

With a flourish, he vanished in a flash of light and a puff of smoke, leaving young Ali alone to further explore his palace in anticipation of welcoming his new bride.

Before the next seven days could pass, the Caliph sent his vizier, escorted by a company of his Black Scorpions, to fetch Ali and bring him to his royal palace. There, they sat together over a sumptuous meal to negotiate the dowry of the young Princess Sheriza. Once again, his muteness stood him in good stead. The Caliph kept offering more and more to the one he believed must be a young prince from some far-off land

In desperation, the Caliph made his final offer of a hundred milk-white camels, all laden with silks, rich oils, and bales of spices; forty-nine pureblooded desert mares broke to the saddle, along with a proven stallion for breeding; ten large wooden chests filled with silver, gold, and an assortment of colored gems of great value. He added a large tract of land near the sea where grew fig trees, date palms, and many orange trees. All this he offered if Ali would accept Sheriza as his wife. The boy slapped the table and nodded, but never uttered a sound as he saw relief wash over the old Caliph's face.

Five days later, they were wed, and the day after marked the Jinn's return to Ali's rich palace, empty of all but Ali and his young wife.

"I have returned. Ask what you will and it shall be granted." The once light but cunning tone had all but faded from the Jinn's wary voice. He seethed with anger at how ancient custom had bound him to the whims of the young mortal for so long a time.

Once again, Ali stepped out onto his balcony and pointed toward the bustling souk of crowded stalls and overflowing shops, pointing to where he knew what he desired the Jinn to give him sat waiting.

The Jinn took his time to scour the area where the boy pointed, trying to see past the bustling crowds and dozens of shops. He considered and then rejected several likely candidates for the boy's wish until he spied the slave pens. He studied the dozens of people who waited under the harsh sun to be inspected by and sold to their new masters. He then looked about at the near-empty palace with none to tend to its upkeep or needs and smiled.

"I see you have no servants. You have none here to clean or to fetch for you. No maids to look after the needs of your new bride, no cooks to prepare the food, or no gardeners to tend the grounds. None to look after the beast in your stables, or guards to protect your home. That must be your wish." He clapped his hands and sent a peal of thunder rolling across the city. Then the palace became filled with a staff of busy servants.

Ali angrily shook his head from side to side while glaring at the Jinn, who snarled in frustration when he saw the boy indicate he had failed to fulfill his wish. The Jinn screamed his fury. He grabbed his scalp lock and gave it a jerk until he pulled it out by its bloody roots. In his fury, he used it as a flail on his flesh, leaving deep cuts that oozed greenish blood, until he calmed and got his temper under control once more as the wounds sealed themselves, as if by magic.

"What has been given cannot be taken away. The slaves are yours, but we are not yet done, mortal. I am drained, but will return in a year and we will complete our business then." With a flash, the Jinn vanished.

The slaves immediately took over the run of the palace. They cared for the gardens, served the meals, and tended the horses in the stables. Ali hired a caravan master and sent him off with a hundred camels to distant lands laden with bales of silk, kegs of wine, and chests filled with rich spices. With the help of his wife, Princess Sheriza, he established a trading house, bought several ships that sailed the coastal waters of the Arabian Sea and stopped in every port to trade goods. As a result, his wealth quickly increased, and his name became known far and wide.

Soon, Sheriza became heavy with child, and in less than a year she gave Ali a healthy son, and all in his house were joyous, especially the child's grandfather. Such had become the life of Ali Za'had, and that's what the Jinn found when he appeared once again on the boy's bedroom balcony exactly a year later.

"I have returned, mortal, to complete our bargain. Now show me what you wish and I shall grant it. Then I will be done with this cursed situation that has been a burden about my neck for far too long." The Jinn roared and ground his teeth so they sounded like rubbing stones. Yet Ali had noticed a tremor in the Jinn's hands, and his once lustrous gaze had become dull.

Once again, Ali looked out toward the souk until he spied the shop where that which had once been the heart's desire of a penniless boy remained, but he couldn't change his wish, for the Jinn's sake. Taking his time, he raised his arm and pointed in silence while he waited for the Jinn to respond.

Wary of all his previous failures, the Jinn took his time to search the section of the city where the mortal boy pointed. He tried to consider what he knew of the greed of the many humans he had dealt with over the long centuries and the hundreds of wishes he had granted those mortals. Power, beauty, riches, and revenge had been the most popular, but he realized that Ali was different. That caused the Jinn to become confused about how he understood the desires of mortals and began to sow the seeds of doubt.

The ashy-skinned giant tried to imagine what the boy truly wanted. He had a palace to live in, a beautiful wife, a healthy son, dozens of servants, and riches beyond compare. What else could any mortal want? Of course, he would want power, but what sort of power?

The Jinn studied the Caliph's palace. The many temples to the gods about the city. The barracks of the Black Scorpions and their parade field where they marched daily and practiced their arms. With a grin, the Jinn turned to face the boy.

"If it is power you want, then power you shall have, as much power as you can wield. I will give you an army large enough and strong enough to go forth and carve out an empire for you and your descendants." He slammed his palms together hard enough to bring forth a thunderous explosion that rolled across the desert.

From the sands sprang up an army such as the world had never seen: rows upon rows of infantry in black-lacquered armor, with needle-like lances resting on their shoulders. Helmets with ostrich plumes nodding on the wind, carrying shields of wood and hide painted with the symbol of House Za'had. Companies of mounted warriors seated upon camels and horses, clutching massive blades or long spears. Behind them, a hundred chariots followed by archers, engineers, and all the support they would ever need to wage war.

The Jinn turned to look down at Ali Za'had, who could only glare up at the Jinn and stamp his foot in frustrated anger as he shook his head furiously from side to side. The Jinn became stricken for a moment. Unable to believe the denial that came from his mortal master.

Then the anger slowly began to boil. Rearing back with clenched fists, the Jinn screamed until the earth shook and lightning cracked the heavens. He clawed at the stone balustrade and left great gouges. The Jinn called the thunder from the sea, and the terrible shattering sounds sent people scurrying for cover for fear of their lives. But Ali stood his ground as he denied the wish the Jinn had taken for granted.

After he regained his composure, the panting Jinn stood on trembling legs in front of the boy, slump-shouldered with defeat before he spoke in a hoarse voice. "What has been given cannot be taken away. The army is yours to do with as you will. I must regain my strength and will return in five years to grant you what is your due." The furious Jinn bowed once before he vanished in a flash of light.

Ali wondered if it could be nothing more than arrogance on the Jinn's part, or a rigid adherence to some unnamed code that kept the Jinn from taking him down to the souk to determine exactly what the boy wished for. With a shrug, Ali returned to his wife so they could jointly decide what they could do with his new army.

Five years passed, and in that time Sheriza had taught Ali to read and write. She also gave him another son and a daughter. The caravan had returned thrice to increase his wealth many folds. Then with his father-in-law's support, Ali used his army to subdue the many wild tribes in the untamed lands of the Sharth Desert that lay between the sea and the Hills of the Prophet. They soon swore fealty to the Caliph and so expanded his empire many times over, bringing joy and peace to the land.

During that time of growing peace, Ali had grown into a handsome young man. His face was no longer beardless, and he had grown taller and broader to become a formidable man. Ali was happy, and beloved by his family and all his servants. He had made many friends in the city, men of power and importance. He lived the sort of life he had never dreamed he could have when he had been nothing more than a young and homeless street urchin.

Then came the day when the Jinn promised he would return. He appeared on Ali's bedroom balcony in a puff of white smoke, just as the sun kissed the western sea and the cool winds blew in, heavy with the scent of date palms and orange blossoms. Ali noted the Jinn no longer seemed so powerful or fearsome, nor so tall now. His gray flesh had grown ashy, and his once-lethal fangs were now chipped and cracked. The talons on his fingertips split and broken, and his eyes had lost much of their lively glow.

"I have returned, Master, and know you this. My failures wear on me; I grow weaker and it takes me longer and longer to renew my power. Make your wish so we may be done," the Jinn announced in a ragged voice.

Ali stepped up to the waist-high railing circling the balcony, still marked with the evidence of the Jinn's last angry visit, and rested his hands upon it. Taking a deep breath, he looked once again toward the souk and its many shops. He then raised his finger and pointed, straight and true. The Jinn groaned in frustration as he tried to focus on where the boy indicated. His glowing eyes raked the souk and the areas surrounding it. But for the life of him, the Jinn saw nothing of note to interest the man Ali Za'had had become.

Sheriza stepped out onto the balcony, her slippered feet scuffing over the stone, and padded over to her husband's side. Ali slipped his arm around her shoulders while she studied the ragged Jinn.

"So you are the one responsible for all this?" She gestured with an outflung arm to indicate the palace and the grounds teeming with busy servants, the stables, and the parade grounds. The high walls were patrolled and protected by a contingent of armored soldiers.

"In a sense, Mistress. I only sought to grant my master his greatest wish, and in that, I have so far failed," the Jinn acknowledged with a bow, but his shaking voice betrayed his feeling of disappointment.

"You have given him much he would never have otherwise. As an orphan of the streets, he would never dream he could reach so high. For that, I owe you my thanks as well. He has been a good husband and a better father to his children. A true and loyal son to my father, as well as a good and generous master to all those who serve him."

"No doubt, Mistress. Even though that had never been my intention, I want him to make his wish, let me grant it and so end our business. Nothing more and nothing less," the Jinn responded. Yet, he still studied the part of the city where Ali had pointed.

"Perhaps I could be of some help then, to aid you to complete your obligation," Shireza suggested, feeling a twinge of sympathy for the bedraggled Jinn.

"Woman, my business is with your husband and none else, and you shall have no say in the matter. He will make his wish known and I will grant it, then we will be done. Then, and only then, will I be free to live my life and do as I will. Until the time comes when I must return to the confines of my prison, where I must wait for another's mortal hand to free me. This is the life of my kind." The Jinn snarled; his temper, never light, now seethed.

"As you desire, oh Jinn. I shall retire then, and leave the two of you to your affairs. Think about my offer before it is too late, for even I see how much your powers have ebbed." Shireza stood on tiptoe and brushed her lips against her husband's cheek. Then she stepped back inside their sleeping quarters.

The Jinn continued his inspection of the city, even as night fell and the stars opened their sleepy eyes to gaze down upon the vast world below. Through the night, he searched, and halfway through the next morning. He asked Ali several times to once again point out what he wished for, not daring to fail again. Finally, he focused on a group of old men who sat beneath the shaded awning outside a small inn. There they dined and watched the rising moon as they enjoyed a respite from the day's heat.

The Jinn finally began to speak. "Know this, mortal. I have given you a home worthy of a prince, filled with faithful servants to tend to your needs and maintain your home. I have given you a young and beautiful wife, the favored daughter of the Caliph himself. Her dowry has brought you riches you have increased with thoughtful and judicious applications of your wealth. You have made many investments and created trade partners in exotic and far-off lands. I have given you an army that has brought power to your hands and peace throughout the land. All things any mortal could ask for, save one: a long life and health, and this is what I now grant to you." The Jinn clapped his hands, and a warm wind struck Ali, wrapping his flesh in its fingerless caress that left him tingling and full of energy

Yet when the Jinn finished, Ali looked him in the eye and gently shook his head once again. Reacting in horror, the Jinn knew the truth of his denial.

Only this time the Jinn did not explode into a paroxysm of rage, or rail against the fates that conspired against him as he once again failed to fulfill Ali's wish. The Jinn stood before the mortal, slump-shouldered in defeat and weary in his mien. Tears trickled from his oval eyes and tracked his cheeks, too weak to rail against the fates.

"What has been given cannot be taken away. Long life and good health shall be yours. I will return in another five years and seek to seal our bargain then." The Jinn all but sobbed before he vanished in a feeble flash and a weak puff of smoke to attest to his fading strength.

Shireza rejoined her husband on the balcony after watching the Jinn depart. Standing side by side, they enjoyed the cool evening breeze wafting in from the sea, heavy with the scent of salt and the sweet smell of the orange blossoms. Together, they surveyed the scattered lights of Qua' Nar. Shining through the doorways and windows of the houses and late-opened shops, the world seemed imbued with an aura of magic. Ali snaked his arm around his wife's waist, and let his palm rest against the swell of her belly, feeling the heat of life as it quickened within.

"One could almost feel sorrow for such a foolish creature. How long will the silly Jinn try to fulfill his obligation to you by granting the one wish you ask of him?" Shireza sighed as she leaned against Ali, to seek comfort from the warmth of his body. "I wonder how he will react if he ever discovers the toymaker's shop in the middle of the souk, where sits a hand-carved camel of wood, resting near-forgotten on the back shelf. It is the selfsame toy camel that had once been a young boy's greatest wish to own and have for his very own—one I bought years ago with the promise from the shopkeeper it would remain there until the Jinn realizes his mistake."

They chuckled together, knowing they had another five years to see if the foolish Jinn could ever grow any wiser.

EPISODE IN AVERNUS

BY STEPHEN WILDER

"You don't have a choice. You are still my apprentice. We're going."

Borgbinjan had decided it was a good idea for Erik Hammersmith, his apprentice, to try to sell some of his "dragon food" at one of the big markets on the first level of the Nine Hells.

Many questioned the wisdom of this decision, but it was Borgby, after all, and he was considered to be pretty wise, as gnomes go. He himself would accompany Erik, and he was hoping he could get Tad to go, too. He would also invite Barney.

"But I don't want to go," said Erik, during one of their discussions of the matter. "Why can't you and Tadmun just take them and sell them, and leave me out of it?"

"Because you're the artist," said Borgby. "If you want any kind of chance of success with this, these are the necessary steps. The customers and potential patrons are going to want to meet you. You have to be present."

"But does it have to be in Hell?! It's...it's *Hell*! I don't want to go to Hell."

"No one wants to go to Hell, Erik."

"You know what I mean. I don't want to set foot there, or spend any time, or sell anything, or meet rich demons, or anything."

"It's not what you think it is," said Borgby. "It's not fire and sulphur and devils everywhere, it looks almost like a normal place."

"Really?"

"Well, no, but it's not like stories. At least, Avernus isn't. I won't lie: the deeper you go, the more 'hellish' it is. But on Avernus, at the market, it's like shopping in the summer at a big fair."

"Oh, really?"

"No, but that's the best I can do. It wouldn't be Hell if it weren't Hell."

BARNULJAN WANTED TO GO, AND SO DID TAD. GOING TO AVERNUS WAS exciting! Tadmun had to promise Minya that he would watch the children for weeks by himself, to get her to let him go. If Minya knew how much he enjoyed it, then she wouldn't let him use it as a bargaining tool anymore.

Barnuljan didn't have to promise Minnifer anything, except that he would be careful. She knew he would go and wouldn't say he was sorry, but he would make it up to her in other ways. After all, he had retired from regular adventuring, and that was a big sacrifice for him to make. Besides, he had made this trip at least a dozen times, and he was more than adept at handling most any situation. She knew this. She repeated it to herself often whenever and wherever he went.

Of course, Theeljanoon wanted to go, but she knew Hell was strictly off-limits until after her dad was long gone. He had said so many times. Nyljadin, on the other hand, seemed to think she was entitled to this trip. She didn't say much of anything, as usual, but she just managed to be exactly where she needed to be seen by Borgby and her pop.

"You know, I expect this behavior from Theelja, not you, kitten," said Barnuljan. "No dear, you may not go to Hell with daddy."

Nylja disappeared, replaced a couple of minutes later by a large, locked box, among the traveling gear.

"Very funny, Dinny. Still not going."

Erik carried several boxes of work over to the other gear.

"Nice! Did you pack everything the way I told you to?" asked Borgby.

"Yes. Triple padded, wound tight."

"Excellent! What about your personal items, you have them?"

"Yep."

"Well go put them back. Why tempt fate? Just food money." When Erik returned, he was pouchless. "Good boy. Ready to go?"

Tadmun, Erik, Barney, and Borgby carried the stuff to the well in the center of town. Tadmun was carrying several giant pillows. He asked, "Is it on?"

Borgby said, "yep."

Tadmun dropped the two largest packages into the well, leaped after and, after falling for a moment, disappeared.

"Perhaps this is the part I am actually afraid of," said Erik.

"Nonsense!" barked Barney. "This is the best part! Just remember to get out of the way after you land." He dropped Erik's trunks into the well, then jumped in.

"This is easy, Erik. You just drop right through, and you land in Avernus. On pillows. Simple. You're next," said Borgby.

Erik got next to the well, sat down on the edge, and spun so his legs were dangling. He started to count to three, but Borgby pushed him and he fell.

§

AVERNUS WAS IMPOSSIBLY FLAT. THE GROUND LOOKED TO BE MADE OF baked mud, but it didn't make sense that there ever could have been water there. There was no break in the horizon - the flat just kept going and going until it disappeared in the sky. Between the flatness, the pushing, and the hard landing on no pillows, Erik was dizzy.

"Why is it flat?" he asked, once he had recovered himself.

Tadmun answered, "Great question, young man! This area is flat, and clear of any bodies or rivers of blood, or craters full of molten lava, because someone wills it so."

Erik knew what he was supposed to ask next but didn't really want to know the answer. "How far to the market?"

"Well, if you look, I bet you will spot it in the distance. Nothing in the way," said Borgby, having arrived suddenly.

"How are you still standing?" asked Erik.

"You only fall if you fall," smiled Borgby.

Erik knew that being hazed by gnomes was a sign of deep affection and trust, but that didn't mean he had to like it. "Mr. Binge!"

Barney said, "Hey! Not so loud, they'll hear you."

Erik got very quiet and asked, "Who'll hear us?"

"No one, he is pulling your leg, these two pull a lot of legs when they are together," said Tadmun.

In the distance, a small black shape with some sparkly bits was just visible.

"We are out of range. If someone were watching for us, I

suppose we could be seen, but we don't warrant that. All eyes on Gehenna," said Tadmun.

"All eyes on Gehenna!" shouted Barney and Borgby, in unison. Erik looked confused for the hundredth time that day.

"Everyone to their gear," said Tadmun, the signal to get going. Each of them picked up a trunk and found there was an extra. They all looked at each other.

"Borg, my brother, how old was I the first time I set foot in this place?" asked Barney, loudly, putting down his gear.

Borgby nodded with understanding. "I think you were around 200, Barn."

Barney opened the box's lock with two flicks of his thumb and a finger tweeze. He yelled into the box, "So sixty and three is much too young, isn't it?!"

Nyljadin climbed out of the box and stared her father down. She was actually rather menacing, especially for a youngster.

Barney knew all of her looks. "Yes, it is. Those are the words you are not saying. I don't care how small and good at hiding you are. Eventually, something always finds you."

Nylja sighed and crossed her arms, widening her stance a little. When she did that, she looked just like her father. Tadmun laughed out loud.

"See, when she does that, any paternity suspicions I may have go right out the window," said Borgby.

"Can you guys manage? I have to carry her home," asked Barney.

"We'll figure it out. Off you go. Sorry, brother," said Borgby. Barney grabbed Nylja and held her very tight, activated the portal with something on his person, and levitated up into it. Barney returned a moment later to retrieve the extra box and disappeared again.

There was a moment of silence, then Borgby said, "... and then there were three!"

⁕

THE WALK TOOK A LONG TIME; THE PORTAL WAS FAR FROM THE MARKET for safety. Erik did his best not to complain. His box was heavy, though, and he knew he was going to have to be presentable and cordial when they got there. He continued to bite his lip.

Before long, he heard music. It was difficult music in that it was made up of many different styles all happening at the same time. It's what Borgby's wife, Thannemeade, would call a "cacophony," and he didn't much care for it. It was as they got closer to their destination that Erik could begin to discern the differences between the disparate sources: one was a group of singers, another was a group all playing the same instrument, the other was a group of several different instruments all playing together. One group was playing fast, the other two slower. One group stopped, so there were only two groups playing. Then one group started again, and another one stopped. He realized that cacophony wasn't so bad, after all. As they got closer, he thought he heard a couple of instruments each playing on their own. One of them had a timbre he'd never heard. He hoped to hear that one up close.

As the party got closer, the usual bustle of a busy town or garrison became recognizable—people walking to and fro, the shouting of barkers—only the size and shape of the passing characters were much more diverse. In fact, diverse didn't even describe what Erik was seeing.

It turns out that there are creatures of every conceivable size, color, and shape, and they all go shopping in Hell.

The first creatures that he fixated upon were two *illithids*. He stopped in his tracks when he saw them. He'd had nightmares about these creatures in his childhood, and his father had playfully used them to tease him when he was naughty. They were gaunt, dark, and absolutely terrifying. The tentacles that surrounded their mouths wriggled and gestured as if they had minds of their own. Borgby had to come to Erik's aid to get him moving again.

"The rules about violence are very clear here, Erik, and they are enforced quite sturdily." Borgby pointed to a large metallic creature, menacing and tough looking. "See that? That's a *marut*. And those ones there, with the robes, are called *kolyaruts*. They punish people who break contracts. You are under contract once you enter the market. One of the things the contract says is that you will not commit violence in market territory. The *inevitables* enforce the contract. So, you don't have to worry about mind flayers, or *neogi*, or even devils trying to harm you. They may try to get all your stuff for next to nothing, but they won't harm you doing it."

Erik looked at Borgby, and said, "I can't believe I let you bring me here."

Borgby laughed and said, "You're welcome."

Erik didn't hear him, though, because he'd just seen another creature out of his nightmares: a *xorn*. It was on a large platform, like a stage, and the stage was floating along, guided by creatures holding ropes. It was just standing there, almost motionless. All three of its slender, radially symmetrical arms hung limp. Jostles suffered by the platform would make the arms move, the eyes twitch. The mouth on top was open and frothing. *Perhaps it was in some sort of stasis*, Erik thought. It was almost enough to make him forget he was in Hell.

He was in Hell.

Just half a year before, he'd been a simple rodmaker's apprentice, but then the red dragon, *Nubaktikiktarai*, had come, and Erik had become an artist at her behest. She had wanted expensive-tasting, gnarly-feeling, artfully crafted creations to fondle and chew, to pacify her, and he had been the one to make them. As it turned out, he had a flair for it; his objects were beautiful, ornate, and completely useless. Borgbinjan had had the idea that the pieces could be sold as fine art to collectors. Erik had gone along with the idea, without complaint, right up to the point where Borgby had announced that the place where he would be selling his objets d'art was the first layer of the Nine Hells.

Of course the idea frightened him. Like every other sentient being, he had heard horrific tales of how souls ended up spending their eternity in one of the nine layers of Hell. He was brought up by his parents to fear Hell and to be nice and good in his life, in order to avoid damnation, just as many other children were. So, it was no surprise Erik would find a voluntary trip to the evilest plane a bad idea.

Tadmun grabbed his shoulder and startled him. "This is your first step into a larger level of being. It will inspire you, if you let it." Tad knelt to talk to Erik's face directly. "Don't let your fear get up above your stomach. If it gets in your lungs, you won't be able to breathe. If it gets in your mouth, you won't be able to talk. If it gets in your brain, you won't be able to think."

"But how do you do that, Tadmun?"

"You draw your breath through your lungs, into your belly. That's what it feels like. You must be able to keep the breath down there while you talk, or walk, or do anything. The muscles in your abdomen become very strong, and you learn to contain your fear, rather than let it take over your body." Tadmun took several deep breaths to demonstrate. Erik tried a couple of times. "Um, it takes practice."

Erik tried some more, and practicing provided a good distraction for him as they approached the market, but there was no way to prepare him for his first glimpse of a devil.

§.

IT WAS VERY TALL. AS FAR AS ERIK WAS CONCERNED, THAT WAS ENOUGH to make it terrifying. Unfortunately, that was only one of its many features.

It had a pair of giant wings, and two long horns on the top of its head. It carried a large spear, with a fancy tip that glowed and spun. He couldn't tell if the creature was smiling or frowning. It was dark brown, but he couldn't tell if it was hairy or scaly, or something altogether else. He didn't want to look at it, but he found it difficult to look away.

He was especially enticed by the tail: it was very active and seemed to be punctuating the devil's actions. It was incredibly agile, and the creature obviously had complete control over it. At one point, the monster scratched its head with it.

The *cornugon's* face was the visage of evil.

As Erik watched the creature glance here and there, looking at things, he wondered what it would be like to match such a creature's gaze, and shuddered.

Tadmun put his hand on Erik's shoulder. Erik suddenly realized he had stopped walking.

"You're going to be fine," said Tadmun, patting Erik, assuredly. "Nothing will happen here. Nothing can happen here."

Despite reassurances, Erik remained anxious and paranoid. He couldn't keep from thinking about the cornugon, right there, so close he could walk right up to it if he chose. The thought made him woozy. Suddenly his legs buckled, and he sat down, involuntarily, with a thud. Tadmun rushed to his aid.

"Um, Erik, you are attracting attention to yourself," Tadmun said, lifting Erik back to his feet. Erik's legs didn't cooperate. "Please, you must stand. This is very awkward."

Erik could see eyes on him - not many, a few beings here and there, curious. It didn't scare him as he thought it might. *They don't look so scary*, he thought. *Not compared to that cornugon, that malebranche.* He glanced in that direction.

The devil was looking at him.

"Stand up, Erik!" said Tadmun in a barked whisper.

Erik whipped his face away from the devil's glance, and somehow, bravely, found the strength to right himself. He coughed, purposefully, emptily. He resisted the very real urge to check if the devil was still looking at him. He examined his pants and tunic, dusted himself off, and then decided he was presentable. He did not look at the devil again.

"Okay, so what do we do now that we are here?" he asked his companions.

IT TOOK THEM ALMOST AN HOUR TO FIND THEIR SPOT AND SET UP THE tables, the tent, and the sculptures. Tadmun handled the two largest objects: a large sphere made of heavy stone, cleaved by panels of aluminum and bronze, and covered in gems, and a mobile-type contraption with a very heavy base in the shape of a pyramid. The balancing arm was long and thin, and dangled smaller, oddly shaped objects from each end. Erik gave him instructions on how to assemble it, and where to put it in relation to the tent.

There were many hand-sized objects, including several gems he had decorated with clockwork. There was a rod that, when activated, sprouted five branches with precious gems at the ends. He had even tried his luck at making a clockwork animal; the type he'd heard about in stories. While it ended up being a very crafty, walky-spinny little thingamabob, it did not look very much like a dog, or any other kind of animal for that matter, except for maybe a modron of some number.

His booth did not immediately garner interest, but every once in a while, someone would walk by and stop to examine a piece or two, and Borgby could see in each of them the moments when they realized the quality of what they were examining. More and more customers came by to look as time went on. They asked many, many questions, some of them more than once.

"Does this really spin?" one customer asked.

"How did you get all of this to fit in there?" asked another.

"Is this real platinum?"

"What made you think of this shape?"

"Where do you get your ideas?"

"So, are these things really for eating?"

"What does aluminum taste like?"

"How do dragons keep from stabbing themselves with the sharp bits?"

"Do different types of dragons prefer certain metals or gems?"

"So, what made you want to become a dragon food maker?"

Borgbinjan took on the job of answering the questions, charming the shoppers, and being amusing or aggressive if necessary. Erik's job was to be mysterious—which, it seemed to him, really just meant mildly aloof. So, he sat on one of the chests and smoked a pipe. He had to be careful not to inhale, though, since he had never smoked before. Every once in a while, Borgby would indicate to him that he should answer a question himself, or greet someone and shake a hand, and Erik would do so, trying to remain in character.

After some time, an incredibly beautiful drow woman in full chainmail, whose long, white hair was tied in a very attractive knot, came by to examine the goods. She was accompanied by a younger-looking girl who may have been her daughter, whose hair was similarly tied. They studied each object separately before speaking.

The adult said, "I think I like this work, but I don't know for sure. This squat man who doesn't smoke: he's not the artist, is he?"

"He is," responded Borgbinjan.

"Hmf. That's too bad, I wanted to like it."

She started to walk away, but her daughter said, "I like it, why can't you like it?"

"Because the context is all wrong," said the mother. "It sends the wrong message."

"How so?" asked Tadmun.

"They were made by a man," said the drow. "And a dwarf, at that."

"Hello!" said Erik, waving.

"Excellent!" said Borgby, smiling wide. "Our artist is naïve, and too young to understand the subtleties of such an argument. Please proceed!"

The drow woman blinked at him. "Really?"

"Yes, please!"

She curled her lip and considered her words. "If these were designed and made by a woman, then they would represent a woman's strength, and the collection would make a statement contradicting the typical ideologies of the patriarchic cultures of the surface. Instead, these works reiterate the hackneyed narratives of the suffering of men, the abstraction of truth, and fear of death. Nothing I haven't seen tens of times on any number of other worlds."

Those present pondered the woman's words carefully, respectfully, until Erik said, quite exasperatedly, "It's food! It's meant to *taste* good! It's made to be eaten by dragons! I'm not saying anything at all about the suffering of men and the fear of abstraction or whatever you said. Dragons are meant to like the way these taste! The shapes give them texture and flair. That's it. That's all there is to it."

Then he took a breath, and said, "Your, *interpretation* of the so-called 'meaning' of these objects is *yours*, and has nothing to do with me," and was surprised by having said it.

There was another thoughtful pause.

"Very good, boy," said Borgby, exuberantly, "if not mildly surprising. Well done!"

"Um," said Tadmun.

The adult drow raised her eyebrow at Erik. "Mmm. Well, that's *forgivable*, I suppose. But I don't see how you get around being bunched with the hundreds, even thousands of other young male 'artists', who are constantly expressing their displeasure with the way things are up top, when in actuality, everything has been designed especially to suit them."

There was yet another pause. Then Borgby said, "Well, perhaps if he keeps his head down and his mouth shut, we can sneak him through."

The drow scoffed, and smiled a sarcastic, irresistible smile. "Mmm, perhaps." She walked away slowly, followed by her companion. "I'll be watching for your work, dwarf," she said, when she was almost out of polite earshot.

When she was well gone, Tad, Borgby and Erik looked at each other. "Good Garl, she was *amazing*," exclaimed Borgby.

Tad agreed. "Um. As a bachelor, I would have walked after her, without a doubt. Even if it were for only the one encounter."

"What in hells were we talking about?!" asked Erik, still exasperated.

"Um, I admit to being as confused as you about the discussion," said Tadmun. "I cannot quite grasp how the same object could mean completely different things, depending on who the maker was."

"Yes you can, Tadmun. If you give a sword to a child, it doesn't pose the same threat as if you were wielding it, correct? That's the 'context' she mentioned. In one context, the sword is not really going to harm anyone, except for maybe the child holding it. In another context, the sword could possibly cut anyone's head clean off with one stroke at any moment. So, the object is the same, but since the contexts are different, the sword has two different functions.

"Erik's work is similar, except he's the maker instead of the wielder, and instead of function, we are discussing meaning. These concepts really aren't that different from each other. In fact, when you think about Erik's objects as food, then they really do have a practical function. As art, the function is to have meaning, or to have no meaning, perhaps. Which is still meaning."

Erik looked back and forth between Tadmun and Borgby, with a hopeless look on his face. He started to speak, to ask a question, but decided not to. He played with his pipe instead.

There were more people standing around their tent now, studying the wares, discussing them in some cases. Some were listening to Borgbinjan talk.

A dignified older woman, dressed somewhat plainly, said to them, "Excuse me."

"Yes, hello, Milady!" said Borgby. "How can I help you?"

"Yes, I'd just like to examine that whatsit there, the big ball of gems."

"Oh! Fantastic. Yes, we like to call it a 'Rainbowlder'," said Borgby. "It's got a heart of cast iron, covered in gems, then a layer of bronze, also covered in gems. We had to cast a spell around the gems so that they didn't get hot while we set them. Quite a trick!" Tadmun picked it up and held it out to her.

"You didn't...heat the gems?!" she asked, excitedly. She took it, and held it in her hands, which should have been impossible. She took a big whiff of it. Borgby blinked and suddenly understood what he was dealing with. His heart started beating a little faster. "You know, if you heat the gems, they don't...they *change*," said the woman. Her eyes were visibly lit up. She licked her lips. "How much?" she asked.

"Well, it's rather pricey, but well worth it. Ten thousand gold." With that announcement, the people in the small crowd around the tent went silent. Some of them walked away, but others seemed to get closer. A couple more people approached.

"Sold!" said the woman. She handed the sculpture back to Tad and produced a coin purse from nowhere. "Will you take platinum?" She reached in, deep in, well past the size of the purse, and produced a solid bar of platinum.

Borgby immediately recognized the worth of the bar and grinned like an idiot. "Young Erik, here's a practical question: at five hundred gold per bar, how many platinum bars would you need to equal ten thousand gold?"

"Twenty!" he barked, then nearly fell out of his chair. He stood and walked to the table to see the bars of platinum, as the woman stacked them.

"It took a certain degree of willpower to save these," she said. "I travel with them in case I get peckish."

"Well, Milady, let me compliment you on your self-control. This amount of platinum makes my tummy rumble, too!"

The woman giggled. She finished stacking the twenty substantial bars of platinum, and then removed her gloves and put them in the pouch. "I'll carry it out, if you please." She smiled greedily.

"Absolutely! I would ask your name, but that would be in very poor taste, especially in such a place as this, but I would desire to contact you with offers on other items, as we make them."

"Oh!" she said. "Well, that would be quite the trick, eh? I'm afraid the best I can do is to promise that I will return here again one year hence. One year local time."

Tadmun suddenly interrupted. "But madam, how is one to tell the length of a year in Avernus?"

The lady's eyes opened wide at the sight of Tadmun. She adjusted her hair with her hand. "Well, it is a subtle thing. You can tell by the tides. The measure I use is the River Otek, at the base of Mount Cyranok. Today, it is at its widest. I shall return again when that river of lava is that wide again. Good day, gentlemen!" And with that, she picked up the Rainbowlder and walked away, briskly.

ERIK ADMIRED THE PLATINUM BARS. "THERE IS SO MUCH OF THIS! I'LL BE able to make lots of stuff out of them."

"Um. Or you could save it, so that someday, you can afford to buy a home, and have a family," suggested Tad. He was playing solitaire with a deck of big, fancy cards.

"Or I could make a big dinosaur!"

"Tadmun, I think he's just a bit young to be thinking about a family," opined Borgby. "Now, back to work, gents. There are customers about."

They made four sales in the next couple of hours. Even the mobile was garnering attention: several potential customers kept returning to view it again. Borgby was very pleased.

Then, all of a sudden, there was a disturbance, far off beyond the gathered shoppers by their tent. The crowd began to part, leaving a wide berth in their direction. And there approached the cornugon.

They could see it before it got close, approaching them with purpose. Erik almost peed himself. Borgby cleared his throat. "Tadmun, I think maybe you should handle this one."

Tad looked up, put down his cards, stood up, and walked around to the front of the tent to meet the cornugon. Borgby marveled at his audacity. "You know, Erik, we are truly blessed to have a friend like Tadmun. Look at him."

Erik wouldn't look. He was staring at his hands, which were shaking, but he, too, was grateful for Tadmun.

The giant beast walked right up to Tadmun and stared down at him.

"Hello. May I help you?" asked Tad.

The cornugon continued to stare down at him. "Do you speak Infernal?" he asked in Infernal, so Erik just heard the sound of a buzzard being torn in half. Tadmun did not understand either.

"I do," said Borgby, from behind Tad. "I will translate for our associate here, his name is Tadmun."

The cornugon looked Tad up and down, deliberately, looking for an excuse to insult him. Tad prepared himself. Some of the customers started to move in, tentatively, to witness the exchange. The devil blinked once, then looked at the end of his own spear, the fancy part. He showed it to Tadmun and pointed at it. He said a few words in Infernal.

"The end of his spear is broken," said Borgby.

Tad looked at it carefully. He brought his hand up to it and looked to the cornugon for permission to touch it. It nodded, very subtly. Tad oriented himself so that Borgby could see him examining the spear's tip. He used his fingers to separate all the moving parts from each other. He suddenly cut his thumb on one of the pieces. He didn't flinch. He looked at his thumb. The devil snickered in a low rumble. Tad raised his eyebrow at it, put his thumb in his mouth, and spit the blood out onto the ground at the devil's feet. The devil snarled at him.

"Tadmun, why don't you bring that over here," said Borgbinjan.

Tadmun took the spear from the cornugon. He saw how the spearhead was attached to the shaft and detached it. He gave the shaft back to the cornugon and handed the spearhead to Borgby. He stood aside, so that the devil could approach the table. He took his place directly behind the enormous creature. Borgby examined the spearhead closely, being careful not to cut himself on it as Tadmun had done.

Erik had finally managed to pick his head up and look at the devil. It was utterly terrifying. He could see now that the creature did have scales, not fur or flesh. He did not want to be looking at it, but he was mesmerized. Then the devil locked eyes with him, and Erik couldn't look away.

The devil was a living myth—a flesh-and-blood nightmare—and he was sitting maybe eight feet from it. Making eye contact with it. He forced his eyes closed.

He tried as well as he could to concentrate on other thoughts. He thought about Tadmun standing up to it, and he thought about Borgby talking to it. He tried to relax. He watched Borgby. He couldn't believe this was the world he lived in. How was it that he had lived so many years with these men, and had never known how rare and miraculous they both were?

Then, amid his examination of the tip of the spear, Borgby seemed to discover the problem. "Erik, could you hand me a piece of the special parchment, and a quill?"

It took Erik a moment to realize he was being spoken to, and then he jumped into action. He found the writing materials in one of the boxes and gave Borg what he needed.

Borgby took a piece of parchment and flattened it out. He reached for the quill, and it hopped into his hand, and he started to write. He spoke in Infernal.

"I am writing down exactly what needs to be done to fix your spearhead. If you take this parchment to an expert jewelcrafter, and they follow these directions, then they will be able to fix it. You should buy the materials. I would do the work myself, but I don't have any of my equipment here.

"I am giving these instructions to you for free. Please take it, and as payment, do not ask any more of us." Borgby finished the parchment and held it out for the cornugon to take.

The devil looked at the parchment and scratched his chin. He looked at Tadmun, and at Erik. He looked at all of Erik's objects. He looked back at Borgbinjan. He opened his mouth, as if to speak, but said nothing. He took the parchment, and nodded, very subtly. And then the cornugon walked away.

There was a palpable relaxing of tensions through the crowd once the devil was gone.

AN HOUR WENT BY BEFORE ERIK COULD NO LONGER KEEP QUIET.

"Okay, this has been driving me crazy, Borgbinjan. Why did you help that devil?"

"We are under contract here, Erik. If someone comes to us as a customer, we are obligated by contract to trade with them."

Erik reacted. "You *have* to sell to them?!"

"Well..."

"But he wasn't even here to buy my stuff, he asked us about jewelcrafting."

"Yes, good point, but it's perfectly obvious that we work with jewelry. Plus, if we refused, then the devil could call for an adjudication. And even if we won, it would attract a lot of the wrong kind of attention. Not worth it. So, I gave him what I could for free, with the stipulation that he not ask us for anything else. It worked."

"Um, the instructions you gave him are worth a pretty coin, I wager," said Tad.

"Yes, well, I'm an expert, what can I say."

THEY SOLD THREE MORE OF THE SMALLER OBJECTS IN THE NEXT THREE hours. One of the customers complimented Borgby on his handling of the cornugon.

"Too right! Can never be too careful, eh? I never would have thought of that, I may have wound up in his service," said the man, a human who may have been a wizard.

"The customer always comes first," said Borgbinjan, picking up a biggish bag of coins. "Erik, why don't you come over here, and talk to this gentleman about the knickknack he's just purchased."

Erik stepped up to the table. "Oh, yes! Well, that took some doing. You see this bit of gears here?" He pointed to a busy section of the little object. "This effect could have been achieved quite easily with a simple spell, but I wanted it to function without. It took me a number of passes, and a couple of weeks to figure out how to create that mechanism effectively."

"Did it? So, I'm getting quite a value, aren't I?" said the man. "Thank you very much indeed!" The man took a small piece of paper out of his inside coat pocket and slid it over to Erik. "Be seeing you around," said the man, as he departed.

"You're having a good day, Erik," said Borgby.

"This card is blank," said Erik, examining the piece of paper.

"No, it isn't," said Borgby.

Then Tadmun smiled and said, "We've got another visitor, look."

Borgby looked up, and said, "Well, here's a distinguished client, if I've ever seen one!"

Up to the table stepped the merchant they knew as Mr. Sturgiss.

"Oh my, isn't this a surprise! Hello, Tadmun, lovely to see you again! And you're... Borgbinjan, yes? And I don't know you, young man, so let's have introductions, please."

Erik stood up and stepped to shake Mr. Sturgiss' hand. "My name's Erik, Erik Hammersmith. Nice to meet you."

"Yes, it is, in fact! You may call me Mr. Sturgiss. I took the name from a tall flower, native to the planet Gryttyk, that emits a beautiful aroma, like lemon rain. That flower is called a sturgiss."

"You named yourself? After a flower? What's a planet?" asked Erik, very confused.

Mr. Sturgiss tactfully avoided Erik's questions. "Borgby, did you make these objects? They are quite remarkable."

"Actually, young Mr. Hammersmith made them. Erik?"

Erik stood up and cleared his throat. "Yes, they are snacks for dragons. These ones. That one's a whole meal, I guess," he said, pointing at the mobile. "So, yeah. People think it's art, so I guess we've got two kinds of customers: the artsy kind, and the hungry kind. Which is nice."

Mr. Sturgiss smiled at him. "That is nice! Did you sell anything today?"

"Yes, we've done pretty well, I think, seven items."

"That sounds like a lot! How much did you make?"

Erik blinked, then looked at Borgbinjan. Borg said, "Thirty-three thousand. That'll pay for the materials!" He laughed.

"With some left over!" said Erik, enthusiastically.

"Yes, Erik, I was being facetious."

"We have very little to carry back," said Tadmun. "That is also nice."

"And how long have you been here?" asked Mr. Sturgiss.

Borgby, Erik and Tadmun all looked at each other. "Ten Eratian hours?" answered Borgby.

Mr. Sturgiss whistled. "Well. I'll buy the rest, if you don't mind. How much for the lot?"

"Wow!" exclaimed Erik.

"Hang on," said Borgbinjan, skeptically. "You're going to resell them at a higher price."

"Of course!" answered Mr. Sturgiss.

Borgbinjan scratched his face. "How much higher?"

Mr. Sturgiss regarded Borgby. "Honestly, I'm not sure. It's a 'feeling out' process. I will tell you, I am going to start very high with that gangly one there." He indicated the mobile.

Borgby thought about it, then said, "Okay."

Erik protested. "Wait a moment, isn't it my decision?"

Borgby and Tadmun smiled at each other. "Of course it is, Erik. Go ahead."

Erik looked around at everyone looking at him, and suddenly felt self-conscious. "I don't want to decide."

"We'll take it!" exclaimed Borgby. "Fifteen thousand for the mobile, and three thousand for each of the others. That's twenty-four."

"I thought the mobile was twelve thousand," said Erik. Tadmun laughed out loud. Mr. Sturgiss joined him.

"It was, until Mr. Sturgiss pointed out that he was going to sell it for much more. I imagine that he will still make a healthy prof-it," said Borg.

"Moradin bless your honesty, young man!" exclaimed Mr.

Sturgiss. "And if I do make a profit, then I can promise that I will be wanting to buy more. How does that sound?"

"Uh, intimidating!" answered Erik, and everyone laughed, including Erik.

As soon as Mr. Sturgiss departed with the rest of their inventory, the fellows were packing up and heading home. Their loads were ever so much lighter this time, for which they were grateful, after a long and intense day. They were exhausted, and there was no resting on Avernus, not even at the mall.

"Well, Erik? Any final thoughts?" asked Tadmun.

"Yes. I am never doing that again," said Erik, firmly.

"Pfft," said Borgby. "Good news, you don't really have to, not for a while. Chances are Mr. Sturgiss will make a nice profit, and he will sell your creations for you from then on. It couldn't have worked out much better! What are the chances..."

"I sent him a message, telling him we would be here," said Tad.

"So, the chances of meeting him there were very good," replied Borgby.

"I'm serious, I don't want to do this any more. I am not going to make any more food. I'm sticking to rods, Borgbinjan."

"You'll still have to sell them."

"But people buy rods, it's a normal thing. I don't have to go to Hell or wherever to find customers. They'll come to where I am."

"It's not that normal, Erik. They cost thousands of gold pieces. It's not like opening a grocery."

"You know what I mean."

"Not really, no. I don't see much difference between selling rods and selling your sculptures. You'll still be relying on an elite clientele."

"Osquip," exclaimed Erik.

"But you have a salesman for your pieces already! And Erik, you're so good at it! It might be your destiny to make these objects," said Borg, enthusiastically.

"Don't talk about destiny! I don't want to have a destiny," said Erik, a bit exasperatedly. "I just want to have a shop and make things and sell them. Why can't it be simple?" He hung his head, over-dramatically.

There was a pause in the conversation. Then Tadmun said, "You fear change. But life is in a constant state of change, Erik. You have to be flexible to survive. This is a fundamental truth.

"There is no reason why you can't have those things that you want, but you have to be prepared to do hard things to get them. This was the lesson today."

Erik blinked.

THEY GOT HOME SAFE, AND ERIK WENT TO BED. THAT NIGHT HE HAD A nightmare about devils, ordering things from him that he couldn't build, for deadlines he couldn't meet. He had similar dreams on each of the two nights that followed.

On the third day after arriving home from the market, Tad came and found him in Borgby's lab. There'd been a message from Mr. Sturgiss: he'd sold Erik's mobile for forty thousand gold, and the buyer wanted two more pieces of equal value.

Erik looked at Borgby. Borgby smiled at him.

"So, this is it, Erik. You can get on with your life, or not. It's your choice now. Congratulations, you're a journeyman."

VANOOCHA
VA
VA
Voom

Lifestyle makeovers, private fashion coordination and personal buyer, brand management consulting. You've seen her in magazines, movies and on the runway for decades. Breaker of a million hearts, winner of Most Fashionable Human in History from Conde Nast, and two-time awardee of the coveted Coughing Marmot at Gstaad Fashion Week. The modeling and fashion sensation, mononymous ultra-model

VANOOCHA is now offering her private fabulosity services to select clientele. Male, female, or Other; young, old, young at heart or an old soul; super hot, merely smoking hot, or only gorgeous. No matter who you are, you can benefit

from VANOOCHA's expert advice and guidance in your personal, professional and spiritual life. Call today for a consult.

$1000 initial consult fee, nonrefundable.

VANOOCHA!

*fee is payable in USD, Euros, Bitcoin or Yugoslav Dinars

A BUTTON'S WORTH

BY XAVIER ANDERSON

The air feels like pudding.

The sensation has little to do with humidity and a great deal to do with the discomfort of stepping between dimensions.

Physicists argue a great deal about how many dimensions there are. Three dimensions plus the dimension of time? Twenty-six dimensions? Thirty-seven dimensions?

Normal humans may roll their eyes at the discussion. Does it really matter how many dimensions there are if you can only interact with four?

For those with magic though? Even just a drop? These compacted, folded up dimensions open up their wonders for you to see. We call them pocket realities, and this particular pocket reality is currently swallowing me whole.

The portal finally spits me out on the other side, and I check myself over. I'm still in one piece. I'm still properly configured. Good.

Inside my mind, relief is warring with giddiness, but I don't have time to see how the battle ends. Right now, I only allow myself to acknowledge that I once again survived the trip, which means I can continue with my mission.

The smell of broasted sand fills my nose. The sun glowers overhead and the sand reflects the sun's heat. I'm baking from both sides. I'm in a very large natural oven.

Deserts are gonna desert, but I somehow always expect more and better from magic.

I shade my eyes with my hand, and turn slowly in a circle, trying to orient myself. I wouldn't have to move slowly—not if I could move any faster—but I'm stuck on slo-mo as the heat saps my energy.

There. Brightly colored structures.

As I trudge, I absentmindedly rub my thumb over the beaten and worn siglos in my pocket. Even after all this time, it's weird carrying around a coin valued at $100. It's even weirder knowing an Ancient Persian once carried this same coin, but it boggles my brain that, to me, it's neither $100 nor a piece of history. It's a PrePass admission badge.

Did I mention you don't actually need to have your own magic to enter these dimensions? As long as you're carrying a magical object or touching someone magical, you'll get through. More painfully, but still through.

Movement in my peripheral vision draws my attention. Tall, scrawny man with dark hair. He's a good twenty feet away, and I still feel half-blinded by the paleness of his skin. He's an indoorsman if I've ever seen one. By my unfounded calculations, he'll be bright red in the space of a few minutes.

I'm not surprised to see him. I saw him outside the portal, speaking awkwardly to a sad-ish blue-eyed blond woman. I suspected at least one of them was coming here.

The structures draw ever closer.

Now, the smells tease my senses. Cumin and caraway, a hint of nutmeg, and the mouthwatering smell of Za'atar. Combined, of course, with the smells of cooking beef and goat and grains, but those smells can be found in many cultures; the seasonings make these dishes unique.

I'm sure music plays in places, while people barter loudly. I can see more than a few customers speaking to each other from that peculiar, slightly hunched posture that means they're complaining quietly about missing some deal. Occasionally because the guy they lost to is bigger, but often the quiet undertones simply help them remain convinced their out-loud lives are stoic and generous and kind.

Maybe it's a sign that all humans are at least a little magic, carrying our own internal pocket dimensions. Sadly, not all pocket dimensions are happy places. It's up to us to choose where we dwell.

I am perhaps the most unmagical of people. Others see the bright colors of flowing silk. They smell enticing spices and herbs. They taste juicy dishes of peppers and meat. They feel the excitement in the air, the smoothness of the glazed pottery, and the softness of the fabrics.

Me? I see the dirt.

I feel the draining heat. I smell other travelers. I taste dust.

I notice the rat poison and bug zappers to get rid of vermin.

That's not all I see. There is beauty in the riot of colors and smells before me, but somehow when intelligent beings try to distract me from the parts they don't want to acknowledge, it brings those parts directly into my focus.

It annoys most people. I suspect it's why my brother left. Before everything happened, that is.

I step into the shade—slats built over the walkways between

the stalls. In the shade, I slowly wake up. I endured the sun, but in the shade, I step into myself again.

Passing close by, a world-weary soldier slumps in the saddle of a fine white charger. If he looks up at all, he surveys the market with a thousand-yard stare, vaguely noticing much, but never truly seeing a thing.

A beautiful woman wanders a little ahead of me, trailed by a man who is either a bodyguard or a bag carrier. Possibly both. He is stocky. Tall. Built. His hair is cropped short, and he scans the surroundings constantly. His gaze never seems to fall on her, but it is clear that he is deeply aware of where she is at all times.

She is oblivious, with the ease of someone who has always been cherished. Deeply tanned, with luxurious black hair, she truly is stunning. Her shirt is delicate and costly, but she values it little. I notice several snags from the ever-changing grip of the monkey she carries on her shoulder. As I watch, she pulls a small piece of fruit from her tote and offers it to the monkey with an adoring smile. I find myself wishing someone loved me enough to look at me like that.

A flock of leprechauns gambol from stand to stand. They look incredibly out of place. I force myself to focus my gaze casually elsewhere. The outside world is a global civilization. You can find people from anywhere, everywhere. Why should the magical realm be different? Why shouldn't creatures of Celtic folklore find their way to a mystical Middle Eastern bazaar?

Is that Baba Yaga wrapping up her purchase of tasty House Treats?

She soon pauses by the silk vendor's stall. She softly strokes a bolt of orange silk. For the briefest moment, I see a look of inno-cent wonder on her face. It reminds me that no one is ever fully lost. There is always a chance that even a murderous grandmother will find a better path. Beauty invites us all to more.

Baba Yaga signals the vendor, and they begin to haggle. For orange silk. Which Baba Yaga apparently plans to wear in a Russian winter.

The bazaar understands. You create an experience, and items sell themselves.

The pet monkey hops from his mistress' arm and wanders. For him, the souk is a pathway in three-dimensions. He runs up a stall and hops onto the shade; then he scampers along it and back down again, elsewhere.

A wine merchant nearly trips over him, spits out an angry word, and then proceeds on his way, giving his mule's lead rope an extra, angry yank. Petty man, taking out his anger on the mule.

It's far from the first time he's done this. I've recently begun tracking him. Now, the reckoning has come...I hope.

Unfortunately, I travel light. Most everything I had of value has disappeared along the journey. I'm human. I need water and food as much as anyone, and let's be honest, the occasional glass of brandy helps when your search continually turns up empty.

I have the siglos, of course, but that needs to stay with me, or my quest is over.

That leaves me with a travel-worn novel and a button that fell off my coat months ago. Silver-colored, with delicate etchings of two rearing horses, facing each other across the buttonholes.

The monkey darts out of a stall with a yellow box, delicately grabbing snacks from the box as he runs.

Right. First things first. I scan the market for a fruit vendor's stand. A mid-20s man bargains for a pomegranate, while nudging his glasses back into place.

I ponder for a moment. He's carrying a notebook, and he has the air of an elementary school nerd on a field trip. Fascination and joy, prepared to write an unassigned essay or two on the topic.

He'll do.

Pausing at the glass vendor's stall, I smile down at a little goblin child who's watching the world with big eyes.

I estimate this child would be the equivalent of a 4-year-old human. At this age, the world is a discovery waiting to happen. Everything is new. Every moment brings wonder.

I pause beneath a hole in the slats. In this heat, the spot of sunshine is uncomfortable; but I need the light. I keep my eyes on the child's parents' stall, casually flipping the silvery, polished metal button and catching it. Up and down. Hand to hand. I let it shine and glint. Pretty. Mysterious. Interesting.

In my periphery, the goblin child scoots closer.

The button falls through my fingers.

That part wasn't planned. I search the ground. This is one of the many points in life when the ability to hear would be helpful. I remember when I could locate a dropped item based on the sound of how it fell.

The child gingerly plucks something from the ground, and gazes at it. Then she very slowly, reluctantly, steps forward and offers it back to me.

I feel eyes on me, and glance at the source. The glass vendor's stall. The child's parents are watching. Good.

I smile at the child and thank her. "You know what? Why don't you hold onto that? I think you'll get more use out of it than I will."

She grins and thanks me, before spinning away in a delighted dance of excitement.

I straighten and approach the glass stall. "Such a cute, bright child! You must be proud."

The vendor at the back of the stall smiles shyly, while the vendor at the counter simply grunts. I can't hear it, but I can see it in the abrupt contraction of abdominal muscles, forcing a burst of air out. Nothing else changes. The goblin stands, straight faced. Noncommittal. Protecting the child by refusing acknowledgment.

I respect it, but I need a little more. Perhaps something along another line.

"I was admiring your work," I continue. "Such skilled craftsmanship. I wanted to get something small as a gift, but I'm afraid all I have for trade is an old novel..."

I smile apologetically, holding up the book. I lay it on the counter.

The goblin at the counter turns his back. Or maybe her back. It's nearly impossible for a human to tell. Especially with goblin costuming—dozens of subtle encouragements for customers to underestimate the faux-ugly, short, uneducated creature in front of them.

Looks like negotiations are over. I reach for the counter and grasp my book. I'm out a button, and no closer to clearing my first obstacle.

The goblin from the back of the stall steps forward. She (it's easier to think of her as she) places a hand on the book. She grabs a small lamassu figurine, formed in blue glass, and offers it to me. I smile and bow my acceptance.

As I step away with my prize, I notice her stealing a few glances into the novel. Goblins are very educated. They just don't want anyone to know it.

I approach the scholar (for what else could he be), just as he starts to work at unpeeling the pomegranate.

"Beautiful place, isn't it?" I ask.

"Gorgeous!" he replies. He's too busy absorbing every detail around us to meet my eyes, but I've placed myself where I can see his lips move, so we're in business.

"Can you believe that most people don't even know this place exists?" I ask.

"Unbelievable!" the scholar agrees. "I have a feeling I can write and write about it, and most people will just think I'm a fiction novelist!"

Interesting. "So, this is your first time here?"

The scholar bobs his head, finally sparing me a glance. "First time! I heard rumors it existed, from my old professor, but I wasn't sure I believed it. And now I'm here! It's incredible!"

I smile at him. "Have you been able to experience much? Bargain and buy and barter?"

He shakes his head, smiling ruefully. "I'm a poor graduate student! I don't have the money to buy, or the items to trade! I barely managed to get this pomegranate!"

I smile indulgently. "Would you let me buy the pomegranate from you?"

He laughs. "You want this pomegranate? Why not ask the vendor for your own?"

I shrug. "Mostly because I don't have the time to haggle. I saw a monkey earlier, eating rat poison. To counteract the poison here, you need Vitamin K. Pomegranates have Vitamin K."

"My heavens!" the scholar yelps. "By all means! Take the pomegranate! Save the monkey!"

He presses the still not-quite-opened pomegranate into my hand.

I accept with a smile and a bow and press my little glass lamassu into his hand. "In gratitude!"

As I move to walk past him, I see him poring over the little figurine like a 3-year-old with a pretty rock, drinking it in and examining it from all angles.

I stroll to the stunning woman who just found her monkey eating out of a box of poison. I assume she's shrieking, based on the breath pattern and tension of her shoulders. There are moments in life when I'm grateful I can't hear.

Fortunately, the monkey is still fine for the moment. It takes time to kick in. Then again, once they kick in, it is much more difficult to get animals to take an antidote, or to have any assurances that their little bodies can repair the damage.

I tap the woman's shoulder, and offer her the pomegranate, along with my explanation. She sobs and hugs me and snatches the fruit. She coaxes the monkey over and offers him more and more of the precious seeds. Her back is to me, so I have no idea what soothing words she might be saying to the monkey, or what she might be trying to tell me.

Eventually, I see her gesture to her bodyguard, who begins rummaging in one of the shopping bags.

"The mistress insists you have this," he says, and presses a ruby necklace into my hand. A queenly gift. Or at least a princessly one.

Yep. I'm once again jealous of a monkey.

"I'm happy to be of service," I bow. "I'm grateful that the monkey will mend. And I thank her for her gift."

The guard nods at me—half acknowledgment, half dismissal. I go on my way, but as I am not positive which way is mine yet, I soon pause to scan the crowd. The necklace is worth far more than a button and a book, but it's not what I need. What's my next step?

The soldier wearily wanders around the booths. He lets his tired, unfocused gaze scan the crowd. It looks as though he's searching for someone he's long since given up finding.

My eyes narrow as I notice the wine merchant round the corner, sight the soldier, and slip quietly back behind the booth he was resupplying. I've already formed suspicions, of course, but it's interesting additional data.

To my left, I see my buddy, the now-pink wizard. I've apparently lost my bet with myself on how long it takes him to turn bright red. He's surrounded by some of the more active vendors, keeping pace with him. I have no doubt they're extolling the merits of this bowl for scrying, and that wand for the most delicate spells, and the distinguished look of a given wizard hat.

Odd.

He moved through the bazaar quickly. This is the pattern of a man who knows exactly what he wants and where to get it, presumably at the best prices. Bargain wizard. His satchel is bulging. He's already gotten what he wanted and is no longer visiting sorcery stalls.

He's looking at...baubles. Beads. Delicate metalwork.

As I watch, he spends a few moments long-distance window-shopping at my old friends, the glass vendors' stall.

Oh! I bet it has something to do with that awkward goodbye earlier, with the blond woman!

A little closer to me, a gaggle of giggling witches wanders past. It's weird to watch giggling on mute.

Even in the shade, the heat is getting to me.

A gust of hot wind blows dust into my eyes. I blink furiously to clear them. Those are my seeing eyes. I need them.

As my vision clears, I notice a one-armed troll lumbering with purpose. He looks like a living gargoyle, his face set in a permanent grimace—either of pain or of anger or both.

My eyes follow him for a bit. Unlike what folklore would have you believe, trolls don't turn to stone in daylight—they're already stone—but they are nocturnal, and prefer the cool temperatures of Scandinavian nights. For him to be here, in the desert, in the summer, in daylight? He's desperate.

Here's the thing: trolls regenerate, but this one only has one hand. There are only two ways to get a one-handed troll, and both are painful for the troll.

After a few more moments, I set the problem aside. It's not a problem I know how to solve and not my goal. I need to get to the wine merchant, and I need a magical practitioner. How do I build my way to them?

I pause. This stall is different.

In the dusty heat, all other vendors taunt and tempt customers with reborn dreams. Remember that desire for love? Wear this attractive bracelet, and you'll be sure to catch a man's eye! Hungry? Taste a free bite of shakshuka. How good would it feel to eat until you're sated?

With cheap baubles, you beam and you mingle and you yell to get customers' attention.

This stall is understated and silent. Everything from the paint job to the awning to the signage indicates solidity, quality, wealth. Translated, the sign reads *Ancient Weaponry*.

I consider the next hour or so of my future and decide a weapon might not be a bad idea.

I pause to look at the wares. The purveyor of antique weapons ignores me, sitting in the shade, lazily reading a novel. Every languid movement, every aloof facial expression, every page turn telegraphs one simple message: He can afford to lose my business.

I glance over the swords. They would look impressive on any number of walls, but I have no idea how to fence. If I'm going to bluff with a weapon, I need a good bluff. Swords aren't it.

Battle axes: also impressive on a wall, also not a good bluff for me. I turn to go.

Huh. I draw up short in front of a truly ancient-looking weapon. It's oddly placed. The display case looks like it's been shoved onto the otherwise neatly arranged counter, knocking over two other racks.

The plaque simply reads "Shurar." I can't help but wonder if it's *the* Shurar.

In ancient Sumerian mythology, the battle axe Shurar was the weapon of a mighty warrior king. He was...enthusiastic, annoying, and somehow both overly optimistic and insanely pessimistic. The battle axe, not the king. Shurar was a talking weapon.

Obviously, when I read my uncle's old mythology books, I knew it was all imaginary. There's no such thing as magic.

Now, I'm an adult standing in a pocket dimension where magic exists. Could any of the old stories possibly be true?

The axe trembles. Before my eyes, the axe slips its blade from between the straps, hops from the display rack brackets, and comes to hover in front of me.

Okay, if this isn't Shurar, it's definitely his descendent. In some metaphorical sense. I hope it's only metaphorical.

You know what, this is Shurar. I have officially decided to believe that, because I quite voluntarily lack the imagination for a different explanation.

"You're remarkable," I murmur to him. The axe tips a little further upright and sways just enough to catch the light. Preening! Ha! "I bet you have lifetimes of stories to tell. Battles. Rescues."

The thought crosses my mind that if I had a self-guided battle axe, I wouldn't be bluffing. I don't know if battle axes get, um, rusty, but even if the axe was bluffing, the sight would be impressive and unsettling.

I glance around. The shopkeeper is closer than I would like for this, but I'm still beneath his notice. I'm not sure if he's listening or not. I focus on the level of vibrations in my throat, trying to keep my voice low.

"I have a question, but I can't hear your answer," I say. Even talking axes have no lips for me to read. "You're intelligent. So why are you in this shop? Are you for *sale*? Or for hire?"

The axe leans ever so slightly closer. He gives the impression of listening intently.

I take it as an invitation to continue. It's a risk. But nothing in this venture is risk-free. I lean still closer, to speak more quietly. "I'm on a mission and I need backup. I can't pay a traditional wage, but if you're for hire, I could give you this necklace, which would be worth something."

The axe tips to the side. I'm struggling to read ancient weapon body language, but he kind of looks like a dog cocking its head. He bobbles slightly—a nod?

And then, he leaps into the air, pirouetting. What is this?

The merchant looks up from his book to glare at the axe. His mouth moves. "Stop it! Be quiet!"

The merchant lunges across the stall and swipes at Shurar. The living myth darts through the air to hide behind me.

If you think it's scary having a drunk Viking run at you with an axe, try having an unsupervised axe race around behind you. I somehow manage not to flinch. I think I even managed to look bored.

The shopkeeper's mouth moves again: "A thousand apologies!"

I incline my head to him.

"I can show you many other weapons!" he offers. "Better behaved ones! Are you looking for something special? Or for a gift for someone special?"

On those last words, he waggles his eyebrows.

I smile blandly. Vendors' livelihoods depend on them being able to read you and offer you the dream you most crave. Right now, I'm a mystery he's trying to figure out.

Thankfully, this pocket dimension has no religious affiliation, and its cultural rules are their own. Still, I imagine very few women frequent his shop, especially unaccompanied by a man.

Yet here I am, without a Y-chromosome. An enigma.

"Shurar should not be talking to you," the shopkeeper efficiently apologizes to me while also threatening the axe. "I display it only to help the most discerning clients make plans for the upcoming auction. Unless I request a demonstration, it is to sit *quietly* on its rack *without talking*. Can I help you purchase anything else?"

I do not fit the profile of the customers he associates with money.

I spare a glance at the rest of the wares and shake my head. "I am only interested in the axe."

The vendor shrugs carelessly. "Then come to the auction next month."

I turn to go, but find my way blocked. Barred by a battle axe. Shurar has spoken.

I assume.

I turn back to the vendor, keeping my face set to bored and vaguely annoyed. "What is this?"

"Can you not hear him?" the vendor suddenly looks intensely jealous. "Shurar says he will go with you, whether you pay or not. He says he is not some common antique weapon to gather dust in a tent. He commands me to take the necklace you bear as payment, or to content myself with nothing."

I glance at Shurar. He bobbles his blade. Which looks threatening, but I'm pretty sure he's nodding.

I choose to trust in Shurar.

I do not trust the shopkeeper. Any goblin who can afford to appear affluent, unblemished, and educated is one with ambition and a whole different kind of conniving. Except he's wealthy, so here we call it 'business savvy.'

"I want a receipt," I finally say. I will not give him any excuse to claim theft later.

The shopkeeper glares at me and Shurar. Though he suddenly becomes much less hostile once he sees the necklace in question. It is shiny, valuable, and most of all, *silent*. Instead of babysitting a barely-cooperating battle axe until the auction, he can get a decent price now and retire from that particular headache.

He writes a receipt. I examine it and demand some edits. Once complete, we each sign and seal both a merchant copy and a customer copy. I finally leave the tent with the single most valuable antique weapon I think exists. Granted, he isn't mine. He has a mind of his own. I have nothing left to trade.

Although... I speak as soon as the thought strikes me. "Shurar, you once defeated a stone army, correct?"

I pause and stare at the axe. The axe hovers before me.

"You have no lips for me to read, bud. I need a yes or no."

The blade bobbles up and down.

"Would you be willing to perform field surgery?"

The axe hops a little higher, bobbing its blade. I take that as an enthusiastic yes.

I head for the stall I'd seen earlier. We ambush the troll as he leaves, carrying a pricy bottle of fine liquor.

I only mean to talk to him, but a battle axe has an unnerving ability to make every unexpected encounter feel like an ambush.

"Excuse me!" I greet.

The troll turns to me.

How do I start this conversation? I've got nothing, so I fumble forward anyway. "That is a fine bottle of liquor."

The troll...speaks. I can tell that much. I stare intently, but I have no practice reading lips made of stone.

I glance around and notice the knight preparing to plod past me. The knight! I needed to talk to him soon, anyway.

The knight is as modern-born as anyone else here, but he's

stuck in the past. Though not in Europe's past. He looks like he's walked out of the pages of *1001 Nights*.

I raise my voice. "Many greetings!"

He stares through me for a second or two, and I begin to fear that he will not talk to me because I am a woman. If he is who I think he is, his nation is more progressive than most in the area, but every country has its fanatics.

"Marhaba," he finally responds.

First hurdle cleared! He'll talk to me.

With a few apologies and explanations, I soon get the knight set up as my translator for the troll.

The troll startled a superstitious Scandinavian peasant. The peasant managed to hack off the troll's hand and then throw acid on the stump before it could regenerate. Why the peasant was carrying acid is anyone's guess. The troll didn't stick around long enough to ask.

The troll tried several doctors, but trolls are solitary creatures who don't become doctors. And the modern human medical professionals prescribed modern pain meds, which don't work on stone. This particular brand of liquor is the only thing he's tried that helps the pain.

"I can heal you," I say.

The troll and the knight look skeptical.

"May I?" I ask, gesturing at the wounded arm.

The troll eyes my hand, and then, ever so slowly, brings his stump up to meet it. I examine it closely.

"I only see acid marks until about here," I gesture, lying through my teeth. The acid marks stop lower down, but I want to be on the safe side.

No reaction. From anyone.

"If we cut your arm off here, you'll be able to regenerate again," I conclude.

The knight looks more in-the-present than I have seen him yet. He looks shocked and disturbed, but truly, presently shocked and disturbed.

The troll just looks thoughtful. After a moment his lips move.

"He says he will try it. He doesn't think it could hurt worse than it already does," the knight translates.

"Shurar?" I say.

From the way he sails into the air, Shurar is enthusiastic.

Also, I really should have planned this better. I did at least pick a spot with a lot of open sky overhead, giving Shurar room to maneuver, but we're beginning to attract a crowd. I believe bazaar amputations, like all amateur medical treatments, should be done in privacy.

Shurar and the troll seem unconcerned. The troll stands with his arm out, and Shurar dives blade-first into it. He must be a bit out of practice, because he severs the arm even farther up than I had indicated. If this doesn't work, the troll will have every reason to pursue a medical malpractice suit.

I glance around. The troll is screaming. Several members of the crowd are screaming. Shurar waits eagerly, and the knight looks both intrigued and disgusted.

For several long, agonizing moments, nothing happens.

Then slowly, ever so slowly, the troll's arm lengthens. Just a little. Then a little more.

The troll sags in relief. His face relaxes. He winces a little with the growing pains, but the haggard look of constant pain has left his stony brow.

As his arm continues to regrow itself, he extends the liquor bottle toward me.

I glance at the knight.

"He says his pain has left him, and he no longer needs his remedy. He wishes to gift it to you," the knight translates.

I bow and thank the troll. "I am happy that our paths crossed, and I was able to ease your pain."

I gratefully accept the liquor bottle. Something to trade!

The knight tugs gently on his horse's reins.

"Wait!" I say. "I think I know where to find the one you seek."

The knight freezes. In his brightening and quickly dulled eyes, I see the moment when hope springs eternal, and I see the moment when he viciously slices hope's legs out from beneath it again. Hope has become an unbearable wound.

Duty keeps him by my side. But I'm glad I have Shurar. An icy, robotic knight isn't much backup for whatever may come next.

I notice the wine merchant again. With most of his original merchandise offloaded, the merchant has stacked a great burden of new wares onto his poor mule. The mule stumbles, and the merchant viciously swats the mule with a cane rod.

The moisture in the mule's eyes looks like unshed tears.

I'm coming for you next.

But first—someone who can guide magic...

The witches are a possibility. They're gathered around a pottery stall, looking at colorful sets of small bowls. Who can blame them? When timing is a potential factor for potions, you need a good mise en place setup, but it looks like they've already found what they need.

As for the wizard... There! He's paused in front of a perfume stall, eyeing the wares from twenty paces. Still trying to find the perfect gift, but not confident enough in this task to approach anyone. That, I can help with!

I visit a silk merchant. I overpay, only having the pricey bottle of liquor to trade, but I get what I need, too.

I saunter up to the wizard, who's too busy contemplating a florist's wares to notice.

"She has the most beautiful blue eyes," I say.

"She really does!" he sighs.

I hold out the new pashmina, silky and blue. "This would really bring out her eyes."

The wizard gives me his full attention now. He looks confused.

I explain. "I saw her when she dropped you off. She was wearing a lower quality pashmina, in a less flattering color. Call it women's fashion sense. She'll love this."

He reaches slowly for it, almost as if he can't stop himself, but he manages at the last minute, his hand falling back. "Why are you telling me this? What do you want for it?"

"A few minutes of your time. A small demonstration of your magic."

His Adam's apple bobs as he considers. "What kind of demonstration?"

"Transmutation!" I say grandly. I hand him a scrap of paper. "I just need you to imbue these words with magic and incant it when I give you the signal."

He still looks wary. "That's it? And then you'll just give me the scarf?"

"That's it."

He agrees, the gleam of adventure starting to overtake the suspicion in his eyes.

I guide the wizard to the wine merchant and his mule. "Direct the incantation at the mule."

The merchant protests, coming toward us threateningly. Shurar neatly intercepts. The merchant tries to step around him, and they begin a complicated and dangerous dance.

I angle myself to watch both the wizard and the mule.

The wizard studies my words on his scrap of paper. Not really my words. I stole them from my studies. I probably could have updated the language but wasn't willing to risk it. Even now, they're only as exact as my memory.

I can sense the magic building around me as the wizard reads aloud: "If the creator of all things did form thee as thou are at present, do not change. But if thou art in that condition merely by virtue of enchantments, resume thy natural shape and become what thou wert before."

The soldier's face hurts to watch. So much raw hope, buried beneath even more not-daring-to-dream. He stands frozen, yearning for the one outcome he believes he can never receive.

The mule collapses on the ground.

The merchant dives under Shurar and ends up on the ground. His eyes are wild. He can't decide whether to rush the wizard, attack me, or crawl away. Shurar keeps him contained.

The fallen mule shrinks, disappearing beneath the giant load he recently carried. I really should have forced the merchant to remove everything before trying this. Live and learn.

The mule's load, sans mule, sinks farther and farther into the ground.

I step forward and lift a corner of the load of baggage. It's all roped securely together, and I strain for a few seconds. Then, the baggage lifts.

At first, I think the knight or the wizard have joined me, but no. The baggage has begun levitating.

The dirty face of a disheveled man pokes out from beneath the pile of baggage.

"I say!" he exclaims. "Anyone got a cloak or some such that I can borrow? I hadn't much use for one, as a donkey, but I'd vastly prefer not to wander through a bazaar in mixed company without some form of garment!"

The soldier stands pale and silent. He blinks repeatedly, and his jaw works. Strangely, I feel like I'm watching him struggle out from underneath an even larger pile of baggage than the one that swallowed his master. Every not-daring-to-hope has frozen a layer of his heart. Now, finally faced with the reality he's pursued relentlessly, he cannot reach out and touch it. A popsicle knight, stuck inside his own personal freezer.

I snag a doodad from the merchant's pile of baggage, make a quick trade, and return with a simple tunic. I've missed the point where the soldier unfroze, bound the merchant, and began speaking with his prince. For a prince he was.

"Jolly good of you!" the prince briefly disappears more thoroughly under the pile.

Then the pile lifts, and he strides out. The clothes are rough, and already dusty. But it barely matters what he's wearing. He's every inch a prince.

It's strange seeing a book character come to life before your eyes. Once I learned magic was real, I knew it was nonfiction. But still. Prince Shakir. Born in a pocket dimension, educated in Britain (at some point in both his and Britain's past). Half-human, half-djinn, erstwhile mule, and the official owner of the treasure I seek.

The wizard all but skips away with the blue silk pashmina, leaving me with the prince's full attention.

"I owe you everything," he says. "Name your reward. If it is within my power, I'll grant it."

I SLOG MY WAY BACK THROUGH THE PUDDING-AIR OF THE PORTAL.

I rest my hand gently, tenderly on top of the satchel I carry. I almost can't believe I finally have it.

One step closer to finding my brother. Like the knight, I struggle against my own wound of hope, unsure if I can face it. Unsure if I can afford to let it live. Yet unable to give up.

I barely notice where I'm going. I seem to float above the

ground. My mind wanders down the uncertain paths of multiple futures.

I glance up at decayed concrete, graffiti, and ragged blanket curtains blowing freely behind panes of shattered glass.

My confused thoughts and unattended legs have carried me straight into the worst area of town.

A pair of thugs eye me, eye the satchel I carry.

I take their measure and dismiss them.

I'm sure I make quite the fashion statement, with a giant battle axe strapped to my back. Shurar has opted to accompany me on my quest. He's not much use here, outside of the magic dimensions. But he still looks impressive.

I also sport a new ring—an additional gift from the djinn prince. It comes with a promise of a favor attached.

I stride toward the most disreputable building, directly toward the door that is always locked.

The rusted metal stings my knuckles as I rap on the door.

A slot in the door slides to the side. As always, there is only blackness behind it. As always, the silence waits for me to fill it.

I place my prize on the ledge before the slot.

"As requested. Am I in?"

A knobby grayish hand appears, swiping the artifact off the ledge. A few agonizingly slow moments leak past. I force myself to wait a reasonable amount of time for the door to unlock.

If it will.

Finally, I stretch out my hand, touch the handle, and prepare to turn the knob...

THE TALE OF IBRAHIM AND THE GHOUL'S GRANDMOTHER

BY URNA SEMPER

O, my Best Beloved, comfort of my old age, when you come to the city of Penesthelia, with its five quarters, its twenty towers, and its one great Market, you will find in the Market's center the fountain flowing unceasing at the top of ten stairsteps of marble and porphyry, and thirty fonts of brass.

If you are like Ibrahim, son of Sulaiman, you will sit on the fountain, peel a limorancio, devour the yellow fruit, and ponder your options. May yours be better than his!

Ibrahim, a tall young man with black hair and eyes, came with a herd of sheep from the downs below the Upper Plateau. Slumbering with them by night at a spring, he dreamed of a great wind blowing like an efreet and awoke to a beautiful dawn with three perfect clouds and not one sheep, each and every having vanished as if they'd never been. Climbing a great stone tumbled there since dry land was the sea's deep, he turned to all of the four winds and saw no flock.

He had hard words for fate, but Ibrahim son of Sulaiman's

225

black eyes shone clear. He knew there was no road open behind, but only ahead: his father and three older brothers would surely beat him to death if he returned without money for the sheep.

He had three broad drachms in his money-pouch and three little dekas in his sash, and he walked through orchards, gardens, and vilaĝos and entered the North Gate. He spent two dekas for limorancios, as you might do yourself. Sitting and eating, he saw a closed and curtained chair carried through the multitude by four strong men. An officer with an ebony staff cried, "Make way! Make way for the high and mighty Shantih, daughter of Tigran!" Two men followed in green-and-desert-brown with long guns on their backs, glaring at everyone tarrying.

"Well," said Ibrahim, "My ruin came this day, so I'll at least see this high and mighty lady and learn if Penesthelian women are lovelier than girls in the North."

He need not stir a step: the chair came to the fountain's foot, and a pale hand stretched out with a silver cup.

One of the men with long guns filled it with pure water and handed it within. Ibrahim watched the cup vanish in a twinkling! But two blue bright eyes gleamed through locks of hair night's color, and as he perceived them, they perceived him. Then the chair was carried away.

Enchanted, Ibrahim followed until the men with long guns spied him. "Back! Rascal!" one bellowed, striking the lad with his gun's butt until Ibrahim's money-pouch of drachms tumbled from his sash. Some beggar seized it, vanishing in the crowd.

"My folly leads me deeper," Ibrahim said. "No sheep, no drachms, and one deka left in my hand. How much more ill-fated is the day?" He turned: the chair was no more visible than the beggar nor the sheep.

But he was a youth of courage. "I may not live to see next moonrise: I may as well see marvels."

226

Every stall flowed with goods: spices uncommon, gems set and unset, shells curious, cloth rich and glittering. Under arches on the market's east side, where night shadows still lay, he paused at a dim stall loaded with wares unnamed: subtle goods and instruments and dangerous things from the lands of the Elbasan in the East. A little man minded it, wrapped in black and brown cloth, narrow face hidden within his hood, gloves on his hands.

"Good day, youth." His voice was like a bird's, thin and twittery.

"Good day, good mercanter."

"Will you buy?"

"I need nothing."

"Everyone needs something."

"What men cannot afford, they cannot need."

"My wares are cheap," said the little narrow man in the little narrow stall. "Look! A mirror you may write upon to converse with friends halfway 'round the world."

"Alas, I've no friends, neither here nor by the farthest sea."

"How of this?" The little man flourished a black box the size of his palm. "This will make a shout like an efreet's voice, opening a hole in a wall wide enough to walk through."

"What wall have I to break, *effendi*?"

"Then this—a silver pen to heal your mind and banish memories of your evilest day?"

"How ungrateful would I be? This is surely my evilest day, yet I have seen great beauty. I would not forget it for all the fortune in the world."

"I had expected no such wisdom in the hearts of men," the mercanter piped. "Perhaps you'd buy your heart's desire?"

"Heart's desire? I see no lost sheep, *effendi*!"

"Is that all your heart's desire, child of man?"

Ibrahim hesitated. "I've seen," he said slowly, "somewhat that my heart desires."

"You've seen a maiden's hand and wrist and bright eyes," the mercanter said.

"How—!"

"Whatever else do youths want? But I've my ways. I can sell you what you wish!"

"You jest."

"I know the face you've seen: the daughter of Penesthelia's richest mercanter, whose caravans groan with gold and silk from far Zarvanipur across Ortrera. A most *delicious* maiden."

"What would *that* desire cost?"

The little man laughed sly. "A thousand drachms for a lifetime of happiness, cheap at the price!"

Ibrahim pulled the sad and battered deka hidden in his sash. "This is all I have in the world."

The little man tugged the chin within his hood. "Well," he said in his whispery, fluting voice, "it's not the only coin I may be paid in if you are bold."

"How do you mean?"

"I suggest this only to the brave..."

"Even if it means my death, I shall attempt to win her."

"Well, then! My aid can be bought by the bold. Leave the city through East Gate, and go to the Penesthelian necropolis. There are tombs of powerful men, each older than the last. The greatest has a stone door carved with a deep-swimming gorgona. Find a stone jar on the lintel above the door in a stone leopard's paws. Curses mark the jar, but you will ignore them. Break the seal to find a red gem in a gold ring. Bring it to me, and I'll teach you how to bargain for this maiden."

"Should I disturb the dead, good mercanter? Are these true, fearful curses?"

"What do the living owe the dead? Happiness and light above ground are yours yet. Strong and young, love protects you. I am old and weak." The little man stretched out his arms, seeming frail in his rags. "I cannot do what young men find simple. There may be danger in this jar, but he who gains the maid will be safe from it."

"What good is this ring?" Ibrahim said, suspicious.

"Merely a sign of a bargain I made, that I require to win my wealth."

"What if I should prefer gold to a maiden?"

"If you say that, your eyes declare you a liar. Wealth is for old, cold men; love and women for the young. Bring the ring and win the maiden; else, never touch her."

"Perhaps I shall do this task," Ibrahim said, "If you promise to help win her."

"I swear, if you bring the ring from the jar, you shall wed her."

"Thus we seal bargains at the foot of the Upper Plateau," Ibrahim said, putting out his hand. "Ibrahim son of Sulaiman accepts your bargain."

"I am called Cassim," the mercanter said, "and the bargain is made." The hand of the mercanter, wide and spade-like in its mittens and wrappings, went in Ibrahim's, and they shook.

"A bargain made is a bargain sworn," little Cassim piped. "Fail not to bring it!"

"I shall return," said Ibrahim.

O MY BEST BELOVED, IBRAHIM STRODE WITH LION'S HEART. LANES labyrinthed through market tents, stalls, and eager traders, leading him as though threads drew him until he passed into cool green streets of fine palacos, arched windows filled with birds and bright curtains.

But in one window, the highest, in one palaco, the grandest, he glimpsed a pale hand reach and twitch the curtain partway. Two bright eyes flashed down, and he and they regarded one another: the eyes in the visage of the fairest maiden he had ever seen.

He removed his cap, bowing. "Lady of the fountain!" he said. "Peace be to you. Permit me to introduce myself! I am Ibrahim, son of Sulaiman."

She leaned, silks blowing in the breeze. "What desire you of me?"

"I would wed you because you are the loveliest woman in Penesthelia."

She put chin in hands, smiling. "What lands or fortune do you have to make this come true? Only the wealthiest husband will marry me."

"I am," he said, "the youngest son of a shepherd at the Upper Plateau's foot."

"Oh? Where are your sheep?"

"Lost, taken by whirlwind or efreet or bandits."

"Have a care," she smiled, "the like happens not to me."

"May I know your name?"

"I am Shantih, daughter of Tigran, oh Ibrahim, son of Sulaiman. How will you win me?"

"I've bargained with the little mercanter Cassim to brave the necropolis and bring him a red gem in a gold ring from a stone jar on an ancient tomb. He promised me in exchange for this, he would compass our marriage."

"One hopes he will enquire of my will also," she laughed, and the laugh was like temple bells, though her eyes were troubled. "But do you not know that the tombs are dangerous by night?

There are jackals from the desert, and some say there are also efreets, ghosts, and ghouls." She frowned.

"I fear nothing with your face in my heart."

"Have you not heard I am a troubled bride? My father has a great debt for which I am the pledge. I cannot wed until it is paid."

"I have nothing in this world, so I fear no difficulty, having nothing to lose."

"I shall let you depart, lest my face make you drunk with love and unable to pursue your labor."

She let the curtain drop, then pushed it aside and called, "Wait!"

He hesitated in the street, and she tossed something to him. He caught a folded fan.

"Put it away, secret! Keep it for deepest need, and it may protect you, Ibrahim, son of Sulaiman!"

It was of ivory and gems, worth all the sheep lost while he slept. But he did not consider what had passed under his heel's dust, only the path before him. He put the fan into his sash, bowed gallantly, and left the city by a great gate blue-tiled.

There were fields, vilaĝos, dry hills and ravines, laden donkeys, creaking carts, a white horse with a blue-cloaked rider galloping hard east, then a sprawling city of the dead, tombs cut into living rock or built tall of marble, some as young as yesterday, some near as old as when men first came from the sky into the world.

One huge old tomb in antique mode had a stone door twice as tall as he, set deep under the lintel, carved with a gorgona's face. A stone leopard above crouched, a stone jar between its paws.

He'd thought little about how to climb to the jar or open it, but now found no way to reach it. The day waned orange over Penesthelia's spires. The quest seemed a worse idea now than earlier, and he tried to shin the smooth doorposts.

"This would be easier with a ladder," he said. "I must think until answers come." He took an apple and bread from his sash, wishing he'd spent that deka on meat, but the girl's eyes made him forget such things.

Night fell across the world, and the river of milk poured down the sky, and the ships of men sparkled on journeys among the pathless stars beyond the sea of air. He often lay with his sheep at night watching glory unfold, but now his hair prickled with creeping dread of dead men and old places.

"There was no going back, only ahead. Now," he added, "there's no going ahead."

Nearby slouched a poor man's tomb, door broken. He crept in, cloak-wrapped, listening to bats and nightjars.

He drowsed until a rattling, a rumbling, a rushing of feet and voices began within the ground. Rolling to his knees, he thought to leap from the little tomb and run. Then he said, "I may be a fool, but I may see wonders yet."

He crept, O Best Beloved, to peek. The stone door swung open, and beneath the leopard rushed forms, murmuring, croaking, and guffawing. They gathered in a ring in the space among the tombs, slapping hands on the ground and chanting.

The greater of the two moons cleared the hills, drenching the city of the dead in pale yellow light. Ibrahim stared, fearful and revulsed.

Like men, they were, but smaller, squat, bandy-legged, with long drooping noses, eyeless flabby faces veiled in rags, hands and feet with mole-like nails, wrapped in filthy shrouds. Thirty? Forty?

The calls grew louder and louder, softer and softer, louder— then silence!

THE SON OF SULAIMAN LITTLE LIKED HIS PREDICAMENT, O BEST Beloved. He knew them to be ghouls, eaters of the dead. Neither beast nor human, they squatted like apes. Many things ran through his mind, not least of all that, as much of a marvel as this was, he was unlikely ever to see Shantih, daughter of Tigran, again.

He lay listening to the wrawling, chirking crew.

"Hungry!" moaned one.

"Starving!" gibbered a second.

"All the bones are dry and dusty!" complained a third. "I'm so hungry I can almost smell flesh!"

"Silence, brothers!"

Taller, like a man, wrapped in cloths and cloaks, another figure appeared. They fell silent.

"Are you hungry, brothers?"

"Yes! Yes!"

It pointed. "Through the tombs from the city comes a man! A fresh man to devour. We hunt!"

They leaped to their feet, eyeless faces grinning. Hissing and gloating, they flowed through the tombs.

"Better," Ibrahim said when deep silence came. "I shall abandon this madness."

Emerging, he found the stone door open, yellow light flowing out.

"Well," he said, "this is a marvel to see, live or die. Maybe some treasure lies here I can win her with."

Hand on knife, he crept in.

The stuffy chamber contained plunder: gold, silver, copper, and gems. Wealth buried with the cold dead was cast in jars and bowls, heaped and dumped carelessly. On the floor sat a begemmed golden lamp with a scented flame.

In the wall, a tunnel bored into solid earth, leading to darkness. He had no desire to see what lay beneath. "The marvel will only be in the quantity of bones. But the ring—that I must fetch from the jar for mercanter Cassim."

He studied the stone leopard and jar above the high lintel. "Less of a trick now," Ibrahim said. "For look! With the door open, I can climb the gorgona's face and reach it!"

He scaled the stone gorgona, swinging his leg over the thick stone door, balancing. The carven leopard stared blankly, paw round the base of a jar marked with warning theurgices that even a shepherd's son knew meant deadly magic.

"He lied not: it is cursed." He hesitated. "I'll dare it! Without love, why live?"

Ibrahim stood atop the door. The lid was coated in cemented lime and dust. He put knife-tip between lid and jar, prising, wondering if it weren't solid stone. Then, the knife pierced a hollow, cracking the coating to split the seal of years. Cold wind moved over flesh creeping with the curse. He knew his death lurked by as a scent of ages rose.

But he remembered Shantih: warmth and courage returned, and the wind passed. He feared neither death nor curses with her in his heart.

The heavy lid scraped and groaned as he wrenched it open. Beshuddered, as you might be, O Best Beloved, your hand placed where spider and scorpion lurk, he groped in the jar, past his elbow, finding filth and dirt...and in the dirt, something cold and hard.

He drew out the ring.

Red stone and gold flickered in moonlight, of curious shape and design, and he shoved it into his sash, grinding the lid back.

Down he jumped to flee, but then heard ghouls moan, gibber, and sough, some from this way, some from the other. He darted behind the tomb to discover shadows clambering through dark sepulchers, squeaking and hissing. Back he went to the front, thinking of diving into his hole again, but loping shapes filled the lane, knuckles in the dust. The space in front of the mausoleum glowed starkly as the second moon rose—

He slipped into the mouth of the ghouls' treasure-house, leaping behind piles of despoil trapped behind jars of oil and pearls

Ibrahim ran with cold sweat. A centipede crept on the sand, and he fought to remain still as its many legs passed over his fingers. The ghoul-clamor approached, washing around the tomb, then in they rushed, smelly, hissing, pattering, stumbling by heaped wealth and into narrow dreadful darkness, like rats plunging into a drain, squirming one against the other with paws and limbs. Last to enter was largest, seizing the lamp and vanishing into the tunnel. The instant its light failed, the stone door crashed shut!

O BEST BELOVED AND DELIGHT OF MY HEART, KNOW THAT WRETCHED Ibrahim, son of Sulaiman, trapped with angry, hungry ghouls, and a priceless ring in his sash, sighed. "I've outlived the two moons rising—how shall I live to see sunlight again?"

The eyes of lovely Shantih were in his mind, but his were clear: there was no path behind and little ahead. He crept to the door in blackness and thrust. It did not so much as quiver.

"Here I am, here I remain," quoth he.

Shuffling and pattering echoed down the tunnel, and a tiny guttering flame appeared. He stepped aside, hand on his knife's hilt. A ghoul appeared, bent over and wrapped around and around with filthy rags, carrying a tiny clay lamp and an oil pot, heading to one of the jars.

He held his breath. The monster, observing him not, filled the pot. Then it raised the lamp. There was no hiding then. He brandished his knife, prepared to die.

"Sss, sss," said the ghoul. "Child of men, what do you here in this deadly place?"

"I am here for love," he replied. "Life is a burden if I do not have what I wish. This is as good a place to die as any other."

"Sss, sss, sell not your life so cheap," the ghoul said. "Not all would slay you so willingly."

"You're a ghoul and eat the dead."

"I am Grandmother of the Ghouls. fetching oil for their lamps. You've no peril from me but will face peril soon."

"I need no one to tell me that!"

"You are here for love?" the grandmother said. "How mean you?"

"A little mercanter named Cassim offered me the hand of a certain lovely maiden if I brought him a certain ring from the jar in the pediment above this tomb, a bargain I made which has led me here to die."

"Rash. What maiden is she?"

"Shantih, the daughter of Tigran."

The grandmother clicked her tongue under the rags hanging over her face. "Ever youth falls in love among the race of men. Do you know her tale?"

"She said something of a heavy debt."

"Unhappy maiden. This Cassim, impoverished though he appears, lent great sums to her father to build his wealth, but the seventh year of the debt has come due with great usury. The day of payment arrives tomorrow, and Cassim will be unpaid: your Shantih is forfeit."

"What of this ring?"

"It's the debt's token. He and Tigran swore their bargain upon it. Cassim presents it to Tigran at the seventh year or fails to recover his money.

"Tigran thought to thwart Cassim: though sealed safely in the stone jar, the maiden's father paid a sorcerer to curse the ring with theurgices, preserving wealth and daughter both. Foolish, greedy man!

"Cassim, undismayed, bided his time for the seventh year, and has found a fool to open the cursed jar for him, as any wise person would guess."

"A fool I am, and bear the curse of death."

"Perhaps," the ghoul hissed. "But the curse breaks if he collects neither debt nor maiden."

Ibrahim pondered these matters. "Will you aid me, Grandmother Ghoul?"

"If you can bargain with Cassim the mercanter, you can bargain with me, Ibrahim, son of Sulaiman. Your life for my desire."

"Anything!"

"'Anything!' Such a large word. Then! If I give you the art to open this door, you owe me a kiss as passionate as any you desire to give Shantih."

Ibrahim shrank in horror, for he smelled the rags, and he had seen the eyeless, wizened faces of two score ghouls, each more carious and twisted than the last, with blank faces and yellow fangs black with unholy meats.

"Come, come, your offer's made, and I claimed my choice. There's no going back on your word."

"My fate is on strange paths since last night," he said. "But my oath I've given."

He put away his knife and stepped forward, but she laughed, waving him away. "We wait, we wait," the grandmother said in her hissing voice. "So eager! No wonder you're in trouble. I'll claim my kiss when I've done my part for you: not before."

He stepped back, relieved. "You'll open this door?"

"Not yet. It is under a power, and the chief of the ghouls is its master. There's no road out but down into the cave of my tribe."

"Then I am lost."

"Give up not yet your hopes. See you that chest of tarnished silver and agèd ivory? Find rags within fit for a ghoul and garb yourself. Then, accompany me."

"Well," Ibrahim reasoned privately, "she could have called for help, so if treason's meant, I shall at least see the marvels of their den first. Very well," he agreed, and found winding cloths and stained garb, and though they smelled of the dead, he covered himself completely, foot and hand and face and broad shoulders.

"Do not show your features," she warned. "You're my niece, come from the distant east to help me in the weakness of my age; you can speak like a ghoul?"

He spoke weakly and chitteringly, satisfying her. "Carry this!"

He took the heavy oil pot from her gloved hand and limped, crawled, and shuffled with goblin steps behind her as they descended into the dark.

O, BEST BELOVED, MY LIGHT OF LIFE, I HOPE YOU NEVER HAVE TO ENTER such a cave, for it is, as Ibrahim, son of Sulaiman, found, a dreadful place. It smelled of ghoul and death, and there were bones, long ones, and small ones, and staring round ones until Ibrahim's courage flagged. Yet he trusted the ghouls' grandmother, for some reason: why, he did not know.

He ached from crouching. His eyes squinted in a dark lit by feeble lamps burning in holes ground out in the walls or by glimmering fat blue insects clinging to roots, shedding unsettling corpse-yard light.

The paths led one way and another, and he knew he could never escape without Grandmother Ghoul's help. The worse for him if her baying people pursued!

"Here we are, Niece," she said loudly over her shoulder. "Here we are, Captain of the Ghouls! I have the lamp-oil."

"It took long enough," the Captain of the Ghouls growled. "The lamp is nearly burned down."

"I shall deal with," Grandmother croaked. "My foolish niece should've been helping, but I found her asleep in a hole." She pulled on Ibrahim's arm and pointed. In the dirt was the fluted lamp of solid gold with only a faint guttering flame left.

He carefully refilled it and trimmed the wick. In its pure light, the hot, breathless room was clear, or as clear as the hanging veils of filthy fabric over his face permitted. Ghouls crouched everywhere, and they mumbled old bones and sucked on their dry, dirty fingers and complained of the bright light and their pangs.

"Hungry!" said one.

"Starving!" said another.

"Hopeless!" croaked a third.

"Silence!" the Captain said. "Grandmother of us, who is this?"

"This? My niece Gulnara, come from the ruins of the city of men called Indrapatha to help me in my infirmity. Niece! The Captain."

Ibrahim had no idea how to bow to a ghoul, but either the ghoul-folk did not know either, or he did well enough: either way, he satisfied the Captain, crouching and bobbing in the dirt.

"Sit behind the Captain and stop your twitching, Gulnara."

"Very well!" the Captain said, waving away Ibrahim in his filthy masquerade. "Kinfolk! Why did you not find this child of men on the road to our house? He was coming. He must have been coming. He must have been there!"

"No man!" said one.

"Clear road!" said another.

"Empty the night!" said a third.

"Bah!" the Captain said in his twittering ghoul voice, striking broad, ghoulish hands on the dirt. "It is you fools who failed and let him slip away unseen."

"Captain of our people and grandson of me, why did you believe he was coming?"

"He was moved by love; he must come."

"Love!" Ibrahim said to himself. "What does a ghoul know of love? What does a ghoul know of my heart?" Deeper chills crept on him than he already knew, and he squatted, shuddering, behind the Captain.

The Grandmother of Ghouls scoffed. "A child of man thinks of love! World-stealers, star-wanderers, fools. Some bumpkin afoot, no doubt, staggering with a skin of wine to tumble by some headstone unseen while these," she waved a paw at the circle of ghouls, "rushed by like jackals."

"We saw clearly!" cried one.

"Not a man was there!" exclaimed another.

"Not a step, not a stitch, not a bone," growled a third.

"Enough! We go hungry. You, you've dug and delved in cold tombs from full moon to full moon of the greater moon and four full moons of the lesser. Reveal the treasures you've stolen so we may buy meats if you cannot hunt man's flesh for yourselves."

Each ghoul came into the lamplight and tossed down what it had found: coins from eyes, rings with fingers still within them, necklaces from throats once lovely, knives of calypscined steel bound with gold wire—a glittering pile mounted at the Captain's ragged shoes.

"Grandmother, what have you brought?"

"Not so much," the ghoul said. She pulled a bracelet from inside her robes and tossed it on the floor by the lamp—an arc of silver with a sapphire. What wrist, once fair, had borne it?

"Ahhhh!" the ghouls sighed.

"Well done!" gloated the Captain. "Learn from Grandmother! Now, you, Gulnara," he turned and patted Ibrahim's shoulder. "A stout ghoul girl! You must have brought something, yes, gifts from the nests of Indrapatha's ruins?"

"Nothing so fine!" Ibrahim muttered, crouching. "Nothing like that."

"You must have something," the Captain said sharply.

"Something! Something!" the ghouls growled.

You bethought you of the deka Ibrahim still had, O Best Beloved. He thought of it. too, but though 'twould be a great treasure for a small child such as thee, and it might feed a grown man bread, it would surely be worthless and insulting to the Captain of the Ghouls. If he sweated under the stinking rags before, he sweated twice as much now.

"Surely Niece has some great treasure about her," the Grandmother said. "Come, Gulnara, fetch it out!"

Ibrahim then bethought him, as you, light of my life, doubtless have also, of the fan of gold and ivory and gems that Shantih had dropped to his hands from her window. She told him it would save him in great need, and as the ghouls slavered and scratched at the stones, he put his rag-wrapped hands under the garments and pulled it out and laid it on the pile of glitterment in front of the Ghoul Captain.

"Oh!" said one ghoul.

"Ahh!" moaned a second.

"Worthy!" growled a third.

"Very fine!" the captain said, prodding it with his gloved hands. "Welcome indeed, Gulnara."

"Sun comes," the Captain said. "We'll have better news from the new day. The man's flesh we'd have eaten tonight would have served us well this day in my plots! But mayhap he succeeded in his errand. If so, all to the good! Tomorrow we shall have untold wealth and better still, we shall dine on *very* sweet meats after next sundown, I promise!" At this, the ghouls laughed, croaking and horrid. The grandmother stood close to Ibrahim, and he felt a tremble.

"If not, I'll make other plans, and our work shall not fail. So! For a little time, we must sleep if we will not eat. Lie down! Be silent!"

The ghouls clamored and groaned but lay here and there on the floor like beasts, twitching and settling until they resembled piles of tattered garments at a rag-picker's. Ibrahim crouched by the wall, wondering how to escape. Grandmother of the Ghouls adjusted the gold lamp so its flame was the tiniest glimmer, no bigger than a peri in a flower.

The ghouls soughed, and the ghouls coughed, and the ghouls sighed, and one by one, fell asleep like beggars in an alley.

Ibrahim waited and listened. The curse the jar released tightened on his heart, and he saw naught but death any way he went in this adventure.

Still, he resolved to find his way to the stone door—but a ghoul stooped over him before he could gather courage.

"Will you be brave?" it hissed, and was Grandmother.

"I will."

"Get the lamp, but be silent."

Ibrahim wished nothing better, as you may suppose, so he took it carefully, thanking his rag-wrapped hands for protecting him from the hot gold. The grandmother ghoul paused by the heaped treasures, which clinked as she snatched two things, then led him with soft, inhuman steps through the twisting goblin burrows.

They hastened, hardly a flicker of light from the lamp or the bugs on the walls. The lamps in the alcoves dug in hard red clay sat guttering or cold and dark. What senses she used to guide herself, he could not guess, but before long they stood in the tomb-chamber. She bade him set the lamp on the floor.

He put his hand on the door, but it did not stir.

"How—?"

"Hush! Now, child of men, recall you our bargain?"

"Yes," he said, reluctant. "I recall, and I would kiss you and more to escape this wretched place."

"More shall not be required at this time." The grandmother sounded amused. "But before I let you free, I would have you kiss me as you did promise, lest you betray your word."

She raised the filthy veils hanging over her face, and pulled him into the foul shadow of her hood, and with not a little cringing at the thought of the mummied thing beneath, he let her draw him close, and—lo!—it seemed that she was not hard and wrinkled like an ancient ghoul, and not smelling of the grave and dead men, but soft and sweet like sudden flowers after desert rains, and he learned she was quite kissable indeed.

When he must break for breath, he said, "I did not imagine that your kiss would be so pleasant, she-ghoul."

"What child of men knows the secrets of my people?" said she, dropping the filthy and bewebbèd veils in place. "We are not the same. You have done as we bargained, now so shall I. The lamp's light shall open the door."

She adjusted the wick, and the flame rose high and smelled pure. The tomb door swung open with a low grating.

"Now," began the ghoul, but an angry voice exclaimed, "What treachery is this?"

The Ghoul Captain sprang from the tunnel, crouching head between his knees, claws cutting the dirt. A long hiss came from the shrouds of his face. "What have we here?"

The Grandmother was at a loss for the instant, but Ibrahim threw off the ghoul-cloak from his head and back and, seizing his knife, wrapped his arms around her and pointed the tip to her throat. "Move not!" he said. "I am leaving this place, but I'll leave her meat behind if you come at me."

The Captain snarled like a cornered fennec. "This is ill-done. A guest of mine, and I knew him not? Man's flesh and I dined not? And you, Grandmother, what excuse have you?"

"I drove her with blade," Ibrahim said. "She did not choose this."

"It is true. Help me, grandson and chief of our people!"

"Pah," spat the Captain. "You either are too foolish not to know your niece, or you betray us."

Grandmother Ghoul turned her face against Ibrahim's breast and whispered, "Seize the lamp and draw me out of here, beloved."

Ibrahim hesitated only an instant. His blade dropped into his sash again. His right hand had the lamp, and with a jerk, he flicked flaming oil at the captain's rags, then threw himself and his prisoner out of the stone door as it swung shut in darkness.

THE NIGHT AIR, O BEST BELOVED, SEEMED SWEET AND CLEAR TO Ibrahim, son of Sulaiman. He cleansed his lungs of the stink of death and the thick burrow smother, shivering at the squeals of rage and pain behind the door, but the Grandmother's mittened hand held him tight.

"There is more than one way out," she said. "We cannot linger. The tunnels run far and wide."

To his surprise, no longer hunched, she put aside her hobbling gait and ran almost as fast as he.

They fleeted past tomb, stele, obelisk, cypress, and palm, past statues faceless and monuments tumbled. The ground rumbled faint and angry, but his legs were long, and hers, if shorter, were swift. Their soft boots rattled over loose stones in the lanes between the looming crypts and monuments. Behind, beneath, came howls.

They halted once: at a trickling font, a broken pitcher and a limp figure lay in the dust. "The ghouls will find this poor soul!" Ibrahim exclaimed.

Grandmother Ghoul stooped over her but straightened, waving him on. "She's insensible, but lives."

"She'll not live long when they find her."

"They will not slay their own grandmother. Cannot you tell by her garments? She also is a ghoul."

"Their grandmother—?"

"Earlier, I struck her down from hiding with a blown powder. We must run!"

In wonderment, he ran.

He expected her to fall behind, but she kept pace until, at the last, she held her side gasping in pain.

Torn, he paused. What monstrous things had she done? What unclean meats had she eaten? Should he leave her to the justice of her kind?

The shrouded face raised to him in such a piteous and human

gesture that he had no heart to abandon the creature. It extended its rag-wrapped paw.

"Do not leave me!" it gasped.

"I will save you." He lifted it in his arms, head on his shoulder, foul cloth in his face as it gasped, clinging to the gold lamp as he carried her out of the necropolis.

"If she's not their grandmother," he wondered as she clung, "is she some other trickster?"

They left the dreadful old tombs on the high road to the east, coming upon grand new mausolea, laurel trees, meadows, along with vilaĝos on each side, with the spires of Penesthelia visible ahead.

At a wood of ilex and dates, she said, "Put me down. No farther! Go on alone."

"Will you be safe?" He put her on her feet

"We're far enough for the moment."

Reluctant, he obeyed. "What will you do?"

"What ghouls must. Go! Perhaps we shall see each other again."

"Perhaps," he said, doubtful. "Peace be to you, Grandmother Ghoul."

"Peace be to you, Ibrahim, son of Sulaiman," the ghoul replied. Like a shadow, she passed into the grove.

Bewondered at the night's marvels and failing to hear a horse's neigh, he strode on, legs and lungs burning, through city farmlands, joining early wains and carts heading to market, girls carrying egg baskets on their heads. At dawn, a white horse rode from behind like thunder, the rider wrapped tight in flowing sky-blue, but he saw no face, thinking only, "That horse passed me before!"

With dawn, he was in the city, with its life and fountains and bright colors, and after he left his ghoulish rags in an alley and washed face and hands in pure water, he could scarcely believe such a sinister den and its cruel abhorrences had been.

Strangely troubled, he checked his sash the twentieth time for the gold and ruby ring safe there. Spake he, "I must find this Cassim and complete our bargain."

He hunted the porticoes of the dark east side of the market until he found the little mercanter's narrow stall.

"Peace be to you," he said. "A fair morning, *effendi*."

"Peace be to you," Cassim said in his whispery twitter. "You went to the necropolis, then?"

"I did."

"Had you adventures?"

"I had some," Ibrahim agreed. "None worth relating."

"Is that so," the mercanter murmured in his hood. "You failed to achieve the ring?"

Ibrahim, son of Sulaiman, revealed it.

"This, you mean?"

The mercanter made a long, slow hiss. "That could be any ring," he said. "Any ring at all. Let me examine it to be sure."

"I took it from the stone jar, bound by time and guarded by theurgices now lying heavy on my heart. It's the ring you wish for, and I'm sure, *effendi*, that you agree. Therefore, when the maiden's hand is in mine, the ring will be in yours."

He crossed his arms, stern.

"A bargain made," muttered the little man, "is a bargain sworn. You! Guard the stall!"

A wizened figure, even smaller and more heavily wrapped, emerged from the shadows of baled goods and hanging fabrics. Cassim led Ibrahim away, leaving it to mind his wares.

O, Best Beloved and the dawn of my heart, if you should go into the houses of the great and mighty, you will find them of ebony and malachite, tile and marble, gold and silver. Even the humblest servants are lovely and in silk, and the fountains run in every courtyard. So it was in the house of Tigran, wealthiest mercanter of Penesthelia, in the great green street from the Market to the East Gates. Thither Ibrahim followed on the limping heels of the little goblin man, bent over so low his nose nearly touched the ground. A tall servant in midnight blue and ivory met them at the door and passed them to a mightier in scarlet and gold, who gave them to one dressed in kingly finery. That one led them on into a great counting hall where Tigran, son of Armenak, sat surrounded by rich and valuable goods of all kinds: cloth-of-gold, silks, precious stones, perfumes, piled carpets, beauteous maids from far lands, bowls of pearls, a golden-collared leopard on a chain, weapons gilded and carved, and devices of mysterious design and purpose. Clad in blue and white and diamonds, he bit his lips.

He rose as Ibrahim bowed, but Cassim stood unmoving. "Peace be to you," Tigran said to the mercanter. "Welcome to my humble halls."

"Humbler they might've been," the little wizened man said, "if it not for sums advanced long and long ago."

"Perhaps," Tigran, son of Armenak, said. "I've paid and paid when paying was needful."

"Needful it is again: today I demand the debt due in gold at the seventh year, or else I take all your fortune and your daughter."

"You've not presented the ring I swore on to prove your debt."

Cassim pointed at Ibrahim, who, now reluctant, produced it.

Tigran turned white, then red, then white again. "It cannot be!"

"You would've cheated me," Cassim said, his thin voice harsh. "You cursed the jar. Yet here the ring is, anyway."

Tigran's mouth worked. "I've not so much money in coin. Give me yet a while—"

"A bargain made is a bargain sworn. You agreed to pay, and here I am."

"How can I fulfill such a bond with my child!"

"Argue with yourself," the little mercanter said. "The debt in coin or forfeit your wealth and daughter."

"You would not take her from me!"

"You would not break your oath."

Tigran stammered, then summoned his daughter.

Shantih, daughter of Tigran, came dressed in green, with gold cloth hanging from her hair and a white veil across the bridge of her nose. Her eyes took in her shaken father, the shrouded figure, and Ibrahim, son of Sulaiman. Seven maidens followed her.

"My dearest Father, what is it?"

"I owe my guest a great debt. He has come to require it of me."

"Father," Shantih said behind her veil, "for a bargain made, you have sworn to uphold it."

"He has come to claim you, my daughter, and all the wealth of my house."

"Indeed. To what end do you mean to turn me, *effendi*?"

"To whatever end I please," the crouched and crabbed little mercanter said, and he made a snuffling noise. "Perhaps you shall be a humble servant to my family. Perhaps it pleases me to wed you to this young man Ibrahim son of Sulaiman of the north, and bear shepherd sons and daughters for him."

Tigran groaned.

"Is this true, young man?" she asked.

Ibrahim could not help but bow.

"What estates do you have to promise me, O Ibrahim, son of Sulaiman?"

"In summer, hide tents and good meadowgrass. In winter, a stone hut."

"I should prefer that to my father breaking his word," said she. "Seven sons and seven daughters I'll bear to you, O Ibrahim, that they shall help build the world."

Ibrahim imagined nothing better, but was shamed that this dwarfish man's power had won this bride for him.

"Maiden, daughter of men, put your hand in his, for he has sworn to pay me a bride price for you."

"A fine thing he should pay you, not her father!" Tigran said angrily.

"Perhaps he shall pay a better price to you than you know," said she, stepping forward to place her cool, pale hand in Ibrahim's.

"Now, son of men, the ring," said Cassim eagerly.

But then he gave a start, as though at seeing marvels. "What is that on your wrist?"

She smiled. "This? My mother's bracelet." The sapphire gleamed in the silver circlet. "Perhaps it can buy more sheep for my new husband."

"I feel I've seen it before," Cassim said grimly, whilst Ibrahim stared, for the last he saw it, it was in a pile of spoil in a ghoul's den.

"I am sure you've not," she said and drew a fan of ivory from out her girdle and fluttered her face.

Cassim recoiled. "What do you hold?" he demanded.

"My mother's fan, sir." Opened, it was picked out in elephants of gems and peacock plumes. "I'll sell it to buy me a stout mule. I need not walk to my husband's hovel in the far north."

"I feel I've seen it before," the mercanter said, sidling back.

Ibrahim looked bemazed, for he last saw it in the hole of the ghouls.

"I am sure you've not." She beckoned, and one of her maidens brought a covered brass salver cunningly worked with gazelles and lions. "But perhaps this might bring light."

She lifted the cover, and the broad gold lamp rested on the salver, completing the little man's confusion. The lamp brought not clarity, but stupefaction and darkness, yet Ibrahim, for his part, began to understand.

Tigran did not. "What does this mean?"

"Father, Cassim is no human mercanter but a dreadful ghoul who bargained with you. You'll find dead men's flesh still between his teeth, and it is my flesh and the flesh of this youth he will devour likewise when he has claimed all of your house and goods. Will you bargain away your daughter to such as he, neither beast nor human?"

Tigran stared at her, then at the little man. "Is this true?"

Cassim hunched even more, palms flat on the patterned marble floor. "The girl lies!" he exclaimed. "I lent you money when no one else would. Where could a ghoul find such wealth?"

"From the graves," Ibrahim said. "I have seen that work myself. I know you now as Captain of the Ghouls!"

The cloth-swaddled head swung from him to her, then with a spring, the mercanter leaped from his cloak, bolting for the triple-arched door, wrapped in gauze and rags and bandages, but with inhuman joints and a blunt, doglike head: a very ghoul indeed, O Best Beloved!

"Stop him!" shouted Tigran, son of Armenak. Two men in tan and green ran in with their guns. Ripping its bandages, the ghoul revealed a wrinkled, pale, blind face and a wide-fanged mouth. He charged Shantih, leaping with froglike bounds. Tigran shouted;

the maidens among Tigran's chattels and wares shrieked; Shantih and her handgirls shrank in horror.

Ibrahim, who'd slain a wildcat leaping at a lamb two springs gone, strode with his blade between them and the ghoul. They struck together, grappling, the Captain's fangs clutching at Ibrahim's breast and throat. Once, twice, the knife flashed. There was black, not red on the calypscined steel, black, not red on the marble floor. With a high shriek, the ghoul spasmed, lay still, and a cold wind blew and was gone. Cassim getting neither money nor maid, Ibrahim's curse passed, and the shepherd's son's heart grew easy again.

He pushed the rumpled, cold form away. "The militia must go to a tomb I'll lead them to," he said. "There's a nest of them there; if they are fled, some of their wealth may remain."

He stood, and Shantih shed her veil. "Father," she said, "I promised to wed a shepherd, have I not?"

"My dearest child, you have promised to marry the man whose bride price for you was the clearance of my great debts and salvation of your life."

"I would be an ungrateful child to say no, then." She took Ibrahim's hands and turned her face up to him.

"Did I kiss you last night?" said he to she, then lowered his mouth to hers.

"Do you doubt it?" she asked after a moment.

"No. No, Shantih, I do not. Yet I do not wholly understand."

"Did you not see a white horse and a blue rider, thither and back?"

"I did. It was you?"

"It was."

"And you knew all?"

She smiled. "Beware! As you see, I am a bold enchantress, O husband-to-be. I knew my father's danger; my art revealed my salvation and true love. My cunning put the true Grandmother of the Ghouls into slumber as she fetched water, and my enchantry led me into the ghoul den and safely out. But your bravery saved us."

"I have guessed! But are not all women enchantresses, Shantih?"

She laughed and kissed him again like flowers, the dew, and the dawn, arms twined round his neck. "I'd expected no such wisdom in the hearts of men!"

So Ibrahim, son of Suliaman, lost all his sheep yet married the daughter of the greatest mercanter in Penesthelia, and in time, they indeed had so many sons and daughters that there was not the counting. So should all our fortunes increase, O Best Beloved!

Also from Raconteur Press

Ghosts of Malta

Knights of Malta

Saints of Malta

Falcons of Malta

Space Cowboys

Space Cowboys 2: Electric Rodeo

Space Cowboys 3: Return of the Bookaroo

Space Cowboys 404: Cow Not Found

Space Cowboys 5: Cattle Drive

Space Marines

Space Marines 2

Space Marines 3

Pinup Noir

Pinup Noir 2

Pinup Noir 3

Your Honor, I Can Explain...

You See, What Happened Was...

He Was Dead When I Got There...

You Again?

All Will Burn

All Will Burn: Fierce Love

All Will Burn: At All Costs

Moggies in Space

Moggies Back in Space

Moggies in Space: A Galaxy Fur, Fur Away

Moggie Noir

Full Steam Ahead

Steam Rising

Giant! Freakin'! Robots!

Wyrd West

Goblin Market

Coffee Adventures

Hooves, Tracks and Sabers

The Big Ones

Alien Family Values

PLEASE, TIP YOUR AUTHORS!

At Raconteur Press, our motto is *Have Fun, Get Paid!* Hopefully you enjoyed the stories in this volume. If you did, please take the time to leave a quick review. Our authors love to hear that people enjoyed their stories and it encourages them to write more like them.

If you liked a story by a particular author, go ahead and find, then follow their author page. This enables you to get notifications about their next release.

To follow Raconteur Press, which you should totally do,

subscribe to our Substack at https://raconteurpress.substack.com/ and you'll be amused by updates from Farnsworth the editing orc, notified of any new releases, and for the low price of free, get special content seen nowhere else.

Printed in Dunstable, United Kingdom

64196911R00157